DOLLAR$

DOLLAR SERIE$

by

New York Times Bestseller
Pepper Winters

Dollars (Dollar Series #2)
Copyright © 2016 Pepper Winters
Published by Pepper Winters

All rights reserved. No part of this book may be reproduced or transmitted in any form, including electronic or mechanical, without written permission from the publisher, except in the case of brief quotations embodied in critical articles or reviews.

This is a work of fiction. Names, characters, businesses, places, events, and incidents are either the products of the author's imagination or used in a fictitious manner. Any resemblance to actual persons, living or dead, or actual events is purely coincidental.

This book is licensed for your personal enjoyment only. This book may not be re-sold or given away to other people. If you would like to share this book with another person, please purchase an additional copy for each person you share it with. If you are reading this book and did not purchase it, or it was not purchased for your use only, then you should return it to the seller and purchase your own copy. Thank you for respecting the author's work.

Published: Pepper Winters 2016: pepperwinters@gmail.com
Cover Design: by Kellie at Book Cover by Design
Editing by: Editing 4 Indies (Jenny Sims)

OTHER WORK BY PEPPER WINTERS

Pepper Winters is a multiple New York Times, Wall Street Journal, and USA Today International Bestseller.

Her Dark Romance books include:

New York Times Bestseller 'Monsters in the Dark' Trilogy
"Voted Best Dark Romance, Best Dark Hero, #1 Erotic Romance"

Multiple New York Times Bestseller 'Indebted' Series
"Voted Vintagely Dark & Delicious. A true twist on Romeo & Juliet"

Grey Romance books include:
USA Today Bestseller
"Voted Best Tear-Jerker, #1 Romantic Suspense"

Survival Contemporary Romance include:
USA Today Bestseller Unseen Messages
"Voted Best Epic Survival Romance 2016, Castaway meets The Notebook"

 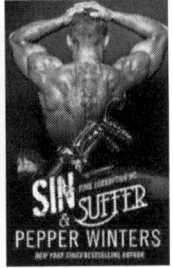

Multiple USA Today Bestseller 'Motorcycle Duology' include:

"Sinful & Suspenseful, an Amnesia Tale full of Alphas and Heart"

AUDIO LOVERS

Tears of Tess / Quintessentially Q / Ruin & Rule / Sin & Suffer / Debt Inheritance / First Debt / Second Debt are available now on iTunes, Amazon & Audible.

Upcoming releases are:
Pre-order DOLLAR SERIES on All Platforms

Pimlico

THERE COMES A point in life where determination supersedes circumstance. Where willpower wins over what should be done.

I'd lived in that point for two years.

I fought my battles silently. I lived in a war zone without a word. I didn't do it consciously; I did it because I had no other choice.

My idiotic will to survive kept me living, even when I wanted to die. It kept me hoping, even when none existed. And every day granted punishment, especially when the dragon-tattooed stranger entered my prison.

He made it worse.

So, so much worse.

But then he came back.

He stole me.

Just in time.

ELDER

ARRIVING AT THE dock relaxed me a little.

Not that I was tense.

Killing didn't faze me. Stealing a bleeding, dying woman didn't increase my heart rate. I'd done worse, seen worse, lived through worse.

It was just another day in my world.

However, during the last few kilometres through downtown Crete, Pimlico had passed out again—either from pain or shock or loss of blood.

Most likely all three.

I didn't intend for my hard work to be for nothing. I wanted her. I wanted to keep her—for the time being—regardless of what it would do to me and the hourly struggle I would endure.

The second I'd set eyes on her, this was the path I'd chosen. It was inevitable for a man like me.

Her strength, her bruises…everything about her screamed for it to end, yet she still clung to hope. That blind faith, tolerance for forgiveness, and stupid belief she could win latched onto the obsessions inside me and made me care.

I didn't want to fucking care. About anyone anymore. It hurt too damn much. But Pimlico…she'd been given a shitty life and somehow still glowed with expectation that somehow, someway, she'd be free.

Free.

I scoffed.

I'd stolen her with the intention of keeping her, not freeing her.

Her blood and silence forced me to answer that misplaced hope in her gaze but only to prove I could keep her alive and deliver a better kind of life, even while still belonging to someone.

Me.

She belongs to me now.

And that complicated my existence a shit ton.

Stalking up the large gangway, I left the dealing of the car to Selix (it had its own berth in the hold below) and strode aboard the luxury yacht valued in excess of two-hundred million dollars. The expensive gleam and untouchable power of such a vessel didn't hold my attention nearly as much as the wraith in my arms.

Her blood soaked through my blazer, dousing me in crimson-wet violence, even as the rigging glittered with fresh white ropes and the timber balustrades gleamed with nautical speed.

Pimlico roused, blinking at the turquoise sea and the sudden flurry of white dressed staff as they flew around deck to cast off. Before, I'd liked their uniforms and how smart they made my home. Now, I hated all things fucking white. Lies and sins and abuse all hid in the achromatic palate. Alrik and his colour preference had ensured I'd change the dress code as soon as possible.

Pimlico flopped unconscious again, the bleeding from her mouth never ceasing.

Taking her to a mainland hospital was not an option. All the doctors in Crete were butchers. I didn't live on the land for a reason. I hated conceited assholes and brain-dead morons who believed their opinion mattered to those around them.

Instead, I'd claimed the sea as my home.

I'd lived on her waves and swam in her belly every day for the past four years. Even when I was on earth, my feet still swayed to the current of the ocean. Being back on the gentle roll stole my escalating worry over what I'd sentenced myself to and allowed me to breathe fully for the first time since I'd disembarked five days ago.

Five days was far too fucking long.

I needed to be far away from here. I needed empty horizons and lonely expanses.

Ignoring the staff who glanced my way then did a double take at the girl leaving ruby droplets in my wake, I entered the first-floor deck and pressed the silver button for the elevator.

It yawned wide as if waiting for such a task and closed silently, descending the moment I touched button nine.

The mirrors on all four walls bounced my reflection back, showing a man who'd stepped over his boundaries of survivable circumstances. Already, the clawing inside me began. The repetitive thoughts of what I would expect from her in return for this. I'd fucked up my own life to save hers.

She owes me more than she can ever repay.

As the lift slowed and the doors opened, Michaels met me.

"Selix called ahead, told me to prep surgery. Give me the scoop." He glanced at the stolen slave in my embrace. He didn't flinch at the blood or look at me with accusation. Mainly because he knew me. He knew I inflicted violence to those who deserved it but did my best to prevent those who didn't.

Selix had once again proven his excessive salary was worth it by streamlining Pimlico's arrival. "Her tongue is partially severed."

"But not fully?" Michaels narrowed his eyes, tipping her chin up with a gentle finger. "That's workable."

His no-nonsense manner was appreciated. I'd headhunted the English doctor from a sabbatical in India. He was one of the best in his field, and his field included most surgeries and other complicated care. I trusted him—especially after what he'd done for me two years ago when my own fucking arrogance almost got me killed.

I clutched the unconscious girl tighter. "Severe blood loss. Multiple injuries—some old, some new. Doubt she's seen a doctor in years."

Michaels nodded. "Right-o. The surgery is all prepped. I'll concentrate on her tongue before doing a full assessment." Snapping his fingers, two nurses rolled a gurney forward, waiting until I'd placed Pimlico on the green material ready for the operating theatre.

My arms ached from carrying her, but I also ached for a different reason. I didn't like that she was in so much pain.

Fuck, get your head together.

If I let sympathy and protectiveness gather so soon into owning her, I wouldn't last a week.

"How long before you've fixed her?"

Michaels scowled, his red hair and white complexion hinting at his Anglo-Saxon roots. "Hard to say until I've assessed what needs to be done. Come back in a few hours, and I'll let you know."

Impatience snarled, but I fought it back. A few hours to halt death and keep her in my world? It was a small price to pay.

With a curt nod, I left the sterile deck of medicine, heading back up to fresh air. It was a ritual I never broke. I had to be at the bow when leaving port.

My hands were slippery with Pim's blood as I strode over an immaculate deck of oak, cherry, and teak. My mind raced with things I should be doing. The urge to take precautions —so I didn't slip backward into my own personal hell—berated me.

Now Pimlico was mine, I had no way of ignoring my desires. She was close. She was on my boat. The sooner I accepted that I had access to her whenever I damn well wanted and put rules in place so I didn't destroy us both, the better.

Not caring her blood stained my fingers, I dragged them through my hair as I stood at the front of the yacht. Engines growled below, propellers chopped the tide into sushi, slowly pushing the big beast into motion.

I looked over my shoulder at the bridge where my captain and his team handled my vessel with expert ministrations. Leaving port on such a big ship was never easy, and my heart thudded as Phantom nudged away from her mooring then leisurely opened up, heading toward the open seas.

As salty air replaced smog and the rock of a movable world deleted the landlocked mundane, I closed my eyes and forced myself to relax.

The stickiness of Pim's blood dried on my skin the faster Phantom flew. I would've given away my entire ill-gotten fortune to leap into the ocean and wash away the gore sticking to my flesh. However, I would have to be patient.

Once we were far, far away, I'd get my wish. For now, I was happy saying goodbye to Crete.

My thoughts turned inward to the dirt I'd climbed from, the mud I'd flung off my back, and the filth I'd invited into my world to survive.

A few years ago, I'd found refuge in alleys, wielding a knife to protect the one person I cared about. Now, I stood on multimillion dollars' worth of prestige with its silken decks, seamless windows, and bullet-shaped hull while glaring at the same mocking sun that'd watched me transform from penniless to prince.

Up until today, I'd accepted the man I'd become to make that happen. I was *happy* with the man I'd become. But Pimlico refused to leave my conscience—taunting me with memories of hardship, hunger, and helplessness.

She forced me to remember things I had no desire to recall all because she suffered the same way I had. Her prison included a home with a monster. My prison had included the streets with gangs.

Our similarities ended there.

Unlike her, who'd begged the devil for death and lived a half-life in a world she couldn't escape, I'd cheated and stolen and built a bridge from destitution to untouchable.

Like her, I'd killed those who wronged me.

I was fucking proud of her for that.

She'd surprised and impressed me when she'd pulled the trigger without any remorse.

She was so bloody strong.

I wanted to see how deep that strength went.

It would be a little while before land fully disappeared, but by the time Pimlico woke up, she wouldn't belong to terra firma anymore.

Not to Alrik or assholes or death.

No.

By the time she woke up, she'd belong to me and the sea.

And there was no escape with water as her new prison and me as her new jailer.

I'm sorry for what I'm about to do to you, Pim.
But you're mine now.

Pimlico

MY FIRST THOUGHT was of water and drinking and thirst.

My second thought was pain.

Pain.

Pain.

My hands flew up to hug my mouth. I wanted to cradle my butchered tongue. But someone grabbed my wrist, keeping me restrained.

"Ah, no touching. You need to keep all foreign items—including unwashed fingers—away from the wound."

My eyes widened as I blinked into focus a man with shaggy ginger-red hair. His eyes were the first I'd seen in so long that didn't harbour sin or evil sickness. His handsome face was normal. He was *normal.* Not an ogre or troll.

He isn't Mr. Prest.

Where am I?

My gaze drifted down his doctor's gown, searching for a nametag.

Nothing.

Not even a stethoscope around his neck or a thermometer peeking from his breast pocket. The only thing marring his clinical uniform was a horrendous splash of blood right over his chest.

He followed my glance. "Yes, you, eh, threw up on the operating table before I could administer anaesthetic." He frowned. "Do you remember the events leading up to now?"

Wait, did Mr. Prest drop me off at a hospital?

Am I free?

My heart bounced in a cheerleading outfit to celebrate.

Taking my wrist, he counted my pulse, not looking at the bruises or rope-bracelets I'd long since grown used to. "You'll feel a bit sluggish over the next few hours, but I'll keep your pain managed with morphine. If you feel any discomfort, let me know, and I'll do my best to help."

Discomfort?

He thought whatever drugs he pumped into the IV piercing the back of my hand muted the agony?

He's obviously never had a partially severed tongue before.

The sensation was worse than any boot or fist. Stranger than any abuse I'd suffered. The muscle was swollen and thick and so different to what a tongue should feel like.

Inhaling through my nose, I instructed the damaged thing to move. I winced in agony as pulls of pressure from the sharp knots of stitches hit me hard.

Will it ever be more than a useless lump in my mouth?

Am I a bona fide mute, after all?

He stood watching, shifting uncomfortably as the silence lingered. Once again, my power over quietness prevailed. I found sanctuary in the pause; I could live in its peace forever.

The only man who turned silence against me was Mr. Prest.

And he's not here.

I didn't know why my pulse quickened with anticipation then slowed with a thread of disappointment.

Why is he not here?

The doctor cleared his throat. "My name is Andrew Michaels. I'm the onboard surgeon. I oversee the small medical team here on the Phantom."

Onboard? So I'm not at a hospital? Not...free?
Instead of worrying about my captivity, I focused on the name that'd sprung up before.
What is Phantom?
I stared harder into his eyes, ignoring the padding wedged beneath my chin to catch any drool and the awful steady throb in my mouth.

Not noticing my mute request for more information, Michaels stepped around my recovery bed and pulled open a drawer to my right by the IV.

His hand disappeared inside, yanking free a pad of paper with the crest of some smoky ghostly design. His fingers vanished again; rustling sounded, followed by the appearance of a pen. Holding both, he turned to me then awkwardly tried to place them in my possession.

I didn't move.

Not because my body ached and cried for all the abuse it'd suffered, but because I honestly didn't remember how to accept a gift that wasn't going to hurt me the moment I reached for it.

"This is so you can talk. I'm sure you have questions." He tried again to pass me the notepad and pen.

I gritted my teeth, amplifying my swollen tongue. The sensation was foreign and so, so wrong. The tickle of stitches itched my palate as I swallowed a rank metallic taste of old blood.

I shuddered.

A panic attack billowed just out of calming distance...a tempest growing with forked lightning and gales.

My soul grew claustrophobic, as if it could shed this old carcass and find a newer, less broken one. I felt dirty and used and useless and not just because I hadn't showered in forever. The past few years clung to me even though Master A was dead.

The memory jolted me.
He's dead.
I killed him.

The quickly forming panic attack paused, swirling with knowledge that I'd finally won. I hadn't had to die to be free of him.

He died.

Goosebumps careened down my spine as I remembered the heavy squeeze of the trigger and the splash of red. If I was strong enough to kill the man who'd done this to me, then I was strong enough to remain brave and figure out what this new future meant.

Wait...

A new memory superseded the murder—something about an ocean and a boat and *him*. Mr. Prest.

Well, that answers that question.

I wasn't free. I was still in the custody of the man who held my life in his palm.

Elder Prest was a lot of things, but he'd taken care of me, given me medical support, and left me in the care of a normal human being who didn't expect sex or screams.

That was enough for now.

I'm lucky to be where I am.

If a half-severed tongue was the price I had to pay for it, then fine.

I reached out and took the notepad and pen. The needle in the back of my hand stung as I curled my fingers around the first ordinary things I'd been allowed in so long.

There was no strike or fist. No laugh or threat. Just a kind smile and nod of encouragement.

The moment the welcoming papyrus filled my touch, I had an unbearable desire to write to No One. To reveal what'd happened and why my future notes would be on paper and not toilet tissue.

He still has my other letters.

My eyes flew around the small, nondescript room with no windows and artificial light feathering up the walls to make it seem day rather than luminescent bulbs. Where had Mr. Prest put his blazer with my stolen stories?

Elder.
He told you to call him Elder.
But why?
He'd been so adamant about Master A not using his first name, yet he'd given me carte blanche to use it how I wanted.
I didn't understand.
"You do know how to write, don't you?" Andrew Michaels cleared his throat. "Judging by your injuries, you've been mistreated for a long time. Did anyone teach you to read? To use a pen?" He cocked his head at the door. "I can get a female to help if you'd prefer? Just occurred to me you might not want a man around."
I let him prattle on all while my fingers stroked my pen and paper gift.
"I was the surgeon who worked on you. I ensured your tongue was repositioned correctly and sutured with internal and external stitches—don't worry, they'll dissolve on their own in a week or so."
A week?
That wasn't long enough, was it?
"Tongues are the fastest part of our bodies to heal. You should have full mobility back very soon. The pain and swelling will decrease every day. However, I can't guarantee you'll have full use of your taste buds and heat sensitivity. That is out of the realms of my expertise, I'm afraid."
My mind whirled with information and questions.
Will I be able to talk?
Will I be allowed to go home once I'm better?
"I also took the liberty to ensure your other injuries were tended to while you were unconscious." He pointed at my plastic cast and bandaged hand and another bandage that tightened around my ribcage every time I breathed. "You had a few heavily bruised ribs, and obviously, you knew the bones in your hand were broken." His smile was gentle but full of authority—just like other doctors in my past. "I did my best to tend to you, but you have my oath, I didn't touch you anywhere

else."

If I wasn't so shocked to have a man doing his utmost to assure me no untoward attention was given when I wasn't awake to even notice, I might've smiled.

I might've reached out willingly for the first time and patted his arm with gratitude.

But all this attention—kind, healing attention—made me nervous. I couldn't stop searching for the underlying hellion who would make me pay for such kindness by beating me bloody.

I dropped my gaze. I wanted solitude so I could investigate my body and patch together the missing pieces of the past few hours.

All I could think about was Elder as he held me tight in his car. He hadn't cared about the blood or the fact he'd committed a crime for me. He'd just given me permission to use his name and then deposited me here.

What does he expect in return?

Nothing was free and killing to give me life was the biggest debt of all.

Dr. Michaels didn't look away as I opened the notebook and clicked the pen to reveal the nib. My brain hurt with unanswered questions and fears. No One was my outlet for such worries. The only one I could turn to.

My fingers itched to write; to scribble as fast as I could and demand freedom and food and fantastical things like my mother to find me and my friends to welcome me back to life. But all I could do was stroke the pristine lined paper and sniff silently as tears slowly spilled from my eyes.

I didn't mean to cry—I didn't even realise liquid had formed until tears tracked unpermitted down my cheeks. I couldn't stop the droplets, just as I couldn't stop the throbbing of my tongue or the battering memories of what I'd endured at the hands of that sadistic bastard.

Long minutes passed where I forgot about the doctor and spiralled into myself. The silence grew too much for him; he cleared his throat again. "I'll leave you to rest. I have no doubt you've been through a lot."

He lowered his voice. "Whatever happened is over now. Don't let the memories haunt you, okay? You're safe."

Patting my hand, he smiled softly. "As long as you're on the Phantom, Mr. Prest will take care of you."

ELDER

"SIR, THE GIRL is awake."

My head wrenched up from the glowing screen of my laptop. Selix stood over the threshold in a fresh suit with his long hair neatly tied. Whether it was a casual day at sea doing office work or tearing through the city with a dying girl in the backseat, his look didn't change. It never had—even our days on the streets he'd been the same. Perhaps, not in a suit, but identical in calculating intelligence and uncut hair.

I respected him for that.

I just wished I exuded the same calm he did. My insides were a tangled mess. My temper harsh with crippling need to tear apart those animals again and again, then force Pim to speak to me as payment.

I've earned it, goddammit.

The silent treatment wouldn't work now she was in my domain. It couldn't. I'd claimed her. My requirements would only get stronger and harder to ignore—only her voice would offer temporary relief.

Reclining in my chair, I gave Selix my full attention. Ever since we left port, I'd used the satellite internet to check the police scanners and crime network for any hint of the bloodbath at Alrik's home.

It bothered me that nothing had been reported even six hours after the incident; and it fucked me off that the third friend who'd been at dinner that first night hadn't turned up to be murdered, too.

He was still out there.

Raping and hurting—polluting the world with his defilement.

I'd track him down eventually and put him out of his misery, but for now, more pressing things needed my attention.

"Was Michaels able to save her tongue?" My voice resembled scratchy granite. I hadn't spoken for hours, and the effects of no sleep made me rough.

"I believe he wanted to give you the report himself." Selix stood to the side, welcoming the onboard doctor into my office. The moment Michaels appeared, Selix nodded and vanished through the door, closing it quietly.

"I trust you're relaxing now you're back home?" Michaels came forward.

"It's preferable to the squalor on land." I jumped to the true reason for his visit; I didn't have time for chit-chat. "So? Tell me the girl's status." I closed the laptop, hiding the software I used to hack my way to illegal answers. I trusted my staff, but they didn't need to know anything more about me than I paid their salaries and expected exemplary service in return.

Michaels clasped his hands over his fresh black shirt and slacks. He must've changed after dealing with Pimlico. "She's awake and lucid. She obviously can't talk, but I've given her a notepad and pen to communicate if she wishes."

"And has she?"

"Has she what?"

What did he think? *Flew?* "Communicated?"

He rubbed the back of his neck. "Ah, no. Not as such. She accepted the paper but hasn't written anything yet." He coughed. "I don't know where you found her, but the abuse her body has been through has aged her considerably. Her spine is that of a forty-year-old, not a girl in her early twenties. Her teeth need care, and some of the bruises have caused internal damage, not just surface discolouration."

"Will she survive?"

"It's hard to say. She's survived this long. She'll have help and nutritious food and medicine, but she'll never be able to do rigorous sports or strenuous exercise without discomfort. She'll most likely endure early-onset arthritis from her injuries; she'll need to be monitored for any signs of stiffening and bone heat."

Fuck.

Not only had years of her freedom and happiness been stolen but she'd suffer long-term damage, too. Hadn't she paid enough?

Shit, life isn't fair.

"And that isn't the worst thing," Michaels added.

I froze. "What do you mean?"

"I mean…how old was she when she was taken into captivity?" He held up a hand to signal he wasn't done talking. "And you don't need to confirm or deny if I'm right. I've seen enough cases like this to know she's been a slave."

My breathing turned shallow. I'd enlisted Michaels because he was the best. But being the best meant he was smart. And he was too fucking smart for his own good.

"It's not your business." I crossed my arms. "Let it go."

"I know it's not my business, but I'm aware you've made it yours. It would be wise to know her history, her family—hell, it would be better if you dropped her off at the nearest cop shop."

Not even Selix would dare be so presumptuous with suggestions.

My hands locked into fists. "Like I just suggested, let it go. She's none of your concern."

"Wrong. She *is* my concern. Her health, at least." His face darkened with curiosity. "Do you know anything about her? The way she stared at the notepad makes me think she can't read and write. She's a starved, broken thing who has no tools for life or much of a future."

My vision hazed red. "She's not broken."

"Well, I beg to differ. She has a few bones—"

"Bones don't make her broken."

"Yes, but…"

"And she's not illiterate."

Michaels paused. "How do you know?"

Because I've read her letters—glimpsed her secrets.

"Again—seeing as you're making me repeat myself—none of your goddamn business."

My temper didn't scare him. He'd worked for me for years and knew how far to push. Cocky bastard.

He continued. "Okay, so at least we know she can talk— or at least write—when she is ready. However, I think it might be best if—"

I swallowed my growl. "If what?"

He sighed, cringing a little as my ire thickened. "If we drop her off at the next port and be done with her—like I said, drop her off at a cop shop. Her body can heal, sure. I'll do everything in my power to ensure she's as healthy as possible, but even cured there's still the matter of her mind."

My hands curled into fists. My patience waned. I had too much shit to do before I could visit my newest Phantom guest, and Michaels was pissing me off by assuming things about Pim he didn't know.

You don't know her, either.

Yes, but at least I planned to. I owed her for reasons I couldn't untangle yet. I didn't intend to throw her overboard just because she might be mentally unstable.

Fuck, *all* of us were mentally unstable to a degree. I wouldn't be a hypocrite and deny otherwise.

She was one of the strongest women I'd come across, and she hadn't spoken a word. That sort of strength…it did things to men like me. It made me want to break her and shelter her in equal measure. It set a war in motion between the devil and angel on my shoulders, and only time would tell what part of me would win.

My gaze narrowed. "There is nothing to discuss about her mind."

"But she needs someone to talk to—"

"*If* she ever talks."

Michaels straightened, as if I'd offended his medical expertise. "I sewed her back up. She will be able to talk. It's a matter of if her *mind* is capable of speech, not her body."

Swiping a hand over my face, I smiled tightly. "And for that, I'm grateful. Thank you for your commendable care once again. However, you do not need to concern yourself with her mental healing."

"Do you intend to do it?" He crossed his arms.

His audacity set my blood hissing. "And if I said yes?"

"I'd say you'd be setting her and yourself up for failure." His head bowed. "No offense, of course."

I glowered at his apologetic stance. "Some taken but not enough to fire you."

We shared a smile.

The tension dispersed.

He said, "I won't tell you how to care for her. It's not my business—like you keep reminding me—but I do know you. I know what you struggle with, and I know what we do in order to manage that. This girl…" He paused, before forcing himself to speak honestly even if I might not want to hear it. "This girl is damaged. And rightfully so. Whatever trick you think you can use to fix a lifetime of abuse? Well, I'm just warning you…it won't be easy. It might not work. And you need to be prepared to get rid of her if her vulnerability makes you relapse."

I stood.

This meeting was over.

Michaels wouldn't get near her again unless it was for strict medical reasons. I didn't tolerate others being close to those I deemed vulnerable. Especially when I grew protective of someone. I'd already doomed Pimlico by deciding her rehabilitation was my burden.

She was mine in both possession and obligation, which meant her health and wellbeing was my concern, no one else's.

No One.

The title of her notes squeezed my gut. Each tissue-square remained safely tucked in my desk. In the six hours since we'd set sail, I'd read each and every one.

Two years' worth of thoughts and pleas.

Two years' worth of research that I would use to break, restore, and ultimately get what I wanted from her.

Her notes made me privy to her secrets, delivering questions I had no way to ask. Yet more complications in the complex restoration of her mind.

"Thank you, Michaels. Despite your concerns, I appreciate your expertise."

He nodded, knowing when to give in. "You're welcome." Moving toward the exit, he placed his hand on the doorknob. "She's been through a lot. Regardless of what I said, I'm glad you found her. You saved her from a tragic situation, and I have no doubt she'll be incredibly grateful."

My schooled features remained calm as he smiled once again and left, latching the door behind him. The moment I was alone, I let my true thoughts paint my face.

Frustration, anticipation…but most of all, disgust. Not at the implied gratefulness Pimlico would feel toward me. But at the reasons Michaels urged me not to do this.

He's right.

I should heal her and let her go.

I should hand her back to the life she'd been stolen from.

Then again, what I should and shouldn't do had always been my biggest downfall.

I wasn't qualified to cure a mind, and I sure as fuck wasn't capable of keeping my own desires from clashing with what was acceptable.

She'd been lucky I saved her from that hellhole. Although, she wasn't lucky I'd been the one to steal her.

Pim was no longer in a tragic situation with Alrik.
She's in one with me.

Pimlico

DEAR NO ONE,

I'll rip this up the moment I've finished as I have no safe place to hide you, but I had to tell you what happened.

I have to give you the good news.

The best *news*.

The news I hoped to write for two very long years.

He's dead.

He's dead.

Oh, God, I'll never get tired of the thrill and pleasure of writing those two words.

He's dead.

They're *dead*.

Every single bastard (apart from Monty) is dead.

I pulled the trigger on Master A.

Are you proud of me? Happy for me?

I want to keep talking to you, but I don't know how much longer they'll leave me on my own. I don't want to be caught. He stole our previous conversations, but he won't steal anymore.

Perhaps, in a few weeks when I heal, I'll be able to whisper my confessions to you instead of scribe.

Maybe then, life will be normal.

I'd just finished shredding my latest note into tiny

fragments and scattering them in the drawer when the door opened. I hadn't budged from the single mattress with its overly starched white sheets and the drip feeding drugs and who knew what else into my system.

I expected the doctor again.

I *wanted* it to be the doctor again. I wanted more time on my own before I had to face my new future.

I didn't get what I wanted.

My first peace in so long vanished the moment *he* prowled into the room.

Our eyes met.

The world once again stopped spinning and flipped upside down. Whatever power he'd held over me in my white room still lingered—stronger and more intoxicating now I was in his home and under his authority.

Elder paused a few metres away, his gaze dropping from my eyes to my chapped and sore lips then to my stark skeleton beneath the yellow nightdress someone had dressed me in.

The cheery buttercup fabric ought to bring light into my dark existence, but it only amplified the greens and browns of my ugly, ugly bruises.

I wanted to be free.

And if I couldn't be free, then I wanted to be naked. Like normal. I didn't like the confines or the mind-twisting conditioning I'd been subjected to where clothes were my nemesis and not to be trusted.

Plucking at the yellow gown, I did my best not to wrinkle my nose. I looked juvenile in lemon while he looked distinguished in midnight. If I had to wear clothes, I craved to don black like him. Black would hide my discoloration and give me a refined power that nakedness and white could not.

His black eyes, almond shaped and regal, trapped mine. His body exuded tightly reined power with simmering lethalness. His strong jaw clenched as I studied him the way he studied me.

My lips tingled, remembering the way he—with all his

masculine violence—had slammed to his knees, cupped my face, and kissed me as if whatever drew me to him drew him to me with equal strength.

A shadow fell over his eyes as he crossed his arms, highlighting ropey muscles and hands ready to inflict danger or death. "I see you're just as opinionated here as you were there."

My eyes flared; my jaw jutting out in question.

What the hell does that mean?

"Don't cock your chin at me, silent mouse."

Don't use my dad's nickname.

The name Mouse did not belong to him, even if my body did for the time being.

He didn't notice my annoyance.

His graphite dress shoes clicked on the white tiled floor as he strode forward. His dark grey t-shirt and faded jeans didn't match the formal footwear.

My eyes drifted to his muscular legs then to the floor where the grout lines and colour were a little too reminiscent to Master A's. I knew it was due to sanitation rather than personal preference, but it still made me queasy.

"I feel the same way about white as you do." His voice borrowed whatever power his body had over mine, slipping through my ears. "It's a disgusting colour and will be abolished from my home."

Hating the persuasiveness he had over my eardrums, I hunched into myself.

He thinks he can read my body language so easily.

It only made me want to hide deep, deep inside when only minutes ago I wanted to look him in the eyes and thank him for all that he'd done. To grab his hand and squeeze so hard with a thousand appreciations.

"How is your tongue?"

The urge to press the agonising muscle onto my palate to see if it was still intact made me wince. The past hour on my own, I'd struggled not to touch it, inspect it. I wanted a mirror to see how close I'd come to being disabled for life.

"I take it it's uncomfortable."

You *make me uncomfortable.*

I had no way to ask him to leave. But I wanted him gone. I wasn't emotionally or mentally equipped for him, his questions, or whatever future he'd already planned for me.

Can you go? For just a little while?

I stiffened at my rudeness and silently added, *I'm grateful. Truly. But I'd also be grateful if you left me to rest in peace.*

He chuckled, not seeing my message this time. "At least you still *have* a tongue."

That's true.

My annoyance at his high-handedness faded a little.

I pursed my lips, flinching as the bottom one cracked from whatever implements they'd used in surgery to keep my mouth open.

I'd grown used to tolerating men in my space even when I screamed for a moment alone—which was good seeing as Elder had no intention of leaving. If he was here to learn about me, to interrogate me for his pleasure, then I would do the same. I would catalogue and pay attention. I would try to figure out what he wanted before his lips opened to say it.

The smug way he crossed his arms antagonised me. "Do you intend to use it? Now you're free?"

I'm free?

I shuffled higher in my pillows.

You mean you'll let me heal and then take me back to London, to my mother, to university and cafes and the mundane normalness of everything I've missed?

He ran a hand through his hair. The sharpness of his jaw, depth of his eyes, and achingly dangerous presence intimidated me. He was the epitome of calculated and gorgeous. A man not to mess with. A killer never to disrespect. "I misspoke. I meant, now you're free from him." He towered over me, his shadow kissing every inch of my skin. "Not free in the general sense. You owe me, Pimlico. I told you I wasn't the hero."

Yes, but you did rescue me against your promise to forget me.

That was progress—if only small.

"Do you need anything?" He paced around the end of my bed, his gaze landing on everything in an assessing distrustful way, as if monitoring an unseen threat.

If I did, I wouldn't ask you.

Not because I had a grudge against being stolen (again), but because he'd already done too much.

He'd given me back my life. What more could I ask?

To free you, of course.

That had always been my end goal. For now though, I had to be satisfied with this change of events and contemplate whether I should fight him, submit to him, or bide my time and kill him.

I didn't know what path I'd choose, but…he was right. I *did* owe him. And I didn't want to owe him any more than I already did.

You could just end it—like the original plan.

The flutter of final freedom washed over me. Elder Prest might've changed my circumstances, but he was still a monster I had to survive. Would it be considered weak to take my own life now or still strong to prevent him from having it?

I'd existed with the idea of death for far too long to relinquish the whisper of everlasting sleep. Suicide was never a spineless option to me but my final hurrah. I wouldn't give that up. Not yet.

"Are you tired? We've been at sea for a while; it's almost dawn." His eyes turned to sharp flint. "Are you hungry?"

His questions went unanswered.

The drip gave my body whatever sustenance it needed—keeping any tummy pangs at bay. Even if I were hungry, how would I eat? My tongue refused to move, and Michaels had warned me not to insert foreign objects into my mouth. No doubt that rule included food for the time being.

I glanced away, clicking the pen open and closed as Elder stopped pacing at the foot of my bed. "I suppose Michaels has already thought about the hunger and hydration issue." He rubbed his jaw, his fingers scratching day old stubble. Indecision etched his handsome face. "In that case, I'll let you sleep. I have a big day tomorrow and need to rest, too."

Striding to the door, he narrowed his eyes in my direction. "I suggest you relax and let me take care of you. You'll need your energy."

My heart stopped siphoning blood, filling my veins with igloos.

What do you mean?

Energy for what?

The sudden tension in my muscles signalled another problem I'd become mildly aware of but was suddenly desperately uncomfortable.

My bladder.

Oh, no.

My gaze darted around the room, looking for a bathroom.

You might have a catheter.

My arms flinched to lift the sheets and inspect below. The thought of peeing while in bed horrified me, but I had been unconscious for a long time. When I'd had my tonsils out at fifteen, the operation had endured a complication. They'd kept me overnight with a catheter so I didn't move from a lying position and disrupt the seared wound at the back of my throat.

Is this like that?

How could I tell?

I could pee and find out the messy way, or I could struggle out of bed and somehow manhandle the drip until I found the facilities.

Either option, I had to wait for Elder to leave before embarrassing myself.

I waited for him to go.

Only, he didn't.

Cocking his chin, he stared at the tension in my shoulders and my bunched hands on the sheets. Slowly, he moved away from the door back toward me. "Are you okay?"

My head didn't bobble; I didn't answer his question—it

wasn't insolence, just a lifetime of self-preservation.

He sighed angrily. "You can give me clues, Pimlico."

Not about this, I can't.

It was too embarrassing.

Leave.

If Michaels returned, I'd write a request for a female nurse to help, or I'd manage myself. I felt strong enough to clamber out of bed. I'd be wobbly from the operation, but I would make do.

Like I always do.

Arching my jaw, I stared at the door.

I owed him my utmost thanks, and he would get it. I would pay him back. I would find a way (even if that way was abhorrent to me) but not now.

Elder growled. "Goddammit, you don't have to be silent with me."

In case you've forgotten, my tongue isn't operational.

A dark smile twisted his lips once again following my train of thought. "I know your tongue prevents you from speaking for now, but your body isn't damaged."

My eyes fell to the ugly bruises and scars.

Not damaged? How can you say that?

How did he look past the grotesque marks on my skin and see someone I'd long since forgotten?

He chuckled harshly. "I didn't mean that you're not injured and that fucking bastard didn't do a number on you. I meant you can wave your arms and shake your head. You can reply to me now you're safe."

Am I safe?

He glowered, lowering his jaw. "Don't look at me like that. If I say you're safe, you're safe. Understand?"

The urge to nod was stronger this time. I ignored it.

Safe from Master A but am I safe from you?

The unspoken question hung like cinnamon smoke, matching the rich spice of his aftershave.

He knew where my thoughts had trailed but didn't answer.

Giving me a piece of my own medicine.

Fair enough.

I could empathize with how frustrating it was to converse with someone who didn't reply. I'd been the receiver of that frustration from Master A long enough.

Alrik.

His name was Alrik.

He's not your master anymore.

I jolted as Elder suddenly strode to the side of my bed and touched my forearm.

My skin tightened and heated beneath his touch.

"You're not telling me something."

I'm not telling you many things.

"I think I know what it is."

I doubt it.

I squirmed a little as his fingers clenched my wrist. The tension in my body squeezed my bladder, reminding me I'd better remove him from my presence soon or risk wetting the bed.

"I didn't let them put one in."

My eyes flared.

One what?

"After everything you've been through and the molestation you've suffered, I didn't want you to feel taken advantage of."

I frowned. I had no idea what he meant.

He huffed, letting my wrist go. He ripped back the sheet covering my yellow nightgown and mottled legs. "A catheter. I didn't let him insert one. And it's been hours since you were in surgery. I know why you're tense and keep staring at the door."

Shit, how does he do that?

"You need to go to the bathroom."

My cheeks instantly scalded. I dropped my gaze, scrabbling for the sheet he'd just torn off me.

Leave. Then I can fix my problem on my own.

"If you think I'm going to let you stand up without

support, you're a fucking idiot as well as a mute." With fierceness and impatience, he placed one arm around my back, dislodging the softest pillows I'd had for years, and slid the other beneath my knees.

"Hold onto my neck."

His command came a split second before he hoisted me from the bed and into his strong, terrifying arms.

I gasped—or as much as I could with padding and gauze stuffed around my mouth—and instinctually slung my arm over his shoulders. The drip cord swooped over his head, stinging my hand where the needle pierced my vein.

"Grab the IV and wheel it with us." Elder pointed at the medication with his chin.

I did as I was told. I had no intention of letting the wheeled contraption scurry behind us with its only anchor in my flesh.

The moment I grabbed the cold steel, he moved.

The only sound was Elder's shoes on the floor and the *pound-pound* of his heart hidden beneath his t-shirt and the impressive sizzling dragon I knew resided on his skin.

It took two seconds to cross the room and another two for him to rearrange me in his embrace to bend and open the door, revealing a small bathroom with a stand-up shower, shallow separate bath, and toilet with vanity.

The sight of porcelain made me shiver with anticipation.

Without saying a word, Elder very carefully placed me from horizontal to vertical. He let my weight shift ever so slowly back to my legs, never looking away from my face.

He made me self-conscious, frustrated, itchy—all manner of things—but not afraid. Having a male touch me made my heart grab its rape whistle and prepare to blow like it always did when Master—*no, Alrik*—came for me. However, no sexual interest was present in his gaze, merely assessment about my health.

His breathing came hot and deep as he took a step away but didn't unlatch his hands from around my shoulders.

When I didn't wobble or black out—even though lightheadedness made my head swim—he grunted, "Once again, I underestimated your strength." Almost reluctantly, he let me go, moving another step. "Even after a long operation and even longer imprisonment, you can stand without support."

The statement was more than just truth but an analogy for all I'd lived through.

"I'll wait outside. Call me—" He smirked, catching himself. "Bang on the wall when you're done, or I'll just barge in when I hear the flush." Pushing a finger in my face, he growled. "Don't get any ideas of heading back to bed on your own. I'm not leaving."

Oh, God, he was going to stand outside and wait? *Listen?* I spun around in mortification, trading lightheadedness for wooziness.

Backing through the door, Elder looked over my shoulder at the small mirror above the silver sink. Our eyes met in the reflection. His shadow lurked behind me, black and sinful with harsh secrets in his gaze, while I stood in sad (not cheery) yellow and random bandages.

We were worlds apart, yet for some reason, he'd not only invited me into his but stolen me to share it. I didn't know why I deserved such an invitation, but I needed him to know just because I wasn't ready to talk, I wasn't ungrateful.

I'd kissed this man.

I'd felt something for this man.

He needed to know I didn't take him for granted.

Blinking purposely in the mirror, I bowed my chin with utmost respect.

He sucked in a breath as he stepped from the bathroom, pulling the door closed. I barely heard his whisper as he said, "You're welcome."

I shuffled painfully to the toilet and prepared to do my business. His scent and lingering presence kept me grounded while my body found comfort once again. Once finished, I stood (wobbling on legs far too weak) to flush.

I tensed for an unwanted visitor. I needed a bit more time to get my thoughts in order and feel somewhat sane.

When he didn't barge in, I used the extra seconds to wash my hands and scrub my face as best I could—avoiding my sore mouth. I couldn't stop the apprehension that I still belonged to Alrik and any moment he would be back to hurt me.

Once I'd slicked back my wild, dirty hair, I turned with full intention of knocking on the wall for him to escort me back.

However, the spin upset the tiny balance I had, and I stumbled.

Falling like a paper building, my knees gave out, crumpling me from proud skyscraper to rubble on the floor.

Bones and muscles protested. A guttural groan escaped, sounding nothing like a girl and more like a severely mistreated dog.

Ouch.

The door smashed inward.

Elder stood vibrating with livid impatience. "I told you to fucking bang on the wall."

I was...I tried...

I hung my head.

He strode forward, towering over me.

Every instinct tensed for a kick, a wallop—something I was used to for disobeying. Instead, he sank to his haunches and tipped my chin up with his finger. "You're mine now, Pimlico, and I'll take much better care of you than he ever did, but if you continue to defy me, if you fight me at every turn, we'll have a fucking war on our hands, and I'll win. Got it?"

I closed my eyes, but he shook my jaw until I reopened them.

"Understand?"

There was no urge to nod this time; it seemed anger elicited the opposite of me. Be nice and ask softly, and the need to reply became almost unbearable. Yell and scream, and I shut down—no longer able to hear questions...just rage.

Elder breathed heavily. "You'll learn soon enough. You'll see."

Scooping me up, he carried me back to bed.

My heart hyperventilated, intensely aware of his bulk trapping me. Placing me back into the sheets, he removed his touch as soon as my weight shifted, as if he couldn't stand to hold me any longer than necessary.

I smarted at the rebuttal even while my body breathed a sigh of relief.

Once I settled, sleepiness crept like poisonous fog over me. Turned out, I didn't have as much energy as I thought.

His voice lost its bite, slipping into molasses. "You'd better get used to invasion of privacy, Pim. I stole you because I want to know you. I want to uncover what you keep hidden. Give me what I want, and this will be a lot easier on you. Don't, and you'll rue the day you refused."

Without a backward glance, he strode away.

ELDER

TWENTY-NINE HOURS had passed since I'd brought aboard a stowaway.

In that time, I'd washed away the death of two more victims and did my best to justify the shame compounding deep inside.

For twenty-nine hours, I'd stayed away because I had no choice.

At Alrik's, I'd been allowed one of everything. One kiss, one taste, one touch. For an addict like me, it was the only thing that helped.

I was allowed to sample the vintage, so I didn't consume the bottle.

Pim didn't work that way.

Every sip left me wanting more and more and fucking more. Her silent strength undermined my hard-earned calmness, hurtling me back to the days when I first stepped from the sewer and claimed my stolen throne.

Focus.
Work.
Don't let your thoughts stray.

The instructions I religiously followed were easily whispered but hard to follow. I turned to another method (one I seldom used) to quarantine my wayward thoughts. However, nothing could prevent the repetition of how warm her fragile form had been when I'd carried her to the bathroom. How my heart coughed in panic and salvation from having her so close and dependant.

She'd almost cracked my self-control.

Michaels is right.

I shouldn't have brought her here, regardless of what I wanted. She wasn't good for me. I wasn't good for her. She was better off under the quiet care of Michaels and his small medical staff—even if he pissed me off.

I would get my answers…soon enough.

I would ensure she paid me back…after she healed.

And once I'd satisfied my ever driving demand, I'd get rid of her so I could find peace once again.

For now, the doctor would be my link to her. He'd given me updates on her wellbeing, and would start her on soft foods at lunchtime.

Yesterday, I'd asked again how soon she would be able to talk.

All I'd earned was an angry scowl. In terms of conversing timeframe, that was up to his patient. I just hoped his patient understood how reckless her presence was in my life, and the sooner she could give me what I wanted, the safer she would be.

Then again, I was afraid she would never talk—even once healed. She'd spent two years silent. Two years of notes to a fictional entity, all dated and delivered in utmost silence.

I wanted a timeline of when she would be physically cured so I could force her to talk if she overspent my generosity.

I'd give her two weeks.

If she hadn't said a word by then, I'd force her.

The captain looked up as I marched onto the bridge. The Phantom was second to none. I'd designed this ship the year my fate changed and put no restrictions on my requirements.

Once the vessel was completed and sailed elegantly out to sea, people took notice. Enquiries flittered around, asking where I'd bought it and how they could acquire such a fine craft.

When they found out I'd designed the one-of-a-kind super yacht and bought the firm who built it for me, orders came swiftly with no marketing or request for their business.

I sort of fell into the trade.

"Good morning, Mr. Prest." Jolfer Scott came highly recommend—not just as a sea captain but also as an ex-military commander with an exemplary track record of sniper shooting and weaponry.

Being at sea was the safest and most dangerous place to live. Safest because humans were few and far between—peace existed in the vast blue beauty and uninterrupted sunshine.

However, Mother Nature could drown us all with a simple storm if she so pleased. Even without a tyrant like Mother Nature as our landlord, living at sea was treacherous because out here, no rules applied. A neighbouring craft could very well be a kind traveller wishing to share a drink and adventures, or a killer wanting to board, loot, and rape.

In the years the ocean had been my postcode, war had found us twice. Both times, the Phantom had been sandwiched by two yachts rigged with antennas and men with machine guns.

They hadn't won.

My death toll had steadily grown.

And the sharks enjoyed a good feast that night as we tossed the pirates overboard, leaving them to sink into the briny depths.

"Anything to report, Jolfer?" I clasped my hands around the old-fashioned helm. That was a design I'd wanted—not because of practicality, but because the kid inside me never grew up.

I'd ruined my childhood and my brother's.

But before that, when life was simpler, I'd loved my brother's schooner that we'd played with in the bath. I loved the steering wheel where we'd place one-legged Lego Black

Beard to steer the endless horizons.

That toy schooner was gone now, just like Kade. And even though I held the real thing, this helm wasn't in control.

Computers were.

Jolfer steered my home with a fully automatic system. Decorating the entire front wall of the bridge was a mirage of blinking lights, buttons, and dials.

"Nothing, sir." Jolfer wiped his hands on pressed navy trousers. His light blue t-shirt was casual but ironed, just like all his navigational team. "Still on course for Morocco. The report for weather on the Med is clear for the next few days with a minor squall coming on the weekend but nothing to concern us."

I scratched my chin. "Good."

Morocco was my next point of call. A Moroccan royal who was the second cousin to the king had a love of water after living in a desert-prone country and had enlisted my help to build him a moderate sized eight-bedroom yacht to entertain his close family and friends.

His requests were the opposite of Alrik's.

Instead of weapons and torpedoes, he wanted sun umbrellas and priceless chandeliers. He also wanted a detachable submarine—which was fairly new to the market and well over half a million dollars—just for a tiny four-person bubble to explore the depths.

I would normally roll my eyes at such extravagance.

If I didn't have one myself.

I'd used it a grand total of zero. I would never admit it, but I didn't install it for recreational use but for the hope of one day finding my family and having gifts to bribe affection.

It was a fucking ridiculous idea.

Selix arrived, squinting at the ten a.m. sunshine streaming into the bridge. "Sir, the girl is showered and prepared as you requested."

Finally.
It's time we discuss a few things.

"Thank you." Giving him a look, I paced toward the exit. "When is our meeting with His Highness?"

Selix pulled out his phone, tapping on the diary where he recorded every deal, open contract, and agenda so I didn't have to. "In six days. We're meeting him in Asilah at a local beachfront restaurant he co-owns."

My mind raced.

Ideally, I would've liked to stop off in Monaco where my boat builders were based and visit the small house where I stored pieces of my past. It was the only place on land where I had a resemblance of home.

But we didn't have time.

The Mediterranean was a busy path of waterways and cruising congestion. We didn't have the luxury to detour.

"I can arrange a small stay in Monaco once we've finished the meeting if you'd like?" Selix asked, reading my hesitation to swing into port.

I bit my lip, contemplating. What would I have done with Pim by then? Would I have earned the answers I needed? Would I have already sold her or would she still be my ward?

Either way, I needed to touch base with my managers. It'd been a few months. And I wanted to visit the things I constantly ran from—the memories I studiously avoided.

"Yes, arrange it. Give us a few days in Monaco after this."

Trusting he would make it happen, I left the bridge and headed below deck to see my silent stowaway.

Pimlico

"GOOD MORNING."

Him again.

My head wrenched up. I tucked the bloody dollar with its scribbled note that Elder had folded into a butterfly beneath the sheets. I'd held onto it all while my tongue was sliced. I'd woken from surgery with it gone. Dr. Michaels had placed the ruined money into the bedside drawer, letting the unfolded butterfly wings breathe with past pain and everything I'd overcome.

It was morbid to clutch such a thing; stupid to try to find comfort in something that had no power to grant any, *especially* when Elder's penmanship inked with the truth: that he'd been willing to forget me but for some reason went against his promise.

Knowing he would've willingly left me didn't grant comfort in my current circumstances.

Why *did he return for me? What made him change his mind?*

It added yet another question to the bubbling cauldron already taking up every nook and cranny of my thoughts.

I gritted my teeth, wishing this episode of my life was over and I was healed and strong and could demand my freedom before I went insane with questions.

Now that he's here…I need all the strength I can find.

My breath caught as he strode into the room, nonchalant and unruffled in a black t-shirt and scuffed jeans.

Even in casual clothes, he reeked of power and money. His dark eyes caught mine. "Time to go."

Go?

Go where?

I had no idea where we were. Where we were sailing. Why. The only thing I'd been able to gather was I was on a ship. The gentle rock caused mild seasickness, but with no window to look out from, I couldn't tell if we were close to land or in the middle of nowhere.

Elder stalked closer, his left hand in his pocket as if preventing himself from reaching for me. "Come."

Beneath the covers, I scrunched up the dollar bill so he wouldn't see and cocked my head. I could take the notepad and write a question. I could finally communicate and ask where he wanted me to go. But old habits were so damn hard to break.

A harsh sigh escaped his lips, answering me anyway. "You're moving."

My eyes flashed around the room I'd grown accustomed to. In this small, sterile space, I'd slept alone for the first time in so long. I'd been warm and comfortable, if not sore and healing. I didn't sleep bound on the floor or collared at the foot of a bed.

This was heaven.

I hunched.

"You don't want to go?" Elder raised an eyebrow. "You'd rather stay in the hospital wing?"

If it means I stay safe, then yes.

My chin rose defiantly.

He rolled his eyes. "Fuck, you push me." Ripping off the sheet like he did yesterday, he muttered, "You can either walk, or I carry you. Your choice."

I shot upright.

The thought of his arms around me again—protecting me while threatening me—was too much to deal with so soon.

I'll walk.
My legs swung out of bed as I glowered.
He smirked. "That's what I thought."
What was his deal? He was so gruff, so pissed off—as if I'd done something to annoy him. It was his fault he felt that way. I didn't ask him to come back for me.
You sort of did.
You begged him—remember? When he kissed you, you gave in. You willingly submitted for the first time...
I scoffed, shutting down those memories. I didn't submit. I dove into pleasure I'd never had before. I gave in because I fully believed I was about to die and wanted to enjoy a splinter of normalcy between a man and a woman before I did.
What was so wrong with that?
Nothing. Just admit you liked him enough to kiss him back.
Never.
This man had intrigued me, but he'd extinguished any affection when he admitted I was his to do with as he pleased. He was just like the rest. He'd killed so easily. What was to prevent him from killing me once the novelty had worn off?
Taking my elbow, Elder helped me stand.
Air hissed through my nostrils as I struggled in his grip.
"Don't fight me, Pim." His features sharpened. "You won't win."
His fingers bit into painted bruises, reactivating the obedience Alrik had instilled in me.
I allowed him to help me out of bed, wincing as my warm toes met chilled tiles.
I wobbled a little, doing my best to stay standing. Elder didn't let me go, but his touch turned gentle rather than commanding.
Dr. Michaels had removed my drip an hour or so ago, saying he'd give me real food once he knew the minor nausea I'd suffered wouldn't make me throw up. He said stomach acid on my tongue's wound would not be good for anyone.
I totally agreed.

I needed to be close to the doctor I felt marginally comfortable with. I didn't want to move in with a man who made my heart gallop when it shouldn't be galloping at all. Not in its current condition.

But he didn't give me a choice.

"Come." Dragging me forward, Elder's grip once again changed from gentle to unyielding.

I shuffled forward, stiff as a plank and uncoordinated. Seeing as I tried to obey but struggled, Elder slowed.

Cupping my elbow, he took some of my weight. "Each step will get easier. Another few weeks and your body will be able to move without pain."

I blinked at how wondrous that sounded.

To move without shin splints, throbbing knees, and radiating bruises. To be healthy enough to exercise and not just stumble in servitude. Even my swollen tongue couldn't detract from that delicious promise.

I took another step.

A crooked smile danced on his lips, but he didn't speak as he slowly guided me from the ward down a long corridor. He didn't yank me forward but he did keep a firm pressure, giving me time but bending me to his will.

Together, we padded down the steel grey carpet with a white monogram of the same ghostly logo on the stationery I'd been given.

Damn, I left the notepad behind.

The pen too.

But not my dollar bill.

My fingers tightened, protecting my crimson-soaked secret.

Coming to a stop, Elder pressed a silver button by a single set of elevator doors. He looked down, catching my gaze. "Pay attention. When you're summoned for a check-up with the medical team, you'll need to remember which deck to go to."

You mean...I'll be allowed to wander around unwatched?

The thought was mildly terrifying.

I'd had free roam of Alrik's mansion, but the cameras kept me heeled tightly on my proverbial leash. I had no doubt Elder would have cameras too, but I didn't mind him watching me nearly as much.

Why is that?
He's still a man.
Still a dominating bastard.
But that kiss...

My mind flittered back to the kiss as the elevator dinged, opened, and Elder stuffed us into the small mirrored box.

My lips sparked as he pressed the button for deck two, and we flew upward. The air in the lift intensified, crackling with awareness.

Would he kiss me like that again? Was that why he'd stolen me? To finish what he'd promised the night he'd let me sleep unmolested beside him?

Even if he wanted to kiss me again, he couldn't. I had stitches in my tongue. I was hurt.

That never stopped other men.

I glanced at him from the corner of my eye. Elder was a lot of things, but the more time I spent in his presence, the more I suspected he wasn't like other men. And if he wasn't like the others, how could I predict what he wanted? How could I ensure my survival if I couldn't mentally and physically prepare for whatever would come next?

The elevator doors opened, spewing us out onto a new deck. This one had rose-gold carpet with bronze accents glinting from subtle wallpaper and pretty sconces on the wall. It reeked of classical money and award-winning interior design.

Elder let me go, marching ahead, expecting me to follow.

My bare feet sank into welcoming carpet, whispering of happiness and a future so much better than my past. My pink nightgown that'd replaced the yellow from yesterday fluttered around my legs.

It was a conscious effort not to tear the material away. I didn't find comfort in the softness, merely torture.

Elder finally stopped outside a rose-gold door and opened it. There was no key or barrier, just an ornate handle in the shape of a clamshell.

Striding into the space, my jaw fell open as I followed him.

A maid jumped as she turned around with a plump pillow in her arms. "Oh, excuse me, sir. I was just making final preparations for your guest."

Elder crossed his arms. "The room looks fine. You may go." His head remained high; his gaze locked on the pretty servant with blonde hair and not the exquisite room with its double doors leading onto a small balcony and cascading sunlight.

She bowed slightly, placing the pillow just so on top of a mountain of identical ones on the bed. The mattress was the biggest I'd ever seen.

"Right away, sir." With a quick glance my way, she dashed from the room and closed the door.

Elder didn't speak. Prowling forward, he opened the French doors and stepped into fresh sea air.

I craved to join him on the veranda and inhale freedom. To witness the rushing waves on the horizon and watch the gushing tide beneath my feet. But I didn't know if he wanted me to follow—if it was an invitation or purely for him.

So, I lingered.

Pressing my stitched tongue against the roof of my mouth, cringing against the pain, I peered around the boudoir.

To my left was a sunken lounge where a couch big enough for eight people rested low enough to jump onto from floor level. An inbuilt coffee table had grooves for cups and racks for magazines to keep things in place regardless of how determined the ocean was at disrupting order. A large abstract painting hung on the wall, and the bed slumbered beneath a canopy of pale cream silk matching the elegant dark chocolate bedspread and ivory lace throw cushions.

Once again, the scent of money oozed from every fixture and fitting. A dining table sat beneath a window beside the

French doors, and a bathroom was visible through a linking door to a full-sized Jacuzzi tub and a two-person shower in the same cream and chocolate décor.

The richness of colour was not lost on me after an eternity of white, white, white.

"Are you going to stand in the middle of the room forever or will you come here?" Elder's voice whipped to my ears with the aid of muggy sea air.

My feet moved of their own accord. My entire body tingled as I stepped outside. I wasn't a mute with a butchered tongue. I wasn't sold into a new nightmare. I was just a girl standing beside a boy in the middle of the ocean.

My shoulder brushed against his bicep as we stood watching the view. Sunshine tinkled like gold on turquoise glass. I'd never seen anything so beautiful.

A million questions unfolded like origami in my mind.

What is this ship?
Where are we going?
Why did you do this wondrous thing and bring me with you?

But the answers weren't needed as much as the kiss of such warm beauty. I'd been denied the outdoors for so long that the slaps of water and the breeze as its fingers tangled in my hair was almost euphoric.

"That's the first time you've looked weightless and not drowning beneath horror since we met."

I jolted as Elder turned to face me.

"I like that look."

I had no snarky comeback. No inner comment. His gaze and the sublime view behind him mesmerized me. Gripping the balcony rail with my unbroken hand, I risked looking directly down at the churning sea froth as the sleek silver lines of his ship cut like a sword through the water.

"I wouldn't get any ideas of jumping overboard if I were you. I'd be pretty pissed if you killed yourself after everything I've done to keep you alive."

My breathing stopped.

He knew about my desire to die? Did he plan to use that weakness against me or did he understand why I'd entertained such thoughts?

Turning on his heel, he murmured, "Come. The balcony is yours; you can stand on it whenever you want. I'll show you around, then I have work to return to."

I trailed behind him.

While we'd admired the ocean, a servant had entered and vanished, leaving in his or her wake a tray full of soft noodles, fluffy rice, and steaming potato soup. A carbohydrate avoider's nightmare, but to my suddenly greedy stomach, it was an oasis of delicacies.

"You're only allowed soft food for now, but if you have a craving for something else, let the staff know, and Michaels will approve or deny."

His eyes fell to my hands.

Between my fingers poked the butterfly gift he'd given me.

His forehead furrowed. "What the—"

Before I could hide my bloody dollar, he'd stolen it once again. His fingers swift and stealthy.

"This isn't sanitary. Why the hell do you still have it?"

I balled my fists.

Because it was a gift.

Elder shook his head slightly. "You want to keep it?"

My eyes locked on the dirty money. I desperately wanted to nod. But then he'd win. When he'd talked to me about first times back at Alrik's and created magic in my blood, making me *want* those things, he'd done his best to make me answer him.

And I did. I'd replied.

I wouldn't do it again...not when I didn't know what he ultimately wanted.

"Well, you can't have it." With a vicious look, he pinched the note between both hands and tore it down the middle.

My heart blazed with frustrated flames. But I didn't let him see—didn't let on that the destruction of something worthless to him but so valuable to me was so damn easy and that terrified me.

His voice fell dark and low. "I told you you are worth more than pennies, yet you cling to a dollar as if it's the sum of your value." He tore the note into quarters with a sneer. "Blood stains everything these days. Even wealth."

My gaze followed the torn pieces as they fluttered to the floor.

"Was it the money you valued or the butterfly? It can't have been the scribbled note." He tilted his head. "I don't understand you, silent one, but I will." His hand lashed out, cupping my jaw. I froze as his thumb traced the bruises on my chin, his eyes lingering on my mouth.

"If it's the money, I'll give you a hundred more."

I exhaled in disgust, curling my lip.

Will that make you feel better? Instead of treating me like a slave, you'll buy me like a whore?

His eyes narrowed. "It's not about the money. Is it?"

I tore my jaw from his hold even as his fingers loosened to let me go.

"If it's the gift..." He cleared his throat. "If it's the butterfly I folded, I can give you another."

My heart plopped onto the pillow-laden bed. How did this man understand me when I'd never spoken a word to him?

He held my gaze as he reached into his jeans pocket, pulled out a money clip, and peeled off a note.

Swallowing was hard enough with a stitched tongue, but as his fingers tucked away the clip and stroked a fresh ten-dollar American bill, I struggled even more.

"I'll allow the silent treatment for a little longer, Pimlico, but fair warning...it will get old very fast." His face tightened. "Especially when I expect answers to questions that are suitable enough for polite conversation."

I bristled.

I couldn't tear my eyes away from the way he pinched the money and folded creases in preparation for whatever bewitchment he would create. The thought of another gift pacified me enough that I didn't bother with the broken pieces on the carpet nor sniff in indignation at his threat.

Leaving me standing alone in the middle of the sumptuous suite, he moved toward the table where lunch waited. "Come."

He likes that word. How often has he ordered me to come like a poodle since I became his?

His command licked down my spine, doing its best to hijack my control and force me to obey.

I'd obeyed for two years without a choice.

Why would I want to trade one prison for another? Even if this prison was colour and sensation when the last had been monochrome and agony?

Fighting the urge, I straightened my shoulders. I didn't mean to antagonise, but I was done being a toy for a man too rich and powerful to be governed by rules and decency.

If he wanted me to comply—if he wanted me to *talk*...well, politeness and civility was the price he had to pay.

Shaking his head, he swallowed a growl. It wasn't anger percolating in his chest but a rare emotion I hadn't seen in so long.

Pride.

He's proud *that I'm standing up to him?*

"Please." Hiding a roguish smile, he bowed his head, his fingers never stopping their folding. "That's what you're waiting for, isn't it? Come here, *please?*"

My chin rose even as I rewarded him with a step toward the table.

His gaze fell on my legs, his smile slipping into a sharp cough of approval.

Why did I get the distinct impression of an endless conversation happening when we'd barely interacted? Was this how animals introduced themselves? Body language and mutual respect?

Respect.

Another emotion I was no longer acquainted with.

Respect for another person or for myself. How many things had I forgotten? And how long would it take to relearn?

Pulling out a chair, Elder watched with a predatory glare until I came close enough to sit. I did so as gracefully as I could with my bruised body and waged war with what to look at.

Delicious food or dangerous man.

The soup curled with flavour; the noodles steaming with savoury tease. But then there was Elder and his sensuous fingers creating a gift for me because...

Wait, why is he making me another gift?

The first he'd given me as payment for the night together. A night that'd ended in horrendous ways. But he'd still earned something from me to warrant his origami present.

That wasn't the case today. Not only had he returned for me. Stolen me. Healed me. Protected me. He now gave me rooms of my own, nourishing food, and most of all, the courtesy of letting me rest with no undertones of evil or malicious expectation.

Is it right I accept another gift when he's already given so much?

The faint whispering of folding linen paper hushed my questions as his fingers flew. Sitting elegantly, he didn't look up from his creation, but his lips twitched. "You eat. I'll fold." His voice flirted with a sensual bargain. "Do we have a deal?"

My tongue ached in upcoming agony even as my mouth watered.

His fingers stopped folding when I didn't move.

"Well?" He raised an eyebrow, looking from me to the food.

Never glancing away, I carefully pulled the bowl of soup closer and picked up a spoon. It didn't go unnoticed that there were no dog bowls or forbidden use of utensils. Here I was human...a girl. Here, I was some*one* not some*thing*.

I just hoped it was the beginning of how my future would unfurl and not a cruel game he was playing while waiting for me to heal enough for his requirements.

Dipping the silver spoon into the creamy potato soup, I

raised my own eyebrow.

Keep being a gentleman and you've got yourself a deal.

He licked his lips as I inserted the spoon into my mouth and struggled with the lack of robust taste or warning if the liquid was too hot. The doctor was right when he said he didn't know if he'd been able to save those senses. It took a second to remind my body how to swallow and winced as the food slid down my throat.

Elder paused his folding. "Hurt?"

I wanted to shake my head. To give him some sign that I was willing to work with him while he was being so kind, but once again, the safety mechanism of my past forbid me.

Tilting my chin, I focused on gathering more soup and swallowing another spoonful.

He didn't ask again, taking my willingness to keep eating as answer enough. Silence fell as he crimped and creased, and I ate slowly, trying to blow on the hot liquid but unable to position my swollen tongue enough to purse my lips.

After a few minutes, Elder spoke calmly but with a cold undertone. "You know why I came back for you, don't you?"

I didn't look up, keeping my gaze resolutely on the soup. He wanted to talk? I wouldn't stop him. But if he was looking for conversation, he hadn't earned that yet.

Taking another sip, I kept my head down but my body relaxed, hoping he understood that I was willing to listen if not participate.

Sighing heavily, he continued in his cool timbre. "I returned because no one should have to live in such a fucking hellhole. I hope you know you'll never be subjected to those conditions again."

My muscles tensed.

But what will you *do to me?*

Do you intend to keep me, free me...sell me?

My current position didn't petrify me, but the unknown future did. How long would he tolerate his boat being a convalescent home? How soon would he expect me to pay him back?

And how?

How *will I be made to pay you back?*

Because everything in this world had a price tag.

"Just because I've taken you for my own doesn't mean I'm like him. I do expect things—the main one being your past and present. I want to know who you are. I want to know your real name, where you're from, and what you would do if you were free. I need to master you, Pim…but in a different way to what you expect."

I jolted.

I ignored the mastering part, entirely focused on the word free.

If I was free.

Not *when* I was free.

I didn't realise how much I was holding onto hope that his intentions were honourable and wherever we were sailing to might've ended with a journey home.

Stupid Pim.

I'd been given safety and sanctuary. I should know by now not to expect anything more—*especially* my freedom.

That had been stolen, and it would remain stolen. I doubted it would ever be returned. I would be forever lost and go from master to master until I was too old, ugly, and broken to be of value.

Elder didn't notice the way I huddled over my soup, doing my best to ignore the crushing disappointment and focus on how lucky I was. I refused to lament over things I didn't have when I'd been given so much.

Biting his lip as he curled an intricate fold, Elder finished the origami then looked up. "All of that can wait. For now, all I expect is for you to heal quickly. I want you to eat when required, sleep when your body tells you, and forget what he did to you."

Those commandments were doable.

I took another sip before my stomach decided it'd had

enough and tiredness settled like a cloak instead.

Elder stood in silent reproach.

I sat taller in my chair, trying to seem stronger than I was.

"Don't fear me, silent one, but don't push me either. When I know what I want from you—other than who you are—I'll let you know. And I'll expect you to do what I want. But until then..." His fingers uncurled, depositing an impeccable sailboat origami by my broken hand. "I won't touch you. You have my word."

Striding to the door, he added, almost too low to hear as if it was purely for him. "I won't touch you for my sake rather than yours."

I spun in the chair as quickly as my bruised ribs would allow.

What do you mean by that?

Pausing on the threshold, Elder said, "I have work to do. Have a bath, a nap, write—whatever you want. I'll summon you when I'm done." Giving me a cool smile, he pointed at the coffee table in the sunken lounge where a black box with a grey ribbon rested. "Your notes to the person you call No One are all there. When you're ready to talk, you can't lie to me. Not after I've had the privilege of reading your darkest thoughts."

I swallowed hard.

Those weren't for you, you bastard.

My unbroken hand balled as he bowed slightly. "Until we meet again." Then he was gone, slipping like a shadow from the room.

His presence lingered, giving me no peace. My anger that he'd invaded my privacy and read my letters boiled over as I clutched the origami boat. The urge to crush it was strong, but the memory of why he'd made it made me pause.

He'd sat beside me and created this gift because he understood what it meant. He'd given me something of value. Yet, he'd also taken something of value away.

He'd robbed me of my confessions. He'd read what wasn't his to read.

Stroking the fine creases of such an intricate little boat, I marvelled at how his brutal fingers had made something so delicate. If he could hold something so gently and twist common into beauty…then perhaps he wasn't like Alrik, after all.

Maybe, just maybe, he spoke the truth when he said he wouldn't hurt me. And if that was the case, then whatever payments he expected in return would be paid, if not willingly, at least less painfully than before.

As the sea rolled beneath my feet and the horizon welcomed with turquoise water, I forced myself to admit that this was just another prison, and he was just another puppeteer, but at least, I was still alive.

I would survive.

Because that was what I was born to do.

ELDER

"SURELY, YOU MUST have a forwarding number."

The woman on the other end of the phone was less than fucking helpful. "No. The home line was disconnected after multiple non-payments. We requested the bill payer contact us on three occasions and never received any answer." Her huff echoed loud in my ear. "That's normal protocol. And like I told you many times, we don't have any forwarding details or reasons why the invoices went unpaid with no further communication."

That was what worried me. Where had Pimlico's mother vanished to? In my experience, if someone disappeared, it was usually from bad situations. Either from committing a crime and running from the law (was she involved with Pim's abduction?) or becoming the victim of such an incident (like her daughter).

Ever since Pimlico entered her home number into my phone at Alrik's, I'd bided my time to use it against her. The digits were as good as a treasure map to who Pim was. And if I could figure out who she was before I lost myself to whatever urges she manifested, the better for both of us.

I wasn't good with secrets. I wasn't good with things I wanted but couldn't have. I wouldn't rest until I'd turned an inconsequential phone number into the truth.

"At least let me know the bill payer's full name. I'll do my own research seeing as you're determined not to help."

"Can't give out personal information."

"It's an old account and of no value to you. If not the name, give me the address."

She sighed dramatically. "Listen, like I just said. No can do."

Goddammit, I hated technology. If I was in front of her, I could've subtly bribed her to give me what I wanted. With miles of ocean between us and a crackly phone line, I had no way of changing her mind. "Is there anything you *can* tell me?"

She chirped smugly, "Nope. Have a nice day."

The dial tone buzzed in my ear as she hung up. That just fucked me off. I respected her doing her job but being rude was not permitted under any circumstances.

Bitch.

I slammed my satellite phone onto my desk and swiped over a holder of pens. "Fuck."

It wasn't often I came up against brick walls, but Pimlico was buried beneath them. I didn't know her real name, I didn't know the town she grew up in or any other details of her life. She'd poured her heart into her notes to No One but focused only on her time with Alrik. She never once mentioned a high school location or favourite club or activity. In fact, the only thing she did give a name to was *Anne of Green Gables* and her love of the show. I'd never seen it, but if it gave me clues…perhaps, I should?

Fuck, I don't have time for this.

And who the hell cared? She was just a girl. A slave. What drew me to her so damn much?

You know why. She reminds you of—

I clutched my head, tugging on black hair to rid such stupid thoughts. I would find out who Pimlico was, and when I did, I'd figure out who was responsible for her capture and treatment. And if it turned out her mother was involved in her captivity, she would pay. Slowly. Painfully. I would make her feel every blow and kick Pimlico had endured.

I couldn't find redemption for myself. But perhaps, I could find it for Pim.

But *why?*

There was that fucking question again.

Why do you care?

Why bother when I intended to keep her in the same role she'd been groomed for so many years? It wasn't as if I would free her. I couldn't. She knew too much about me already. The longer she was mine, the more incriminating knowledge she would have.

So once she's fulfilled her purpose, you'll trade her for something else that benefits you?

Why chase down her family and find out the truth if I had no intention of returning her to the life she'd been abducted from?

The answers danced on the back of my mind, elusive but teasing, letting me know I was more human than I wanted to admit. More in tune with broken things than I ever wanted to believe after what I'd done to my own family and the circumstances that followed.

Falling from grace and trading a home for homelessness had shaped me from kind to heartless. Ever since then, I didn't give a shit about anyone else. Why should I? I was the cause of contamination.

Looking at my hands—the same hands that'd touched Pim and stolen her from her dead master—I snorted at how wealth had given me freedom but imprisoned my skills with more money than I could ever spend.

What the fuck was I supposed to do with that?

Where had the fun gone from stealing when I had everything I ever needed?

Not everything.

Growling under my breath, I shoved aside yet more traitorous thoughts.

Maybe that was why I wanted Pimlico's secrets. Because if

she turned out to be as bad as me, if she harboured some awful confession that meant she deserved her fate…then that would grant me peace.

Peace to stop butchering myself with guilt.

Relief that even a girl in torment wasn't innocent.

Because if she wasn't innocent, then it didn't matter what I'd become.

And I could forget the shame that I could never shake.

Pimlico

CAWING OF SEABIRDS was my alarm clock, wrenching my gaze open to a scene I didn't recognise.

Where am I?

Instantly, my heart buckled its running shoes and prepared to sprint, to hide. Where was the white? Where was the mansion where my blood was spilled daily? Where was Master—

He's gone.
Dead.
You're Elder's now.

That knowledge scattered goosebumps over my arms, injecting me with adrenaline. Sitting up in the softest bed with the warmest blankets, I clutched the sheet to my naked chest as sunlight dappled the inviting space. Chocolate, cream, and lace were decadent reminders of who owned me now.

The gentle swaying spoke of a warm body of water beneath me rather than a cold mountain of dirt.

"Morning, miss." A maid popped from the bathroom to my right, her arms full of the towels I'd used last night. I didn't want her picking up my laundry. That was my task. Who was I to deserve to be waited on?

She gave me a gentle smile, scooping up my discarded nightgown from the floor.

The moment Elder left last night, I'd done what he'd suggested. I'd drawn a bath, and while the tub filled with lazy bubbles, I'd gazed out to sea, clutching my origami boat, wishing I could somehow turn it into a larger vessel and sail far, far away.

The kind generosity in which Elder treated me with weighed on me more and more. The kiss we'd shared. The way he'd watched me. His tattoo. His temper.

Every snippet of interaction layered me with fearful hesitation. I couldn't stop worrying as I'd wriggled from the cotton nightgown. Up until now, I hadn't attempted to shed the gown even though the itch to fling it far away grew more intolerable every hour. I didn't because Dr. Michaels expected a woman who needed to cover up after her ordeal. To camouflage her scars and pretend it never happened.

The opposite was true.

Nakedness had been used as a weapon against me. To strip me bare; to teach me I had nothing of my own—no value but the skin I lived in. My body was the only thing I would ever call mine, but in that simplicity I found power. I never had to suffer ropes or chains made out of silk or velvet. Never had to suffocate in elastic or zippers.

I was free.

As the muggy air licked my skin and the warm bubbles of the bath crept up my legs as I gingerly lowered myself into it, I found some sense of normalcy after so much strangeness.

I wished Elder had told me at lunch what he expected. Was it sex? Entertaining his friends? What would he make me do to pay back the delicious meals, vanilla-scented bed sheets, and pretty maids bustling around keeping my room—the room he'd given me—clean.

"Breakfast is on the table." The girl brushed aside a sable curl that'd stuck to her pink cheek. "Porridge with brown sugar, I believe."

I'd never had porridge in my life. The thought of opening my aching mouth and inserting food for my mangled tongue to push and swallow was too much.

I was hungry but not hungry enough to activate more pain.

Especially for porridge.

However, the maid didn't need to know that. I smiled. I didn't nod as that would be overstepping my communication guidelines, but I ensured she understood I was grateful.

She moved toward the door. "By the way, your wardrobe has a few sundresses and other nightgowns inside. Once we dock, I'm sure Mr. Prest will send one of his assistants to buy you more if you wish."

One of his assistants?

How many does he have?

My gaze travelled to the walk-in wardrobe that I hadn't ventured into. I smiled again, knowing full well I wouldn't wear any of the given items while I was alone in this suite. If I explored the ship like Elder said I could, then perhaps I would cover myself for the sake of his staff, but the moment I was alone…

I might've killed Alrik, but he'd killed any reminder of the girl I'd been before I was his.

Hoisting her armful of laundry, the girl grinned. "You'll like living on the Phantom. It's amazing to wake up every day to a new view, new ocean, new port." Cocking her chin at the unenticing breakfast, she added, "He told me to warn you to eat. The doctor, too. He sent some more painkillers; I put them in the drawer beside your bed."

My arms ached from clutching the sheet. The mention of a new view had impatience siphoning in my blood for the girl to leave. I wanted to look out the window and see.

Silence fell; the maid coughed self-consciously. "Is there anything you need before I go?"

A question.

Those, I couldn't answer.

However, despite myself, my chin moved left and right ever so slightly.

What the hell are you doing?

Already the steely resolve to remain mute was fading. Was I truly so weak that a few hours of unmolested sleep and a kind face had me abandoning my crutches so fast?

She beamed. "Okay, great. See you tomorrow morning!" She bustled out, leaving me in comforting silence and the freedom to kick off the covers and stride naked onto the balcony.

After living in an air-conditioned mansion for so long, the muggy heat was an aphrodisiac on my skin. I wasn't cold. I wasn't afraid. I wasn't hurting from a fresh punch or kick.

The sensation was far too foreign and earned yet another lick of terror for what I would have to do to deserve such luxury.

Looping my fingers on the metal balustrade, I let the wind be my dress and the sun my shawl. The view of lolling swells and the occasional sequin of light glinting off the epic blueness granted my first unforced smile in years.

Payment for this would be astronomical.

But I might as well enjoy it before that day came.

* * * * *

Nine hours I was given.

Nine hours where I relaxed in my room, dozed in the sun, wrote a quick note to No One before tossing it into the swiftly passing sea, and did my best to ignore the swollen tongue pounding inside my mouth.

My other injuries took a backseat, barely noticeable after living so long with such agony. Even my broken hand didn't bother me now it'd been properly strapped. I'd often wondered if I'd grown so used to pain that I would miss it. That if a time came when I had no black and blue contusions, I would no longer feel real.

I couldn't remember a time when agony didn't hunker inside like a gremlin ready to attack. Would Elder let me experience such a phenomenon or was he merely curing me of Alrik's misdeeds so he could inflict his own?

The sun had set in a blaze of orange glory, setting fire to the ocean in a patchwork of golds and apricots just as a female staff member dressed in a smart navy dress entered my room.

It didn't escape my notice the door had no lock and the staff attending to me were all women. Was that for Elder's benefit or mine? Her gaze landed on my naked breasts where I sat curled up on a chair three times the size of me looking out to sea.

This suite was the epitome of luxury, yet there was no television, no laptop or key to the outside world.

Just the view.

And I was addicted to it. Obsessed with the moving scenery after being chained to a hilltop for so long.

"Oh, I'm so sorry!" The woman turned sharply, averting her eyes.

The long-forgotten urge to tell her not to worry—to be socially acceptable and put her at ease—made my lips part. My useless tongue spasmed, before remembering speech was not something it was used for these days.

With her gaze locked on the carpet, I couldn't catch her eye. Grabbing a cushion from behind me, I positioned it over my front and kept my legs tucked up tight in modesty. I patted the arm of the chair, signalling she could look.

She did, slowly.

Her gaze landed on the cushion as her eyebrow rose, but she didn't say anything. If she wondered why I sat here naked, she didn't ask.

Moving forward, she held out a small envelope. "You're summoned to dinner."

Our fingers grazed as I took it. I sucked in a sharp breath. Not because I was afraid of her, but because she was the first girl I'd touched since my mother. Tears dared to stab my eyes as I looked down and fought such idiotic hurts.

Elder had given me his first commandment.

I could curl into a ball and refuse to go. I could be the slave he thought I was and cower. Or I could remember how to stand straight, how to walk and talk and glower with confidence. I'd steal his secrets by watching his habits—learning him all the while he thought he was learning me.

This is just another test. I will not fail.

"Inside is a small map of the Phantom. He's waiting for you on the main deck in the dining room." She sucked on her bottom lip before blurting, "He didn't mention a dress code, but can I suggest…at least, covering up a little?"

I tore open the envelope and pulled out the laminated map of a super yacht. So this was Phantom. A boat big enough to house hundreds of people.

"He said he expects you there in fifteen minutes." The girl took a step back as I stood and tossed the cushion onto the chair. She gulped, keeping her eyes on mine, forcing her chin high to avoid my nakedness.

If she wasn't so nervous, I would've smiled.

All this time, I'd been the scared one, the one holding her breath whenever Alrik walked into the room, the one cowering in submission when he decided I overstepped my bounds. Here, in Elder's world, there was innocence still. Innocence enough to turn bare skin into an uncomfortable situation for his well-trained staff.

Power that I'd done my best to cling to sprang to life.

Beneath my bruises and memories, I was still Tasmin. Still a girl who wanted to go home and hug her mother. Yet as I strode to the walk-in wardrobe and selected a black shift that tumbled over my head in a whisper of finery, I feared I teetered on a very unstable edge.

My vulnerability was twisting, changing. After two years of being someone else's toy, the same evil I'd been hurt with had infected me. I was no longer soft or hopeful but hard and cynical.

If Elder wanted me, I couldn't do anything to stop him. I just didn't know if I would be able to remain the girl I'd been or if I'd evolve into a complete stranger when he did.

Pimlico

"I'M IMPRESSED. YOU found me." Elder cocked his head, holding a small glass of clear liquid. If I hadn't watched him at Alrik's and noticed he refused every drop of liquor, I might've thought it was vodka. Armed with the tiny piece I already knew of him, I suspected it was just water.

His black eyes slid over me with a lethal calm. "I see I'll have to order dresses a few sizes smaller."

I didn't stroke the black cotton encasing my body like a normal girl being inspected might. I'd had that stupidity beaten out of me. I stood military still, accepting his assessment. I didn't let him know that I liked how big it was, how loose and floaty. The black straps barely clung to my shoulders as if apologetic to touch me while the size allowed air to provide a buffer between my skin and the material.

"You can come closer, you know." Elder placed his glass on the wooden table.

My fingers fluttered over the small map of his home. I'd taken a few wrong turns down luxurious corridors and peeked into opulent drawing rooms and suites, but I'd made it in time.

Taking a small step toward him, I glanced at the decadent spread of fresh grapes, watermelon slices, and crisp green apples on a platter in the centre. Everything about this was the opposite of my previous world.

Walking had been tiring due to my healing body, but I wasn't riddled with pain. The carpet beneath my toes was thick and springy, keeping me warm rather than padding on cool marble tiles. If I were made to kneel in this place, at least my bones wouldn't splinter when the order came.

He stood as I neared the table. I didn't look away as he reached forward and plucked the map from my grip. My heart hissed like an adder as I tracked his large palm, hating that I tensed for a hit and was almost confused when it didn't come. He just placed the map on the table and pulled out a chair for me.

I didn't trust him.

I didn't trust his calmness because I tasted the things he kept hidden. I remained stiff as I slipped into the offered seat, resting my hands on my lap.

Wordlessly, Elder moved back to his chair at the head of the table. He'd positioned me next to him. The rest of the long table was merely a runway for food, not offering any space between us.

Catching my gaze, he frowned.

What was this? A game before the true fun began?

A door slid open from behind me as two staff members entered and placed a bowl of green soup in front of us. Nodding respectfully, the head waiter said, "Tonight, your entrée is cold pea and cucumber soup with saffron butter. Please, enjoy."

Bowing, the staff retreated, leaving Elder and me to stare silently at each other.

Neither of us reached for a spoon, not prepared to be the one who looked away first. Slowly, Elder reached for his glass, raising the glittering crystal to take a sip. His powerful neck rippled as he swallowed then cocked his head, studying me harder.

"Something's different about you."

I stilled.

Was I not permitted to change?

I didn't even understand what *had* changed. I just felt...off. Not myself. If I couldn't describe it, how could Elder already see it?

Depositing his glass, he rubbed his jaw. The five o'clock shadow was darker, as if he hadn't shaved since the day we met over a week ago. "Are you okay? Minus the injuries and your tongue, of course?"

I picked up my spoon.

"I don't understand it..." He trailed off, copying me as he pinched the delicate silver utensil. "But when you look at me, something's disappeared."

Disappeared?

Was that what'd happened? Had my dependency on being abused been deleted? Had my fear vanished?

No, the fear's still there.

I checked inside for the remnants of the girl who'd been a pet, a possession. I still struggled, but Elder made me brave enough to look *at* him rather than avoid him.

The fact he let me get away with it encouraged me to be bolder, brazen. Was that what was happening? Had I finally had enough of merely existing and begun the process to claim myself again?

A headache looped around my temples, squeezing with heavy questions.

I don't know anything anymore.
I'm tired.
I'm lost.
I'm alone.
Even No One can't help me figure this out.

Angry tears once again tickled my spine. I spindled tighter, a shrapnel detonation just looking for an outlet to explode.

I need...help.
I need time.
I need...

I didn't know what I needed. But it wasn't him. It wasn't this life. It wasn't even kindness anymore.

I'm past that.
I'm screwed up.
I'm angry. So damn angry.
I wanted to take that anger out on someone. I wanted to rip and tear and *scream* at what I'd endured and what I'd become.

My breathing escalated until my lungs burned and my entire body trembled. My spoon hovered over the soup (soup I didn't want because it would add yet more pain), doing my best to stuff down the overwhelming insanity brewing like lava in my blood.

I need to leave.
I need to be alone before I snap.

Gulping back the tsunami of messy rage, I clamped down on my shaking and waited for him to say something—*anything*—to distract me from my rapidly twitching madness.

But he didn't.

He merely watched me with that deadly poise—noticing my shaking, my breathing—most likely seeing the fire incinerating my brokenness inside.

"Take it easy. Nothing can hurt you here."

Wrong!

My eyes shot to his as the lava bubbled and popped.
You can.
And you will.
Stop lying to me.
Tell me what you mean to do with me.
Put me out of my goddamn misery.

Elder stiffened, his body becoming ice-calm. "Whatever you're thinking, it's making you upset. I suggest you stop."

Stop?!
When did that word ever mean anything?
When did Alrik stop?
When did you stop?
When will all of this fucking stop!

A panic attack slithered around my ribcage, waking from

its sleep to torment me. The soul-sucking terror licked its way up my throat, squeezing...*clawing.*

My fingers latched around the spoon. The room etched with darkness as air became a much-needed commodity.

"Pim...stop. Relax."

I couldn't relax. Not now. Not now the itchy panic had multiplied in size and dribbled into my belly as well as my throat.

I flinched as Elder leaned toward me.

I gasped as he narrowed his eyes.

"Talk to me. Tell me what you're dealing with."

My spine shot stiff.

Tell you?
Speak to you?
Why?
You won't understand.
You won't help.

Stampeding tears blurred the world, making him dance and jig.

"Okay, if you're determined not to talk, what do you need? I've given you food and clothing. I've given you a bed and peace. What more do you fucking want from me?"

His roar hacked through my whirlpool of hysteria, dragging me back from the suffocating clouds.

Pointing at my quaking body, he snarled, "You're acting as if this is a torture session. It's not. It's just dinner. Remember those? When people talk over food and answer questions when asked? Fuck, Pim. Stop looking at me as if I'm him. I'm not fucking him. Got it?!"

My gaze turned sniper sharp. Contorted snowflakes filled the holes left by my panic attack.

Excuse me if I'm not comfortable.
Excuse me if I struggle to see only dinner and not a game to play.
Excuse me if I'm not eloquent and your perfect guest!

Elder rolled his eyes. "While we're on the topic of normal behaviour, let's talk about that dress. It's a goddamn sack on you. You need to eat, and I'll buy you better fitting clothes. Just because you were a slave doesn't mean you have to look like one."

Air hissed through my nose. Snowflakes turned to ice picks, dying to stab him over and over again.

How dare you!
My skinniness is abhorrent to you?
Why fucking rescue me then?

Elder continued, his own anger blind to mine. "He might've starved and beaten you, silent one, but I expect you to resemble a woman, not an animal. Next time we're in port, I'll arrange for underwear and other clothing. But in the meantime, I expect you to trust what I goddamn say and stop flinching whenever I raise my arm and *speak* to me. Fucking get over your silence and grow up."

My back locked in revulsion.
I'm an animal now?
My panic attack switched to an erupting volcano of hate.
I'll show you what an animal I am. I won't grow up. I am grown up. I'm older than you'll ever be. And if you try to make me wear underwire and tight lace after a lifetime of scars and bruises, I'll kill you.

My teeth ground together.
You hear me?
You want me to wear tight clothing? You want to destroy me?
No!

Rashness overrode my brain. My hand soared up, yanking off the strap clinging loosely to my shoulder. It slid down and down. My fear-hardened nipple was the only thing keeping the weightless garment from revealing my full breast.

Elder froze, his gaze locking onto the bruised skin. "Christ, what are you doing?"

I bared my teeth.
Being an animal.

"Fuck, you really don't understand, do you?" Smooth as syrup, he leaned forward and plucked the strap from my elbow. His fingernails threatened my paper-thin skin, slipping the strap slowly, ever so slowly, up my arm to rest on the hollow of my neck and shoulder.

His face was obsidian with no sign of light or sanity. "Don't push me. I warned you, Pim. I'm doing my best around you, but if you pull a fucking stunt like that again, I won't be responsible for my actions."

His palm cupped my shoulder, his flesh kissing my flesh. His face came millimetres from mine. "Whatever issues you're going through, don't take them out on me. Otherwise, I'll have to return the favour and take my issues out on you." He chuckled with black undertones. "And if I do that, you'll know the truth about me. You'll know that Alrik was playing make believe while I'm the true villain."

Saliva dried up. My tongue swelled with pain.

For the first time, I believed what he said. For the first time, he didn't hide whatever he battled. He let me look inside him, and I didn't like what I saw.

He wasn't a gentleman. He wasn't refined.

He was chaos and uncultured and dying to be free to invoke whatever calamity he needed to inflict.

No...

Goosebumps scattered as his fingers stroked my shoulder, reminding me he still held me, still owned me. Terror transformed to horror as my eyes flickered from his lips to his gaze.

He didn't move, letting me draw my own conclusions—to read between the lines of what he would never say, but I felt. I *felt* every word, every threat, and it didn't pacify me, it made me want to bolt from the room and throw myself into the sea.

Running his finger under the strap, he bent and kissed my shoulder. He'd touched me before. He'd kissed me before. Yet that simple readjustment of my clothes was more erotic than anything we'd ever done.

"You still want to go to war with me, silent mouse?" Elder leaned back in his chair, making the ornate wood creak with his large bulk.

Don't call me mouse!

"Are you so repulsed by me that you're willing to push me until I push back? Is it so bad to be cared for when the entire time I give you sanctuary, I want to take so much more in return?"

I stopped breathing.

He buffed his fingernails on his t-shirt. "I didn't want to have to be so stern with you, but it seems I don't have a choice."

My sniff made his black eyes sharpen. "All I ask of you is politeness, obedience, and eventually your voice. Three things that won't hurt you or reduce you to something you're not."

I shivered at how easily he delivered his terms. How simple he made them sound when they were some of the hardest requests for me.

"You do that, and I'll be able to keep my distance and treat you kindly. Don't, and you'll regret it."

You're hiding behind obscurity.
Don't threaten with vagueness.
Tell me what you'll do.

Gritting my teeth, I plopped the spoon into the soup and swirled it around. I had no intention of eating. My tongue was a constant reminder of what I'd almost lost by being brave. Elder had made it his mission to heal and cure me. But for what?

It was the not knowing that burrowed like a mole through my mind, bringing dark tunnels of recklessness. Bravery no longer had anything to do with it.

It was a matter of survival.

My previous questions came chugging back on a steam train, railroading me with coal smoke and speed.

What do you want?
Tell me.
Right now.
Tell me you'll sell me. Hurt me. Use me.
Tell me you'll free me.
Tell me what you'll do if I disobey.

Just tell me so I can decide if I want to fight you, obey you, or throw myself off the bow of your ship and end it once and for all.

I wasn't aware my anger had overflowed physically until the spoon shot from my fingers, splashing green goo all over the pristine table.

My shoulders rolled as I hunched for a beating. It would be a good one. I'd never been allowed at the table for this exact reason. I wasn't worthy of human tools because I was too dim-witted and merely an animal to be used when it suited its owner.

He called me an animal.

Whatever attraction or pride I thought I'd seen in his gaze was gone now we'd finally been honest.

Elder didn't move.

The gentle rustle of his black t-shirt was the only noise as he breathed deep and evenly, never taking his eyes off me. "What were you thinking about to warrant wasting your food? Food, I may add, that should be in your stomach to replace everything you've lost from being with him."

I dared to look up, staring, *staring* at the mess I'd made.

I couldn't make myself care what would come next. I couldn't bring myself to bow in apology or beg in forgiveness. The anger that I'd kept locked up so damn tight for years poured from the vault where I'd banished it. The foreign tightness—the strange daredevil baring its teeth inside me—it all embraced me as if to say *'please never forget again.'*

Never let yourself merely exist.

Fight.

Or die.

No more surviving.

No more accepting.

My fingers dug into my palm as my fists squeezed—even my broken hand did its best to curl with rage at how long I'd lived in hell and how much I hated myself for letting it continue.

Why didn't I kill myself sooner? Why didn't I kill *him*

sooner?

Because he took every option away!
You tried, remember?

Time already clouded the past, making it seem like I had other options than the truth. It shattered me because it made me even weaker when I'd believed I'd been so strong.

There was nothing you could do.
But now, now it is *different, and you will* not *bow to another.*
Not again.

If Elder expected me to serve him, fuck him, and be at his beck and call. I would jump overboard tonight. Not because I had nothing left to give but because I was finally brave enough to say *no*.

Even if it meant saying no to any more tomorrows or yesterdays.

No more!

Elder murmured, "What's going on inside that mind of yours?"

I snarled.

He stiffened. "You look as if you want to go back and kill him all over again." He cocked his head, inspecting my every inhale, exhale, and twitch. "Are you angry that I came back for you? Do you wish I hadn't, so you could've ended your life, rather than face something new?"

You don't know me.
Get out of my damn head!

"So that's what this is about. You're angry."

I wanted to tear out his eyes at how condescending he made it sound. I was more than just angry. I was rage itself. I was the harbinger of vehemence.

You think you can scare and belittle me?
Wrong.
I'm done with these parlour tricks.

He smiled coldly, no kindness left in his face. "Anger is expected after what you've lived through." He leaned forward, whip sharp and brutal. "But if you think for one fucking moment you can take it out on me, you'll be severely disappointed."

My chest rose and fell as I breathed harder than I had in years. My bruised ribs bleated with agony.

"If I didn't recognise that fire in your gaze, I would think you missed that godforsaken hellhole."

I froze.

You think I liked being beaten?
You think I enjoyed being a slave?

Elder pushed his fork with his index finger, sedate and sly. "You knew the rules there. You knew everything there was to know about the bastard who called himself Master. You knew what to expect and when."

His black eyes locked me against the hard chair. "You miss predictability even if that predictability would've killed you, either by his hand or yours."

Silence fell, littered with secrets.

He didn't speak for a few seconds. Running his hand through thick blue-black hair, he whispered, "You pulled the trigger. I watched you take his life happily. You threw off those invisible chains even while you bled out from the wound he inflicted." His voice dropped to a murmur, "But that wasn't the moment you ended predictability, Pimlico. You did that before becoming a murderer."

I sucked in a breath as he stroked his lips with feather-soft fingers. "You did that the moment you kissed me back."

My tongue twinged as I swallowed hard.

"You changed your future the moment you let me into your bed."

I didn't let you.
I had no choice.

Licking his bottom lip, Elder smiled coldly. "I feel you trying to read me, silent mouse. I feel you probing me, watching me; don't think I don't. You want—no, you *need*—to know what I'm going to do to you. Your questions are so fucking loud they're making me deaf."

Standing, he pushed away from the table and paced, looking between me and the spilled soup. "But you won't learn who I am until you give me what *I* want in return."

Determination suddenly etched his face as he stalked toward a sideboard holding a massive candelabra with eight tapered candles and wrenched open a drawer.

Two seconds later, he slammed down a matching notepad and pen. Pushing aside my bowl, he stabbed his fingers at the fresh paper. "Speak to me."

I cringed but didn't hunch. I couldn't keep track of my thoughts. Yesterday, I'd drowned in gratefulness for what he'd done for me. Today, I suffocated in suspicion of his true agenda. And anger. So. Much. Anger. Rage licked me faster and faster, turning my thoughts to ash.

"Talk to me, Pimlico. That's the least you owe me for what I've done for you."

Done for me?
What are you going to do to me?
Let's talk about that!

My fingers itched for the pen but not to speak to him. To speak to No One. To ask my unknown, unseen friend what I should make of this new prison and master. Should I run? Should I kill? Should I do neither and submit instead?

The longer Elder kept me wrapped in safety, building my debt to him with every breath, the more I spiralled out of control. I'd lived with such fierce unbreakable boundaries for too long. I knew how to survive Alrik. I knew how to read him. I knew how to prepare for punishment. And I knew how to glue back my shattered pieces afterward. That was it. I didn't know how to endure anyone else.

And why should I have to persevere with another?

I didn't know how to be Pimlico in this new world. I had no idea who I'd end up becoming. How could I be something Elder wanted when I had no idea what that was?

Then don't be Pim.
Be someone else.

But who?

I needed to become someone who could outlast, outsmart Elder Prest.

But I don't know who he is!

Trembling began again. Swift and severe.

My body betrayed me as more and more confusion plaited with anger. I hated that I had a psychical reaction to Elder as he loomed over me, his hot breath fluttering my eyelashes, his demands crushing me.

"Write what it is that you want." He took the pen, ripped the lid off, and grabbed my hand.

I didn't flinch as he inserted the cool plastic between my fingers, making me grip it. "Write what you're thinking. Write one fucking word, and that will be good enough for now."

He stepped back.

I held the pen, but I didn't attempt to obey.

Words flew from my head. Spelling no longer part of my education. The trembling grew and grew until my teeth chattered and bumped against my swollen tongue. The unfinished panic attack howled with fresh freedom.

I flinched as pain hit from sharp incisors followed by the faint taste of blood.

"Christ," Elder hissed. "I'm not going to hurt you. How many times do I need to tell you that?"

That's a lie.

You just admitted it!

I threw the pen down, steeling myself to look up at him. My teeth clamped again on my swollen tongue by accident. My gag reflex reacted as another wash of metallic made me grimace. A small trickle of blood escaped my cracked lips, staining my chin and splashing in accusation on the notepad.

He inhaled sharply, staring at the bright red droplet.

He wanted a reply?

He'd earned a reply.

In blood.

"Stand," he barked.

I obeyed, pushing my chair back a little. Having his wrath finally unleashed was…not comforting but known.

This is what I'm used to.

I could handle his anger because I could predict what came next and could turn off my mind. Self-preservation kicked in, and soon, I'd be free. Soon, my soul would clamp down and vanish deep inside.

Thank God.

It was the thinking that was making me change.

The free time and questions making me worry.

This…I knew this.

Elder bristled, his hands curling into fists. "You think bleeding in my presence is appropriate? I've done all I can to *stop* you bleeding. Is that a slap in my fucking face, saying I'm not doing enough?" He prowled forward, his chest almost touching mine.

I sighed heavily as I gave into his power.

Down and down I swirled, blank safety beckoning.

I hated that I accepted his rage so much more easily than I ever could his kindness. That I went searching for his animosity because I would never trust his calmness.

Not looking up, I kept my eyes respectfully on his shoes. With my unbroken hand, I pushed off the black shoulder strap, followed by the other, and let the dress slither over my body until I stood naked before him.

The room howled with masculine rage as Elder whipped upright and took a staggering step back. "What the fuck are you doing?"

What I've been taught.

My mind had retreated to where it couldn't be touched. Hidden and protected, finally at peace after chasing its own tail with endless questions.

My body was in charge now, and my body was a creature of habit.

Falling to my stiff and gristly knees, I bowed at his feet. He'd stolen me.

He might as well start using me the way he intended. It was better for both of us to know our places so I could return to the shell I'd made my home.

I thought I was strong enough to return to the real world. I thought I wasn't broken enough that if I ever found freedom I could walk from the shadows and laugh and speak and love like any normal person.

But I knew the truth now.

Elder's strange care had made me come to terms with something I never believed was possible. I *was* broken. All my inner speeches of being so strong and merely biding my time.

They were fiction.

I'm a liar.

My head bowed harder, my hair spilling over my shoulder.

And still, Elder didn't move.

The door opened behind me, footsteps shuffling with the aromatic scents of the second course.

Everything exploded.

"Get the fuck out!" Elder bellowed.

A plate smashed to the floor, followed by the thud of a rolling baked potato. Muttered apologies fell then the door clanged shut and silence once again reigned.

Elder took a step closer to me, his black boot nudging my naked knee.

I didn't shrivel or back away. My mind had flown free, leaving whatever remained at his mercy.

I didn't care.

His joints didn't make a sound as he slid to his haunches and grabbed my chin. "Under no circumstances are you to do that again, do you hear me?"

I looked blankly past him.

He shook me. "Pay attention. Don't disappear on me. Don't treat me like that bastard. Don't make me become something I've fought so fucking long to avoid. I won't slip. Not for you. Not for anyone." His fingers dug into my cheeks. "As much as you expect me to and as gratifying as it would be,

I said I wouldn't hurt you. And I meant it."

Words were cheap.

I knew how lies worked.

With a heavy growl, Elder stood.

My stomach muscles clenched, waiting for his kick but nothing came. Instead, he scooped me into his arms and picked me up just like the day he'd carried me bleeding and mostly dead from the white mansion.

Kicking open the dining room door, he stalked through the boat, taking the stairs rather than waiting for the lift and carrying me gruffly back to my room.

Every step was a full stop to the confusing conversation we'd shared. Every breath was a bracket around the truths we'd revealed and then smothered just as fast with falsehoods.

I didn't know what was real anymore: what threat was truth and what truth was a lie.

The moment we were behind closed doors, Elder shoved me on the bed and paced away, jerking both hands over his face. "Goddammit, I don't know what the fuck I'm doing."

I lay there, naked and waiting, knowing enough not to move.

He continued pacing, muttering to himself. Finally, he prowled back. His large hands landed on my hips, dragging my body to the edge of the bed where he wedged his jean clad legs between mine. "*This* is what you want? To be fucked against your will? To be used against your permission?"

His fingers left bruises. It was nothing new.

"Tell me why? Why do you want pain when I want to give you safety? When I'm doing my damn fucking hardest to be a better man—to protect you from myself just like I protected you from him."

I barely heard the question in my protective bubble.

I didn't blink or swallow, merely stared back unaffected.

"You know what I think, Pimlico?" He used my name as if it was a witch's curse. "I think you're lost. For the first time, you have permission to rest and relax with no threat of agony on the horizon. You finally remember how life should be, and it fucking terrifies you how much you want it."

He squeezed me harder. "And when your mind started to accept that—that, yes you deserve this and, yes, this is how it could be from now on—you became fucking petrified." He bowed over me, wedging his hot, hard muscle on top of my breakable body.

He didn't hide the erection in his jeans, pressing it against me unashamedly. "You're weak. For all the strength I saw in you, all the power and unbreakable courage, you let questions strip that away. You let the unknown steal who you truly are, and you've slipped back into the only role you know. I fucking pity you."

His lips trailed over my cheekbone, his tongue tracing the shell of my ear. "I could fuck you right now. I could kiss you, hit you, string you up, and do all manner of disgusting things to you, and you wouldn't fight me. Hell, you expect me to do it, and that's what's so bloody sick about this. I gave you my word that I wouldn't touch you, and you didn't listen."

His hips rocked, pressing against me.

It didn't feel good or bad. It was just pressure. Pressure I'd long since grown used to while I curled into a nonreachable ball inside myself.

"Not only did you not listen but you didn't believe, and I have a good mind to do exactly what you expect. I want to fuck you." His hips thrust again. "I want to hurt you." His teeth nipped at my ear. "Because then you might stop looking for the worst."

His heat made my skin prickle with sweat.

I couldn't breathe with his weight, but I wouldn't shift or beg. If he wanted to smother me, then that was one of the easier ways to welcome death. A kind way to go compared to so many others.

But then he was gone, folding off me, rearranging the steelness in his trousers.

"But that would be too easy. You think you can control

me? Get me to do something I would never do? Become someone I've fought all my life never to be again? Well, fuck you. Fuck you and whatever conditioning that's ruined you."

Striding to the door, he jerked a hand down his t-shirt as if preparing himself to enter a room full of well-dressed diplomats. "Until you have the balls to accept that I won't lay a finger on you; until you've addressed what that cunt did to you, you won't see me again. I don't have time for broken things; especially slaves who I believed were so much stronger than what they turned out to be."

He turned and strode out the door without another look.

Silence fell like a guillotine as he slammed the wood into place.

For a second, I didn't breathe. I remained locked inside and safe, able to ignore the smarting agony of what had just happened. Of the degradation of what I'd become, the shame of what I was, and the guilt that I wasn't as good as I thought.

And then rage came again, hurling me from my bubble, dragging me back into liveliness.

For so long, I'd tempered my anger so it curled around me but never exploded. There was nowhere for it to explode, no sobs I could shed, no screams I could utter.

But here, as I lay naked and vulnerable with far too many wounds and far too little strength to rebuild myself, I let loose.

I lost it.

It wasn't sweet, obedient Tasmin who shot to her feet and snarled at the finery. It wasn't timid, broken Pimlico whose claws latched onto the decorative cream silk from the ceiling and yanked.

It wasn't me (whoever that was) as I hurled off the bed and threw cushions and pushed over chairs and smashed sea life figurines.

I let two years' worth of tears spew forth.

I hiccupped and howled and gagged as my tongue pounded in agony.

I lost myself.

And I no longer cared if I ever found my way back.

ELDER

WHAT THE FUCK am I doing?

The question had run a track inside my mind for the past two days.

I should just pull up to shore, drop her off with a lump of cash, some clothes (which she would probably refuse to wear), and say good fucking riddance.

I didn't have time for this. I didn't have the luxury of going down a path that had taken me so long to run away from.

I had my own issues to deal with let alone shoulder hers.

Did you expect her to snap out of it the moment she was yours?

If I was honest, yes that was exactly what I bloody expected. I envisioned myself as the saviour and her smiling in gratitude and finally opening that bruised little mouth to say *'Thank you, Elder, for saving my life. What would you like to know about me? I'm an open book for you, read my pages, pry away.'*

I dragged my hands through my hair, digging my elbows into the desk.

Nothing was going according to plan. And seeing her struggle only made me realise how much *I* fucking struggled. How much I shut down and pretended I had everything I wanted—that my business kept me whole, that I wanted for nothing more than wealth, my boat, and the sea.

It was all a bloody lie.

I smothered myself with rules and trickery to prevent the addiction inside me from taking claim. She'd made me snap and admit some of my darkest truths at dinner.

That wasn't how it was supposed to go.

I was supposed to crack her, not the other way around.

Fucking woman.

Even in her despair, she had the bravery to show me just how much I confused her.

Lying in bed after throwing her back in her room that night, sleep had refused to come. I recalled every word she'd written to No One, doing my best to put myself in her shoes and figure out how I would've coped.

The thought of someone physically and mentally abusing me was too abhorrent; I couldn't fully comprehend what it would be like to live with such a monster. I'd done my fair share of hardship, but it had been my own doing, not from some corrupt bastard who thought he could own another.

Old memories sprung up, threatening to drag me under.

Digging my fingers into my skull, I held on.

Don't fucking—

Too late.

I couldn't stop the memory from stealing me, hurtling me back to a time I couldn't run from—eighteen years ago where it all ended and begun.

My mother cried.

She'd been crying every night for four months. And because her tears were my fault, my heart drowned with every salty droplet. The shame wasn't new. Guilt wasn't, either. But I hadn't meant to do what I did. If I could rewind time and fix the catastrophe I caused, I would.

But I accepted my punishment: her disappointment in me, our removal from our home...I bowed beneath the penance because she needed me to suffer. She needed to know I felt the weight of my actions and accepted that I'd been the reason for everything.

And I did.

Crap, how I did.

"Okaasan...please." Glancing around the dirty alley we'd stumbled

upon three nights ago, I ensured we were alone before dropping to my haunches beside her. "I'll make it right. I promise."

She tore her body away as I placed my palm on her shoulder. Her rebuttal of my affection cut me but not as much as it had at the beginning.

Our first night on the streets had been the worst in my entire thirteen years. I missed my room, my cello, my comfortable, if not rich life. But it was all gone now. My brother was gone. My father. Our house.

The only thing I'd been able to save besides myself was my mother, who cursed the very ground I walked upon.

"How can you make it right? We have nothing! No one will take us in. We're alone." Her sobs crushed me deeper into the dirty concrete where I'd laid a few cabbage-stained cardboard boxes from the dumpster behind us.

"I'll get a job. Someone will hire me. We'll have a home again." I swiped at a piece of torn newspaper as it blew down the wind tunnel that was our accommodation for the night.

New York was not a kind innkeeper to those who found sanctuary on her streets—especially in fall. The leaves had switched from green to rust, and it was only a matter of time before the frigid mornings became frost and snow.

I have to fix this before then.

My mother cried harder into the crook of her elbow. Her black hair glistened in the faint lights of the cheery apartments above us. Craning my neck, I looked up the sides of the buildings we sat between, watching shadows of people cooking dinner and laughing with loved ones.

My stomach growled, tearing through the silence with empty ferocity. We hadn't found decent food since yesterday morning.

What I'd done...it was unforgivable.

Overwhelming hatred for myself swirled with humiliation, thicker and thicker as my mother sobbed beside me. Her pretty blouse and jeans were now grubby and tattered. Her closet full of patterned kimonos and my father's freshly ironed suits turned to ash and rubble.

My fingers flew over the newspaper I'd snatched from the wind. Folding it into a square, I tore off the ragged ends and set about transforming the crumpled inked page into something better.

As my mother cried herself into a catatonic coma like she did every night, I sat silently, turning rubbish into origami. My fingers shook as I smoothed the petals of a blooming rose before slipping it gently into my mother's balled hands.

Wrapping her in a hug, I vowed, "I will fix this. I don't care that I'm too young to get a job. I'll find money and a way to fix what I've done."

My mother sucked in a shaky breath, not believing me but accepting my origami rose as a peace token. Her head rested on my shoulder as her tears slowly dried.

She didn't speak, but she didn't need to. Her doubt, disappointment, and despondency spoke loudly.

She didn't believe me.

I didn't believe me.

What could I do? A stupid boy trained in cello and origami?

As the moon crept over the sky and the temperature plummeted until our breaths became ghosts in the night and cardboard boxes became useless blankets, I stared at the talented hands that'd given me nothing but grief.

I'd been proud of my hands—of the skill they wielded. Now, I wanted nothing more than to cut them off.

But…

Wait.

Holding two palms and ten digits in the New York City gloom, a plan began to form.

I could strum a cord before I could run. I could curl the finest crease of paper before I could write. If I had such agility in my fingers…perhaps they could learn another trade?

A better trade?

One that would ensure our survival and drag us back to where we belonged.

I'd brought badness into our life. It was time to become bad to free ourselves from it. I wouldn't be a useless brat who only thought of himself.

No.

I'd be a pickpocket.

A thief.

And I'd steal every damn thing from every damn person to ensure my family forgave me.

I shuddered as the memory finally let me go. Cold sweat drenched my spine.

When my life had changed, giving me food instead of starvation and tailored clothes instead of tatty dumpster rags, I'd thought I'd be forgiven. That I'd erase the shame I'd brought on our name and be welcomed back.

I wasn't.

I wasn't just shunned—I was given the worst kind of punishment. I was called a ghost. Doomed to be familyless and disowned for the rest of my days.

I'd become lost, just like Pimlico.

And I turned to the only thing that had saved me—accepted me.

Crime.

Petty theft turned to illegal enterprises, and no matter how I tried to untangle myself, I only sank deeper into the sticky webs, crawling further into the underworld.

Each dark step I took ensured I was one step closer to my ultimate goal.

And where I was going, there was no room for a mute prisoner no matter how much she toyed with my emotions.

Stop thinking about her.

The command echoed in my skull, heard but utterly ignored.

Closing my laptop, I stood and massaged my nape. I needed a good session with Selix in the ship's ring or a long swim in the ocean. Then, whatever thoughts about Pimlico would vanish, and I could refocus on who I was and what the fuck I was trying to do with my life.

Striding from my office, I undid my shirt as I went. It wasn't far to the bridge and at this time of the evening, Jolfer, the captain, would've signed off, and Martin would be in charge.

He was a safe navigator and obedient.

I wasn't in the mood for a martial art fight with Selix, but fuck me, I needed a swim.

Heading over the expanse of deck, I peered at the stars above in velvet black. Only the flaming galaxy lit up this place. No city lights, no houses, no cars.

Just the Phantom and her pretty windows dancing on the calm tide.

Yanking open the door, I strolled in and immediately spotted the man I needed. "Martin, stop all engines. Hold position."

Martin was older than Jolfer and his snow-white hair was almost as bright as the stars. Even at sixty, his face was barely lined; somehow avoiding the crags and furrows that a life spent in salt and sun tended to cause.

"How long for this time, sir?" Martin asked, already pressing buttons and radioing down to the engine room to reverse direction and hold.

"Two hours. I don't want to rush."

"No problem. Take all the time you need." He smiled, knowing exactly what I was about to do. All the crew knew because their boss liked to go swimming at odd times and strange places.

Middle of the Pacific? Sure, why fucking not.

An hour before sunrise when the world still slept? Shit, yes.

I'd swum with humpbacks, dolphins, even a whale shark or two. I wasn't afraid. I'd hover on my back, cradled by seawater, and watch the sun blink awake.

That was the beauty of sailing.

"I'll visit again once I'm done." I turned to leave.

"No need, sir. I'll send up a lackey to make sure you're safely onboard. It's too deep, so we won't set anchor but will hold position with the engines."

I understood what he was telling me. "I won't go to the back. I'll use the side ladders and avoid any chance of a riptide caused by the propellers."

Martin chuckled. "I know you know that, sir, but it's force of habit to warn, I'm afraid."

I threw him a tight smile. "Nice to know you take your job and my life seriously." I headed back outside and didn't bother going back to my quarters to change.

My black boxer-briefs would do. After all, in the pitch black yonder, who was there to see me?

Walking to the side of the vessel with its thirteen floors to the unforgiving blue glass below, I unbuckled my belt, kicked off my shoes, and tore off my shirt.

The moment I was free from human costume, I opened the railing and dove off the side.

Pimlico

YESTERDAY WAS BRUTAL.

Once I let go—once I allowed my soul to take over and weep for everything I'd been through, I couldn't stop.

All night, I sobbed.

All day, I wept.

And by the time the sun rose and then set again, my face ached, my tongue throbbed, and my head howled with dehydration.

Staff members had tried to get me to eat, ignoring my naked form sitting on the floor amongst a destroyed suite to ply me with cake and feel-good food.

I didn't want a single crumb.

Feathers from the pillows fluttered around the space thanks to the sea breeze. Curtains hung haphazardly on their rails, side tables rattled on their sides as the boat rode gentle waves.

I hadn't been able to flip over most of the larger furniture—bolted in place for high seas or hungry storms—but the soft furnishings hadn't escaped my wrath.

I knew I was only harming myself by exuding so much energy in tears and refusing to eat or drink. But I *needed* to hurt myself. For the first time, *I* was the one in charge of the pain and the discomfort suffocating me.

I took ownership of that. *I* controlled that. It was liberating to be the brute for a change, even if it was me, myself, and I who I hurt.

Exactly forty-eight hours after Elder had left me, the only other male I was allowed contact with entered my annihilated room.

His kind eyes widened, taking in the destruction before pressing his lips together and crossing the space to the bed where I huddled beneath a salvaged sheet.

"Hello."

I squeezed my eyes, knowing exactly why he was here and ready, but not quite ready, to accept his help.

"I hear you've had a rough couple of days." Standing close, he rubbed the mattress beside me. "May I?"

I didn't open my eyes or give him permission, but he sat anyway, carefully keeping his body from touching mine. "Do you want to talk about it?"

Such a simple question but loaded with far too much. My gaze flew wide even as my tongue stung from where I'd bitten it by accident two nights ago. Even if I did want to talk to someone, to remember what it was like to hold a conversation and purge this filth inside me, I couldn't.

Not yet.

Not until my tongue was knitted back together.

Dr. Michaels nodded in understanding. Looking at the tumbled bedside table and the scattered items on the floor, he pointed at the notepad and pen strewn haphazardly. "I meant, do you want to write it down? We can discuss it that way?"

I merely stared.

He cleared his throat after an uncomfortable minute. "Okay, we'll leave therapy for another day, how about that?"

Therapy?

I wrinkled my nose. Was that what he thought I needed? Was I mentally ill? A basket case who needed rehab from life?

Wouldn't my mother love that?

She'd jump at the chance to be my psychologist. The more

screwed up her patients, the better.

He held up his hands. "Wrong word. Sorry, professional habit. You don't need therapy in the normal sense. But I do think you need to talk to someone. You've been alone for so long—or at least I think you were alone." His face whitened. "Were there others? Did Mr. Prest save more than just you?"

His questions fell on appreciative ears that he was willing to chit-chat, but I had no interest in replying. I hadn't even had the energy to write to No One during my crying purge. The thought of others living what I had hollowed me with grief. I rolled over, tucking the sheet tighter against me.

What happened to the girls I was sold with at the Quarterly Market of Beauties? Were they still alive or mostly dead by now?

"Okay, I know when a social call isn't wanted." Michaels rubbed his thighs. "However, before I go, I must ask you to sit up. I need to inspect your tongue and discuss a few other medical issues."

I looked over my shoulder. Now I'd stopped crying, all I wanted to do was sleep. Sleep for decades and wake up a better person, a saner person, and someone who had no aversion to speech so she could blurt out her story and move on.

"Please?" The doctor motioned for me to sit, even grabbed a pillow from the floor (only half unstuffed), and fluffed it against the ruined bedhead. "If you don't mind, we'll get it done as quickly as possible."

Not wanting to disappoint him, I slid upright and settled against the pillow. The sheet fell around my waist. I didn't think anything of it.

Michael's gaze flickered to my chest for the barest of seconds. He cleared his throat then resolutely locked eyes with me. Any sign of a normal hot-blooded man vanished under the authoritative presence of a doctor who had seen patients in all stages of undress.

"May I?" He scooted closer, hoisting a bag I hadn't noticed onto the bed beside him.

I didn't nod, but he must've seen approval in my eyes because he reached forward, running his hands over the glands in my neck and gently prying my mouth open.

I allowed it, holding my breath as he inspected my stitched tongue.

I watched his face carefully, wanting to catch any worry or concern he might have on the status of my healing.

His face tensed.

I stiffened in response.

"You have a cut on the left. Did you bite yourself while eating?"

If there was a time when I should start answering questions, it should be now, but my body language remained silent.

He let me go, grabbed a pair of rubber gloves, and put them on. Once hygienic, he gently opened my jaw again and touched my tongue, running expert fingers over the hack job Alrik had done, and hopefully, the stitch job that would ensure it would be as if it'd never happened.

"The swelling has gone down but not as fast as I hoped." Michaels drew back, his face softening. "Not coping is understandable after everything you've been through, and it's best to get it out. I'm glad you gave yourself time to do that. If you want help sleeping, I can prescribe you something, and if you have intolerable pain, I can help with that too. However, what I can't help with, and it's entirely on you, is how fast you wish to recover by eating well and resting often."

A fatherly scowl illustrated his face. "You need to eat if you're to regain your strength." His eyes tracked to my belly, ignoring my naked breasts. Black and purple painted my skin; bruises disappearing under the bandage still wrapped around my ribs. "You're underweight, undernourished. To put it frankly, you're dying."

I froze solid.

To hanker after death was one thing. To be told it was creeping over me without permission was entirely another.

"I didn't mean it like that." He tried to soothe. "I meant, you're in a bad way and need to help yourself. I can only do so much. It's up to you to decide if you want to stick around. And if that decision is yes, then you need to start taking better care of yourself."

I swallowed, tasting the faint rubber of his gloves.

But what if I don't know what I want? What if I'm still afraid that if I accept life, Elder will steal it from me in some other way?

Michaels didn't wait for me to answer him. He took my broken hand, inspecting the plastic splint and bandage, making sure it was still secure. "Now you're coherent and not in a hospital bed straight out of surgery, I'm going to be honest with you. Do you think you can handle that?"

A huge exhale exploded from me.

Truth.

Honesty.

Yes, I want that.

I need that.

It was frank truth I was missing. Wrapped up and given my own space with no rules or expectations wasn't good for me.

"That's what you want? No matter if it's scary? You want the truth?"

Do I do it?

Yes, that question was worthy of breaking my silent oath.

I nodded just briefly.

Michaels beamed. "Okay, now we're getting somewhere." His face fell a second later. "Not that I should be happy to tell you bad news, of course."

Bad news?

What bad news?

I shuffled forward, clutching the sheet in my lap.

He sighed. "I'm going to be frank and not sugar-coat it, okay?"

What the hell? I'd nodded once. Another wouldn't hurt.

I tilted my chin down then up.

"All right then." He rubbed the back of his neck. "Your body has been through a lot. I don't need to tell you that. Even with you eating and resting like you should be—" he gave me a commanding glare —"you'd still have months' of recovery before you're on the mend." He pointed at my mouth. "Realistically, your tongue is the least of your worries. That will heal as long as you keep it clean and don't bite it again. Your hand will heal now it's bound, and your ribs will be fine as long as you don't ransack your room every night."

His head turned to survey the damage but didn't make a comment on the mess. "What won't heal quickly are the injuries you never had tended to. Older broken bones that mended but incorrectly. Your feet, your fingers, your leg. The bumps and abnormalities will only become more troublesome as you get older."

I swallowed again, feeling smaller and smaller, more and more fragile.

"Some of your teeth are loose from being struck. Your blood-work shows a few vitamin deficiencies. You need your eyesight tested along with many other examinations to ensure you'll be okay."

He patted my knee almost subconsciously over the sheet. "The body is a miraculous thing, and if you give it time and patience and the tools in order to knit itself back together, it will. Even with the other things I've mentioned. If you agree to let a dentist look at your teeth, and an optometrist to ensure your eyes are good, even a neurologist to check your nerves and brain function, then any future complications can be managed."

Silence fell.

Somehow, I knew that wasn't the end of the lecture. Slowly, because I knew it made him uncomfortable, I raised the sheet, covering my breasts and tucking it under my arms.

He gave me a half smile. "You don't have to do that. I've seen enough human forms not to be embarrassed. Although, you've just proven your biggest injury to overcome."

I waited for the awful verdict. A verdict I'd already realised after turning into mayhem and demolishing the lovely suite Elder had given me.

"Your mind," Michaels murmured. "Your mind is going to be...messed up for a while."

Tears clawed the back of my eyes as someone finally acknowledged what I feared. It shouldn't make me so relieved to have confirmation that I was going mad. Having him understand...God, it was as if I had permission to give into the psychotic breaking inside. That I could somehow swim to the other side and still be whole when I got there.

Michaels held out his hand, palm up, as an offering of support.

The urge to take it—to have someone squeeze me in comfort rather than in pain—was overwhelming. But I didn't reach out. I hugged my sheet and myself, drawing comfort from my body the way I'd done for so long.

He nodded, linking his unwanted hand with his other. "I understand why you trashed your room. I understand why you haven't eaten. I'm not saying I've ever been in your situation, but I've done papers on how the mind works and want to tell you whatever you're feeling...the explosive anger, the deplorable rage, the unexpected grief, even the hopelessness and looking for a way out, let me tell you...it *is* normal. You're allowed to be topsy-turvy. You've been through hell, and your brain is only now coming out of protection mode and starting to sort through the past, try to make sense of your present, and figure out if it should be afraid of your future."

Yes. Exactly.

The tears I fought won.

They spilled over my cheeks, stinging a little from old salt tracks from crying all night. To be told I wasn't going insane—that I was allowed to feel this way...it helped. So much. Even though I'd known everything he'd said. I'd studied such conditions. I was a textbook case for people suffering an emotional breakdown.

But he delivered the news in a way I could accept rather

than run from.

Michaels reached into his pocket and handed me a clean tissue. "Let it out. Don't hold it in. I'm glad you gave the decorating team something to do. If it made you feel better, do it again. I'm relieved you cried and let yourself be sad. You should be sad. You should be in mourning. A part of you was stolen, and you might never get that back. But what you will get in return is someone so much stronger than the rest of us. Someone who has lived damnation and survived."

He grinned, almost vicious with conviction. "You, my girl, are a warrior, and even warriors are allowed to be afraid."

My neck bowed, tears splashing onto the sheet despite blotting them with his tissue.

"What you aren't, though, is a girl who can afford not to eat. Okay? You need to give your body time to heal while your mind does, too. Will you promise me you'll try?"

When I didn't look up, he nudged my knee. "Nod for yes. I'm not leaving until you do."

It hurt this time. The third time.

But I obeyed and nodded.

"Good." Standing, he patted my head. It could've been condescending, but in an odd way, the weight of his hand on my scalp was...nice.

Clutching his bag, Michaels added, "There is one more thing."

My jaw came up; my eyes making him fuzzy with tears.

"I know you're afraid of him. That you expect him to be like the others who stole you." He lowered his voice. "But don't judge a man just because he has a past he can't outrun. Don't expect the worst because, by expecting the worst, you're inviting it to come true."

He took a breath, pondering how to phrase his parting wisdom. "You don't need to know what the future holds. No one does. After all, no one can truly know or predict what their next day will include. All you need to know is right now. Can you survive *right now*? Can you survive today? If the answer is yes, then keep going. Who cares what other people's agendas are? You can't control that. You shouldn't weaken yourself by worrying. Accept that you are strong enough to endure the present. The rest doesn't matter."

ELDER

THE OCEAN WAS cool.

The water wet and welcoming.

For an hour, I powered through the gentle swell, circling the Phantom, giving the back end a wide birth. The low hum of the engines keeping her bulk in place added depth to the sea-silence, infiltrating the wave's licks and laps against the hull.

My arms burned, my lungs shredded.

But I didn't let up my pace.

I needed to feel the pain because it kept me centred, kept my thoughts on me rather than on her. Rather than on the manic, debilitating urges I constantly lived with. Urges I'd learned to control but had broken multiple times since I'd brought her aboard my home.

Just this morning, I'd found myself repeating the same thing over and over because I became fixated on an idea. The previous night, I'd returned to the dining room after leaving Pim in her suite, ignoring my unwanted erection by cleaning up the mess of pea soup and baked potato.

The staff had tried to help, but I'd turned them all away. The desire for cleanliness and order overrode my normal ability to let it go.

And it's all her fucking fault.

The reports of what she'd done to her room yesterday made me storm to her quarters. I'd wanted to punish her for bringing pandemonium into my world and force her to fix what she'd damaged. I was half-way there before I'd ordered myself to turn around. If I saw her again—before I got myself under control—it wouldn't end well. Plus, I'd meant what I said. I didn't want to see her again until she stopped watching me as if I was that fucking bastard.

Waiting for me to strike her.

Expecting me to kick and fuck her.

The fact she wasn't wondering *if* I would but *when* fucking gutted me. I was many things. I wouldn't deny I had impure urges when it came to her, but I would never hurt her as bad as that motherfucker did.

My intentions were…different.

Slowing my stroke, I rolled onto my back and let the ocean cradle me. The engine hum echoed underwater louder than in the sky. A shooting star blazed overhead, bright and unapologetic, burning to death in its moment of absolute freedom.

Pim was a shooting star. She wasn't free, but she was beautiful in her quest to find peace. I'd hoped once I'd stolen her, the thoughts of suicide would fade from her gaze, but they remained.

What the hell was I doing that was so bad? Why did she cry for twenty-four hours straight when the only things I'd done were give her medical attention and a bedroom to call her own?

I clenched my hands in the salt, my heavy inhale breaking the water skin as my body became extra buoyant.

Something flickered to my right. Turning my head a little, careful not to roll too much, I looked up at the colossal beast of my floating home. Phantom poised on the sea like a swan ready to take flight. Its portals and twinkling lights so homely and welcoming.

I'd built a large boat, not because I needed to live in

something monolithic, but because I'd hoped it wouldn't just be me living on it. I'd sent invitations. None had come back.

The flicker came again.

Kicking my legs, I turned from horizontal to vertical, treading the tide. In the distance above, Pimlico drifted between rigging lights, blocking them as she passed before their brightness illuminated the sky once again.

Where the fuck is she going?

I tracked her as she wandered along the deck. Moving toward the railing, she ran her fingers over the smooth mahogany, her face pensive as she peered into the darkness.

She wouldn't see me down here, so I took the opportunity to study her. To assess the way she carried herself. The anger mixing with residual fear.

Perhaps, I was too hard on her. Expected too much, too soon. Our fight at dinner had been destructive at worst and juvenile at best. I'd said things I wished I could take back.

I was supposed to be the saviour here, not the aggressor.

Michaels had told me as such—warned me that incidents like this might never heal. The wounds on her body might fade…but her mind, that might never be fully complete.

My gaze danced down her figure.

At least she'd worn another too-big-for-her dress and not wandered around naked. It fluttered in the night breeze, a soft lavender style one of my assistants had picked out. I didn't want to admit it, but even from here, the colour set off Pimlico's dark hair, making her seem otherworldly.

Pushing off from the railing, she disappeared past my line of sight.

Something tugged inside me, but I ignored it. I'd already let Pimlico affect me more than I should. I fucking refused to let her eat away at me. Not when she expected me to be a monster.

I *was* a monster.

Just one she'd never come across before.

Pimlico

THE COLD ALMOST made me turn back.

I hadn't brought a cardigan (not that I'd probably wear one), and the chilliness reminded me too much of being constantly freezing in the white mansion.

However, something was infinite and majestically calming about the night sky. Instead of running, I commandeered a bollard where a massive rope—damp with sea and reeking of salt—coiled heavily, waiting to be used.

Perching on the top, I tugged the hated dress and wrapped it around my knees.

My ribs hurt to crunch up, but it was comforting sitting outside after two years locked in a house.

For a while, nothing moved. No stars. No birds. No life.

It was just me and the vast blackness both above and below.

I grew weary, lulled to relaxation by the sway of waves and whispers of night. The mania of the past few days finally calmed, and I was able to breathe without anger or confusion.

Other emotions that'd been hidden inside slowly crept into acknowledgement like woodland mice. Regret for the way I'd pushed Elder. Grief for the way I'd reacted—not because I'd wanted to but because my mind was so riddled with rot, I didn't know any other way.

I needed to apologise to him and myself. Michaels had given me enough confidence to reach out with tentative fingers and take the first grasp of whatever Elder was offering without peeking beneath the kindness and searching for cruelty.

I need to live in the moment.
The future I cannot control.

I tipped my head back to the moon, allowing the silver light to recharge and forgive me. Forgive a woman who was still a girl even if she thought she was ancient. Forgive a slave who had no notion of pleasure or happiness in a man's company.

My education in submission was not welcome here, and it hurt to have to shred up those lessons and be open to learning new things—especially when I didn't know what things Elder would teach me.

I sighed again, expelling another windstorm of gathering questions, doing my best to stay calm.

A crack and small thud wrenched my eyes wide, waking me from my unsuccessful meditation.

I blinked as hands appeared on the railing followed by arms then dripping wet hair and dragon-tattooed torso.

Just like the first time I'd seen his skin art, it stole the very breath from my lungs. The inked creature snarled and snapped, coming alive in every contour and muscle shadow.

Elder didn't look up, climbing the last rungs of a ladder I hadn't noticed and stepping onto the deck with endless authority and confidence.

Raking his hands through his hair, he threw his head back and exhaled. His stomach rippled, his dragon hissing with smoke.

For a second, I sat in the darkness, watching. Wishing I could tear away his secrets and understand who this man was.

He had a temper. He had secrets.

But that doesn't make him evil…does it?

A breeze whistled down the deck, unlocking my dress from around my legs, sending it fluttering like a purple flag.

Elder froze.

His eyes narrowed on me. "I thought you'd gone in."

I stiffened.

You saw me?

My brain worked, trying to decide how I felt about being spied on just like I'd been spying on him.

Against my wishes, my eyes travelled south, taking in the way his black boxer-briefs glued to his body. The masculine bulge spiked my heart rate despite me hating that part of a man. Elder had done his best to switch some of my aversions the night he'd kissed me. Even two evenings ago when he'd pressed his erection against me, I hadn't coiled in disgust.

I hadn't wanted him.

But the thought of sleeping with him was marginally acceptable because at least he'd given me things in return.

Seawater continued to rivulet down his legs, catching in dark hair before pooling over his toes. Everything about him was exquisitely formed and perfect. Even his feet were in proportion to his height and build.

"Have something to say to me?" Elder smirked, not caring my eyes stalked over him. "You can, you know. Say whatever you want. I won't get mad."

I scowled. Was he going to bring up our fight or let it go? I was prepared to follow his lead, but once again, his wet body and chest tattoo drew my attention. The inked illusion hinted that the ocean had been allowed to swirl around his organs thanks to his ribs being exposed beneath his dragon.

Does that smoking thing have a name?

Why a dragon?

And wait…what is he doing swimming at this time of night?

At least my questions were saner and related to less harmful topics. I didn't know if I'd evolved or just been successful at focusing on easier to handle queries.

When I didn't respond, Elder strolled to another bollard holding yet more rigging and scooped up a towel wedged down the side. He never took his eyes off me, somehow stroking me with his vision in a way that evoked yet more goosebumps. It seemed my skin reacted whenever he was around.

I don't like it.

I don't like feeling this way.

What way?

Hugging my knees closer, I tried to answer that.

Like a girl with a boy and not a slave with a master?

No, that wasn't quite right. Elder would never be a boy, and he was far too dangerous to drop my guard and allow whatever remnants of the kiss we shared to have an effect. He was just different. And different people, scenarios, and locations were all taking a toll on me.

"Did the darkness give you the answers you were looking for?" Rubbing his face with the towel, he dragged it down his torso, before tying it around his waist. "Or maybe you've decided to give me the benefit of the doubt and behave?"

My teeth ground together.

Behave?

He chuckled, a lot more carefree than I'd seen him. A rogue droplet trailed over his pec; his dragon licked it up. "I'm not going to apologise for the other night. And I don't expect one from you. I pushed too hard. I'll try to be more understanding."

I sat up in shock.

I'd expected a warning, not a vague admittance of equal guilt.

An uneasy silence fell, which for me was almost as foreign as the way my belly warmed while looking at his half-naked body.

Elder cleared his throat, his fingers twitching by his sides. "I hear Michaels came to see you this evening."

Does your staff report everything I do?

"Not everything about you has to be such a bloody secret, Pim." Rolling his eyes as I crossed my arms, he moved to shut the side of the ship and leaned against the railing. "I also heard you didn't approve of my décor and decided to do a bit of home improvement. On an empty stomach, I might add."

My arms tightened around myself.

Is that a crime?

I didn't know why I antagonised him. If he hadn't hurt me yet, why push and push, waiting for him to do the exact thing I didn't want him to do?

What would a psychologist say? What would my mother?

It didn't matter that I was raised with the matters of the mind. Sorting out another's issues was easy, guessing their concerns wasn't nearly as hard as diagnosing my own.

Elder looked me up and down. "I'm fully aware that your tongue isn't healed and speech is still impossible. But you could give me what you gave Michaels."

My legs jerked, causing one of my feet to slip off the bollard.

He'd told Elder I nodded for him? What happened to patient confidentiality?

"He didn't tell me what you discussed or even how you communicated. He just said you answered his questions." He rubbed his head again, dispelling another shower of sea. "I want to know how you answered him and why you won't answer me."

My shoulders hunched even as my swollen tongue itched. I'd done what Michaels had asked of me. After he'd gone, I'd eaten every mouthful of soup and bite of fluffy rice that a friendly faced maid had brought in.

I even sucked down a berry and banana smoothie and forced my very full stomach to tolerate the chocolate mousse. So much food. Much of it too sweet. But the range of savoury, sweet, and starch did wonders for my depleted system.

Within an hour, I didn't feel so jittery or teary-eyed. My sad confusion faded, leaving curiosity in its wake. Hence my hesitant exploration and expedition onto the deck of Elder's prized yacht.

"Pimlico." His growl echoed in the night. "I asked a question. Answer me."

My nostrils flared.

It didn't work like that. Michaels had found me at my weakest. He'd been kind to me, and I respected that kindness. It wasn't a weakness to answer him.

A curse fell from Elder's lips. "I'd hoped not to see you again until your tongue was healed. Do you know why?" His gaze shot me with ebony arrows.

That question demanded a yes or no answer, but still, I remained mute.

"Because," he snarled, "if I knew your tongue was better, I would force you to speak. You expect me to hurt you? Well, perhaps I will if it means you'll finally tell me what I want."

You do, and it will make you just like him.

I bared my teeth, showing more emotion than I meant.

You do, and I'll clamp up and never utter a word to you.

He sighed, his face softening. "That would make me just like him, wouldn't it?"

I breathed hard as he battled for calmness.

"And then I wouldn't deserve your voice." Pushing off the rail, he came closer. The moon shone behind him, etching him in silver silhouette. "Fine, silent mouse. Keep your quietness a little longer; let me prove to you I *do* deserve your voice."

Ever so slowly, he took my hand, pulling it away from my knee with a sharp tug. I couldn't fight him, even though I tried.

My suspicions about his intentions flared. Was this the first point of initiation? Did he hate that I'd trespassed on his time out here and would make me pay for it?

Only, his fingers slipped through mine—cool and slightly sticky from sea water. "This isn't working…for either of us."

I sucked my bottom lip as he curled his hand tighter, holding it like any normal introduction—like the introduction I'd refused when Alrik had ordered me to shake his hand.

"I think we should start again, don't you?" His fingers tightened around mine, activating the warmth inside me into a scalding heat. "I think you should stop doubting me. Learn to know me with no judgment clouding your mind."

I tugged, but he didn't let me go.

"In return, I'll give you the time you need. I won't force you. And I won't get angry when you deny me my answers." His lips pulled into half a smile. "For a short while, at least."

Our hands grew hot, searing together the longer we touched. Fire licked down my arm, tickling and foreign, hissing through my spine and into my already hot belly.

"Do we have a deal?"

Just like the decision to nod for Michaels was hard, this was even harder.

Harder because there was no going back from this. It wasn't just a nod but an oath to trust him, and I hadn't trusted anyone in so long. Those I had trusted turned out to hurt me the most.

Don't fear the future.

Only endure the present.

Michaels' wisdom was what made me squeeze his hand in return and very reluctantly nod.

Elder sucked in a breath, a sinful smile on his face. "Thank you. For finally agreeing to give me a chance."

Memories of him coming back for me, of his livid anger at my bleeding tongue, and tender strength as he carried me out of hell wrenched through my doubt.

In my twisted emotions, I'd forgotten one thing.

How to be grateful.

He deserved my thanks, and I hadn't given it to him. I'd been rude and distrustful and ruined his property. Yet, he hadn't raised a hand to me.

Trust would be very hard to earn from me, but short-term thanks wouldn't be. My mother had raised me better than that. I had manners...somewhere. I just had to remember how to use them.

Pulling my hand from his, I paused, then, ever so hesitantly, I placed my fingertips on his damp chest, right where the snout of his dragon protected his heart.

I let thanks fill my gaze. I tightened my fingers a little,

sinking my fingernails into his skin. Not to draw blood but to show the depth of what I wanted to say.

Thank you…Elder.

He shuddered beneath my touch, his black eyes an eclipse.

He didn't remove my touch, barrelling his way through our locked gaze as if he heard every syllable I didn't utter.

Finally, his lips smiled in the darkness. His voice wrapped around me, promising a better tomorrow now we'd drawn battle lines.

"You're welcome, Pimlico."

* * * * *

Lying in bed that night, I couldn't stop Elder from starring in my thoughts.

After we'd lingered under the moonlight and he'd accepted my gratitude, he grabbed my wrist and pulled my touch away. Without a word, he strolled down the deck and disappeared downstairs.

I followed a few minutes afterward, still lost and afraid but not quite as rageful as I'd been.

Unable to fall asleep, even after an emotionally draining few days, I pulled the notepad and pen toward me and poured my heart to the one friend who I trusted impeccably.

Dear No One,
My life has changed.
How many times did I wish for that?
But what happens if the change wasn't what I expected? What if I didn't get to go home to my family? What if I now face yet another trial, another man, another ownership?
Was it stupid of me to admit that if Elder stole me to protect me from Alrik, I would be content to be his? Is it wrong of me to back out of such an admission so soon?
I have so many questions, No One, and nobody to ask.
Who am I anymore? Who do I want to be? What will become of me when my tongue heals and nothing but my stubbornness keeps me silent?

The moment I scrawled the last question mark, my eyes drooped as if my mind had only kept me awake to spew out the disease-like questions.

I didn't even place the notepad and pen on the bedside table. I did the only thing I could.

I sprawled out on the pillows and fell into a deep, delicious sleep where Elder waited…promising not to hurt me.

ELDER

A TRUCE HAD formed.

Too fucking bad I had to leave before making it solid.

After leaving Pimlico on the deck last night, I'd checked my emails before retiring and found an urgent one from my warehouses in Monaco. I was needed for an issue the manager did not wish to discuss via electronic correspondence.

So as any good CEO and leader would do, I replied saying I would be there first thing in the morning and made the arrangements with the pilot on staff to ready the helicopter.

Anger curdled my stomach wondering if this was the moment my past caught up with me. I'd been hunted before. Had I been found again?

By nine a.m. we were airborne over the Mediterranean, flying to my ship builder empire and the port I'd wanted to stop in but didn't have time between our commitments.

At least, I had wings this time. Wings were faster than sails, and it meant I could do both with no ill effects.

Knowing Pim was on an armoured yacht far away from whatever mess I was about to walk into, I disembarked the helicopter and stepped onto firm ground.

A mixture of repulsion and relief flooded me.

I liked it here. In fact, Monaco was the only place on land where I genuinely felt at peace. However, I was never fully free without the undulating power of water beneath my toes—especially if my sins had finally caught up with me.

What if you don't return?

I shut that thought off immediately.

It didn't matter that I'd left without a word. It didn't matter if I never went back for her. Pim wasn't my equal. She didn't need to know my whereabouts or me to ask fucking permission.

But the truce...

The truce would stand.

In fact, the time away would only work to my advantage because her tongue would have another few hours of healing before we met again.

Nodding at my manager, Charlton Tommas, I strode from the helipad and into the huge warehouse where floating dreams were made.

"What seems to be the problem?"

Charlton gnawed on his bottom lip, his eyes darting away in panic. All thoughts of Pimlico vanished as he whispered, "There's been a murder."

Pimlico

HE LEFT WITHOUT a word.
He stayed away for two nights, three days.
In that time, I had good hours and bad.
I ate what was delivered, and each meal was slighter easier than the last. Dr. Michaels visited me again to ensure my tongue was healing, and the swelling continued to abate as my body rehabilitated.
I wrote notes to No One before tossing them out to sea, as if the ocean had become my own personal wishing well for things I could never have.
No matter the peace I was given or the safety in which I hovered, I still didn't trust those around me. Even the girl who came to clean my room and dole out fresh towels was kept at a distance. However, if she didn't like to natter while working—nerves caused by my silence—I would never have known Elder had left and wasn't just sulking somewhere on his giant ship.
I'd never heard the helicopter take off (I didn't even know there was one), and once the maid left that first morning, I'd sat on the balcony, staring at the sky, looking for a speck of the returning craft.
Thoughts of pillaging Elder's office for clues on how to end my captivity taunted me. I remembered the password he'd

had me type before calling my mother on his phone. I had a way to contact the outside world…*I think.*

I desperately wanted to know more about him.

The second afternoon, when I'd given into the stupid urge to snoop, I'd spent hours stalking the corridors for his work space. But I hadn't found it thanks to locked doors and no skills at lock picking.

And even if I *had* managed to break into his domain and read his emails or understood what he kept hidden, what would that achieve?

We were in the middle of the ocean.

Apart from knocking out countless staff and learning how to fire a flare or call the Coast Guard, I wasn't equipped to go to battle with him.

I wasn't lazy or fearful…I liked to think it was smart to bide my time and let Elder grant more snippets of his life. Already, he'd given me clues in the way he acted and the respectful way his staff went about their chores even though he wasn't here to oversee.

They worked diligently because he deserved it not because he commanded it.

A tyrant wouldn't have such loyalty. And I was willing to give him more time before I made up my mind. Everyone was worthy of that, even men who owned another's life—*especially* a man who'd saved another's life.

I was aware my thoughts were a walking contradiction.

By the third evening, when the Phantom had passed inlets and peninsulas and other yachts nowhere near as fine sailed through our wake, the faint *whop-whop* of flying machinery sounded.

As the sun set over the sea, a sleek helicopter appeared on the horizon, slowly growing larger the closer it came.

My heart did a weird pole vault dismount. I couldn't decide if it was a death roll or a somersault of expectation. Either way, Elder had somehow gotten under my skin without even being here.

The helicopter hovering over the stern of the ship was deafening even with the constant hum of boat engines. Leaving my spot on the balcony, I padded naked across my bedroom to head upon deck and witness the arrival of the man who called me his.

I cracked open my door and came eye to eye with a young steward vacuuming the corridor, I looked down at my state of undress. He gaped like a mouth-breathing idiot, and, as much as it amplified my discomfort to wear clothing, I had to start accepting the habit for other's sake.

Closing the door, I headed to the wardrobe and selected the oversized black dress I'd worn to dinner. Holding my breath, I slipped it over my head. Fighting the disgust as the soft cotton cocooned me, I pulled out my hair and let it drape down my back, hopefully hiding some of the whip marks and heavy scars left there permanently.

Now suitable, I left my suite and headed down the corridor to the lift. Once the mirrored elevator arrived, I pressed the top button for the outside deck and waited impatiently, pressing my tongue on the roof of my mouth, activating a tiny sliver of sensation.

A few levels higher, the lift spat me out on a glass-fronted walkway. I left springy carpet, and my toes kissed polished wood as I left inside for outside.

The helicopter was still winding down, its rotors barely still.

Crew dashed around, placing ropes and pulleys, strapping the machine to this mega water city. A few noticed me, one even waved, but no man with hair as black as nightmares and eyes as lethal as snipers appeared.

I waited to see if the cabin door would open, but squinting in the twilight, I saw only one person remaining: the pilot.

Elder had arrived and already vanished.

I didn't let myself sigh with disappointment. Instead, I sucked in a breath and headed back the way I came. So what, I hadn't seen him? What did I expect? That I'd welcome him home like some besotted lover? That he would want to see me after my desire to be left alone?

As the lift opened its maw, welcoming me into its belly, I changed my mind. I didn't want walls and ceilings to swaddle me anymore. I wanted the wildness of the sea, the snap of the wind, and the freedom of air and sky.

Pimlico

I WOKE TO the strangest smell.

Something that reminded me of bad decisions and stupid teenage recklessness.

Sweet and pungent and wrong.

My eyes cracked as the caw of seabirds heading to roost echoed across the night sky.

Night?

When had it become so dark?

Unfurling myself from where I'd napped in a wrapped up lifeboat, I stretched. The canvas covering the boat made a perfect hammock; I'd commandeered it after forgoing the lift and staying up on deck. It was only supposed to be for a few minutes, but it seemed tiredness had other ideas.

I don't remember falling asleep.

Chills scattered over my arm, coldness heavy in my blood.

A noise made my ears twitch as my nose wrinkled against the familiar sweet stench. Holding my breath, I looked over the side of my twilight hideaway.

There, haloed by deck lights and stars, was Elder. He stood with his elbows on the railing looking out to sea, one ankle cocked over the other. He wore black slacks and a cream shirt with the sleeves tugged to the middle of his forearms.

He looked powerful and refined, but all of that was a lie

judging by the cigarette between his lips and the cloud of smoke dispersing overhead.

He smokes?

Why had I never smelt tobacco on him? Another whiff of earthy flavour hit my nostrils.

Because it's not tobacco.

Marijuana.

So he doesn't drink, but he smokes pot?

Could there be any bigger contradiction?

"I know you're there." His voice was low but carried weighty on the breeze. "The captain informed me of a woman dressed in black sleeping in his lifeboat." Turning around, he inhaled more smoke, grey fog slipping erotically through his lips. "I told him I'd check it out. Make sure we had no unwanted stowaways."

I sat up, shifting to position myself on my knees.

My tongue was half the size it was the day he left but still tender as I fought a yawn and stared instead.

He followed my eyes.

"You can ask." His face darkened. "In fact, if you open your mouth and ask me what I'm doing with marijuana, I'll give you the honest to God's truth. I'll tell you more than I've ever told anyone just by asking that one question."

Silence was heavy and potent between us.

What was his truth? Why hadn't he told anyone? What secrets could he possibly be harbouring?

Attraction that I'd ignored webbed tight around us. He breathed hard as if afraid I'd take him up on his offer while part of him begged me to. "Go on. No one knows what I am, what I've done. You ask, and you'll be the first and only." He pressed the joint against his lips, inhaling deep. "You hold all the power in this situation, Pim. One little word and all my fucking secrets are yours."

My lips stretched to form the words, but my tongue sat heavy and unwilling. Shaking my head slightly, I looked away, doing my best to ignore the way the curling smoke from his mouth made me feel.

I never thought of smoking as sexy.

I'd grown up in an age where every establishment banned cigarettes and the culture turned it into a nasty, awful habit that was killing, not only them, but also their loved ones.

I agreed with it being a death stick, but Elder was smoking weed, a plant...he smoked it in such a way he looked like he needed it, not just used it for the sake of using.

His head cocked, waiting for me to find the balls or overcome the pain to ask.

I doubted he'd give me an opportunity like this one again. I had the power to skip ahead—to jump the superficial getting-to-know-each-other and steal his biggest confession.

After all, he owed me. He'd read my notes to No One.

He knew how I thought and reacted to pressure.

I had no idea how his mind worked, and now, my curiosity was even worse because weed was a relaxant, a painkiller in the medical world—given to those who needed help to survive.

Was he in emotional or physical pain?

And why did I want to know so badly?

He said no one else knows.

No One.

The fact he'd chosen to tempt me with the title of my salvation wasn't lost on me. Was it a trick or the first honest to God raw reality he'd shown?

Climbing from the lifeboat, my feet didn't make a sound as I padded toward him and clutched the railing, my eyes locked on the empty blackness all around us.

He didn't say a word, merely dragged deeper on his home-rolled cigarette, encouraging the end to flare red, before exhaling and clouding the moon with vapour.

We stood like that for moments, wrapped in quietness and for once not caring.

He never offered me a drag, and I never asked. I doubted Michaels would approve of smoke inhalation when my tongue was healing so well. However, I inhaled whenever Elder exhaled, stealing a little of the sickly sweet—willing it to numb me a little, to steal the questions driving me insane, to grant me a little of the syrupy calm.

Finally, when the joint had become too small to hold, Elder flicked the butt into the ocean. The small red dot twirled and twirled until it hit the water below. The second it extinguished, he turned to me, his eyes shredding mine.

"You wouldn't break your silence to make me talk, yet you're still here." He licked his bottom lip. "Why is that?"

I kept eye contact, not moving.

"Did you miss me?"

I gave him a tight smile.

"I take that as a no."

I blinked.

You're wrong.

No, you're right.

I had missed him in an odd way. My dreams had featured him, and my days had been fraught with thoughts of the way his fingers manipulated paper as I stroked his origami sailboat. I'd suffered unwanted questions of what it would be like to be touched by fingers that could conjure life from dollar bills.

My body repelled against the fleeting curiosity even as my heart put on its armour and prepared to do whatever it took to find out.

I didn't miss what you represent. But I did miss the fragments of the man behind the monster.

"Fuck, this is harder than I thought it would be." His hands curled over the railing. "Look, I've had a rough few days. Normally, I wouldn't smoke, but it's the only thing that works around you."

Around me?

That admission made my belly clench. No man had ever admitted I'd made them weak just by existing.

His face tightened, the anger I'd witnessed at dinner returning. "Don't think you can use that to your advantage, Pim. It only puts you in a precarious position." Pinching the bridge of his nose, he muttered, "It's only fair to warn you I won't be good company tonight. In fact, you should go."

Go?

Why?

His jaw hardened, seeing my question in the jolt of my shoulders. "I can't guarantee I'll keep my promises if you don't."

My heart stopped.

Promises to keep me safe? Promises not to touch me?

The moon cast his face in silver sin. His brow shadowed his eyes until all I saw was black matching the black around us.

"Leave, Pimlico. I wish to be alone."

My feet glued to the deck. Why did he want me to go? Because he had a tyrant inside him he couldn't control? Would he snap and hurt me after he assured me he wouldn't? If the demons I sensed inside him were closer to the surface tonight, I should run. I should hide.

But that would only make the future worse. I might have agreed not to worry about what tomorrow would bring, but if I could find out the worst now—so I could stop fearing—then it would be better for my sanity.

Puffing out my chest, I stood my ground.

He growled under his breath. "You truly are the most stubborn woman I've ever met."

Woman. Not slave. Not orphan or pet.

Woman.

"Have it your way." Reaching for his shirt buttons, Elder undid them with dexterous fingers. The moment the cream material flapped around his sides—once again revealing that magical dragon protecting his bare ribs and internal organs—he dropped his hands to his belt.

He gave me a wicked look. "Fair warning, silent one. I've been away for three days. I only went prepared for one. Know what that means?"

I swallowed as his fingers undid his belt, followed by his zipper.

The flash of skin was a shock after expecting underwear. "I didn't take spare boxers with me." Holding his trousers with one hand, he kicked off his shoes and tugged off his socks. "Run now, unless you secretly want to see me like I've seen you? Do you want to see what I hide under clothes, see the true beast I am? Is that why you're more comfortable naked? Because the truth can always be concealed in trousers and suits, and nakedness it can't?"

My heart plucked ancient glasses and put them on, ready, despite myself, to gawk. My gaze kept skittering from his face to the waistband he held up.

"Fine. You won't run? I won't make you." Without a care, he dropped his trousers, stepping out of them like a royal prince.

My mouth parted at his size. He wasn't erect, but his cock hung heavy and dangerous, protected by a manicured area of black curls.

"Strange to be on the other end." He smirked. "Odd that I'm naked and you're dressed, and for some reason, I feel like I'm the one with all the power." He lowered his head. "Perhaps that's why you like to be naked. Because you enjoy the way people are distracted by you."

Striding past me, his scent and the cloying aroma of marijuana trailed after him as he unlocked the railing that revealed the ladder.

His ass didn't have an inch of fat, firm and tight, graced with the rest of the dragon's tail on his left cheek.

I expected him to turn to face me and climb down the ladder like a rational person from such a height.

He bared his teeth over his shoulder. "If you have any balls left, girl. Come join me."

His arms spread, his legs bunched, he threw himself off the side.

I rushed over, just in time to see him somersault and dive into the black crystal below.

ELDER

FUCK YES.

The minute the cold slap of water splashed over my head, the tension of the past few days dissolved. The awful memory of hard asphalt and dirt receded as my body once again remembered the beat and rhythm of the sea.

Letting the depths cradle me, I held my breath until my lungs screeched for oxygen. Not for the first time, I wished I could dive and dive and never come back up. To somehow find a way to exist in the inky blackness and start a new world where no one knew what I'd done and no family disowned me.

My business on Monaco ought to have been, if not fun, then marginally enjoyable. But that was before I'd arrived to find a boat carver had died thanks to a slash to his neck with a rasp.

If the murder of one of my staff was retribution for my past, I wouldn't rest until I'd killed or been killed.

My manager, Charlton, had been the one to find the corpse. He hadn't informed the police or anyone but me. He'd done well. And I'd be the one to create another corpse in response to the crime.

The first day was spent with the dead man's family, enquiring about grudges and enemies. The second was spent stalking a certain newcomer who was friends with the man's son. He'd been caught stealing the dead man's grocery money the week before.

It was a simple matter after that of giving the young murderer enough rope to hang himself.

I didn't know if I was grateful it was a simple greed attack or pissed off that it wasn't in relation to me. I'd been waiting fucking years for this farce to be over and face them.

After an interrogation that started off cruel and ended in brutal, I learned that this minor disagreement was the cause of a spineless coward who thought he could take things that didn't belong to him, including a life. I wouldn't be surprised if he'd done this before. But now I'd found him and he would never do it again.

I killed him.

The same way he killed my master boat builder.

I ignored the similarities over him taking what he wanted and me taking Pim. I never said I was a saint, but at least I'd cleaned up my business before it became messy.

Once I'd washed the blood from my hands and ensured my factory ran like clockwork, I boarded my helicopter and came home.

To her.

Pimlico

DECIDE, PIM.
Right here, right now.

Elder had given me a choice as he plummeted into the abyss. He'd laid down a challenge that until a few days ago, I would never have risen to.

But now...now, I was more Tasmin than Pimlico. More daring than afraid.

It's time for me to start believing in myself again.

My hands shook as I tore off the unwanted dress. My head fell back as freedom kissed my skin. And panic washed over my healing tongue and down my throat as I moved to the edge of the yacht.

Right here, right now.
Decide.

My toes inched over the edge of the deck.
I took a deep breath.
And leapt.

ELDER

A SPLASH WRENCHED me from the deep.

Kicking hard, I broke the surface, earning a face full of sea froth as something landed beside me.

What the—

Moonlight and stars were a sorry excuse for lights, but the ghostly glow of the yacht gave just enough illumination as Pimlico erupted from the ocean, her dark hair now black, her skin white, and fading bruises marble and slate in the night.

My mouth opened, pouring uninvited salt into my lungs.

Holy fuck.

She jumped.

She'd had the guts even from such a height.

This girl who battled me silently and somehow unravelled my level of control yet again surprised me.

I couldn't take my eyes off her as she spat out a mouthful of ocean and spread her arms to stay afloat.

After everything she'd been through, she was still one of the most beautiful women I'd ever seen. Her very injuries were what made her fucking stunning.

The delicate starkness of her collarbone. The arch of her chin and resolute distrust and unfailing strength in her blue gaze.

In the three days I'd left her, she'd eaten and rested. Her

skin had taken on a porcelain glow, no longer sallow or unwell. She was healing—accepting my care, even if she did continuously search for what I would expect in return.

"You jumped." My voice was thicker than I'd intended as my gaze travelled to her mottled chest where that fucking bastard had hurt her.

The dark water hid everything else, but my mind remembered how willowy she was when naked, even while on her knees or hunched for a reprimand. When she was nude, Pim was no longer a recovering slave but a goddess slowly learning to live again.

It fucking hurt that the obsession inside wanted to take that life and bend it to my will—to use her strength for my benefit. To master her power for my own.

I'd hoped the joint I smoked would've taken the edge off tonight. Having yet more blood on my hands and the intolerable urge to rip Pimlico apart to learn her secrets drove me insane.

I didn't smoke often but the thick lethargy that normally came from inhaling cannabis was muted tonight. Yes, it affected me a little. I'd meant what I said about her not being safe around me. However, the slight buzz in my veins meant I could tolerate her being close without risking myself or her—for now.

Pimlico twirled in the water, facing the behemoth looming over us. Her lips parted as if shocked she'd actually done it.

Goddammit, I wished I hadn't been underwater. I would've killed to see her standing there, naked and poised, battling her fear and winning.

Brushing away droplets from my eyes, I grinned. "Was it frightening? Or exhilarating?"

She turned back to face me, pride shining in her gaze. She obviously hadn't thought what jumping would mean. That she'd be down here, swimming with a man she shouldn't trust.

"What made you do it?" I treaded water, keeping a couple of metres between us. "Was it the thought that you'd survived worse than heights? Or the fact that if you landed wrong, the worst that could happen would be a broken back?"

Her eyes widened.

"Perhaps you hadn't thought about the broken back."

Her lips pressed together.

I wanted to order her to open her mouth, to show me how her tongue looked. I'd done my own research on tongue injuries, and according to medical papers online, that particular muscle healed faster than others.

Her swelling should be mostly gone. She should be able to talk…soon.

The tide whipped us this way and that with gentle currents—some hot, some cool. Pimlico tired quickly, her arms waving in the water, fighting to stay buoyant.

"How long is it since you've swum?"

Her eyes narrowed, but her blue gaze shot answers. Answers that signified a long time.

Other questions trailed on the back of that one, but I let them go.

I could interrogate her later—when she wasn't using her energy to stay alive.

Kicking, I propelled myself forward, closing the couple of metres separating us. "Every day, you surprise me."

Her gaze widened, her eyes trailing from my nose, to my lips, to my chin. The way she watched me made my body harden beneath the waves. Perhaps, by admitting that, I'd surprised her in return.

"Are you feeling better?" A current pushed me forward, closing the final distance between us.

I'd been in her company enough now not to expect a reply. However, her barely noticeable nod overrode the pot in my system, making my heart race.

"I'm glad." We stared at each other, neither of us looking away.

Either fate was working with us for once or Pimlico deliberately swam closer. So close, her body heat warmed me through the tide only centimetres away.

We both sucked in a breath as the ocean bumped us together.

Bare skin to bare skin.

Pim silently gasped, her arms spreading like wings to push away.

I didn't know if it was the relaxant drug or my intolerable urge to know her, but my leg moved forward, wrapping around hers.

She jolted as I pulled her forward, my ankle curled around hers. My left arm came up, looping around her lower back.

She shuddered as the rest of the ocean was deleted, sandwiching our nakedness together. I gritted my teeth as her soft breasts and tiny form wedged against my bulk. "Fuck..."

Her gaze glittered in the dark as her hands landed on my shoulders, pushing me down to keep herself above the waves, trying to break my embrace.

I just held on.

My legs worked harder to keep us afloat, but I had no intention of releasing her when she felt so goddamn good.

We didn't say a word as we hovered in the water, glaring at each other, trying to decide what should come next. I'd toyed with her at Alrik's. I'd asked for a night with her because I was fucking attracted to her—not to her skinny body and abuse, but to the soul inside. The soul that'd almost flickered out.

I wanted her.

So fucking much.

My heritage spoke of contradictory things. There were arranged marriages in my family and then there was true love. My great-grandparents had been an arranged marriage. But my mother and father...that had been kismet and the ideal on which my childhood fantasies about love were based.

They were born for each other.

No question.

Which was why I was cursed for what I did.

Pimlico wriggled in my grip. My dulled senses couldn't

prevent the exquisite sensation of her warm skin interspersing with cool liquid on my body.

I groaned. Loudly.

I was so bloody thankful I'd smoked before she'd found me. There was no way I could've tolerated holding her this close without losing my goddamn mind.

Even with the thick fog of calm, I still struggled to keep the addiction at bay. To avoid admitting that I'd wanted this girl since I met her and that desire wasn't fading…it was only amplifying.

The one kiss and touch I'd permitted myself were no longer enough.

Not at all.

She licked her lips, questions drowning her that I wanted her to ask so I could ask my own.

"Is this another first for you, Pim?" I whispered, reminding her of the intimacy between us when I'd kissed her that night. How I'd touched her and painted erotic images in both our minds about delivering pleasure she'd never had.

"The first time a man has held you without sticking his cock inside you the moment he could?"

The sexually violent question made her muscles lock. She flinched, digging her fingers into my shoulders.

I should let her go. I shouldn't ask such things.

I couldn't help myself. "You never answered me what other firsts you've been denied. I think it's time we deleted a few." My eyes locked onto her lips. "I brought you here for a reason. Perhaps that reason was to fuck you out of my system."

Her breathing caught.

My cock hardened at the shock on her face, followed by a contorted mix of disgust, loathing, and fear.

I'd never had a woman look at me with such a recipe of hate.

Shit, it turned me on.

My leg tightened around hers, forcing my aching dick to press against her hollow stomach.

She gasped, turning rigid in my arms.

"Don't worry. I won't break another promise tonight." I traced my fingertip over her forearm. "I've already broken a few by touching you. Best to keep the rest for another time."

Her foot kicked, doing its best to dislodge me.

"Doesn't mean I won't take other things from you, though."

I knew the right thing to do would be to let her go. She'd requested in her silent way to end this.

And I would, just not quite yet.

Cupping her nape, I brought her forehead to nudge against mine. Nuzzling her with my nose, I let go of my self-control, allowing the intense intoxication I always lived with to escape. "Do you know what I'd do if your tongue was healed?"

I didn't know if it was her, the pot, or the night swim, but I was free for the first time in a very long time.

Her nostrils flared as if expecting me to request her voice again.

However, that wasn't the reason I wished her tongue was cured. Not right now.

Sandwiching her breasts against my chest, I breathed, "I wish it was healed so I could kiss you."

Her gasp was audible this time, sending my heart bucking.

So she does have vocal cords.

She could speak. How had stubbornness and silence kept her alive for so long?

She stared harder, fear, mistrust, hatred, even annoyance crossed her face. Her gaze darted to my lips as I deliberated kissing her despite her denial.

Some of her annoyance faded, replaced with feathery breathing, brushing her nipples against my chest.

I swallowed my groan as the same hint of vacancy overrode her mistrust. Shutters clamped down over her soul, protecting herself the same way she did with Alrik, while at the same time, sacrificing herself to whatever I wanted.

It doesn't work that way.

Not with me.
My free arm cut angrily through the water. "You think you can compartmentalize your feelings? That you can give me your body but not your mind?"

She bit her lip, her dark hair swirling in the tide. I didn't like the judgmental way she watched me, already condemning me to hell.

Bringing her face closer, I whispered harshly, "When I kiss you again, you'll *want* me to kiss you. You won't look as if I'm taking something from you. You'll beg me to give you something you desperately want." Dragging my lips over her salty-cheekbone, I ordered my body to behave even as our legs bumped and my cock jerked to sink inside her—if only to prove a point.

To show her sex felt fucking awesome.

Even if she hadn't experienced such ecstasy yet.

She's not ready.

As much as I wanted to rush ahead and take her, I refused to damage her psyche when her thoughts were more valuable to me than her body.

My fingers looped around her seaweed hair, tightening just enough to wrench her head back. "I order you to forget everything that that bastard did to you. None of that was sex. That was abuse, and it won't happen again. You're a woman beneath whatever slave he turned you into, and when I fucking kiss you, I expect a woman to kiss me back not a slave to shut me out. Do you understand?"

She flinched, her eyelashes sparkling with droplets. Her jaw worked, but beneath her rage, the mildest form of agreement glowed. She wanted to be normal. Despite her fighting me, she secretly hoped I'd smash her cage and teach her how to be free.

Well, I'd help her be normal.

But not tonight.

Her body softened infinitesimally as she licked her lips. My cock immediately reacted, understanding her message. In some small part of her...she wanted me to kiss her. Tongue stitches, black ocean, and whatever chaos existed between us be damned.

Fuck.

It took all my strength to shove her away from me. "Goodnight. I trust you can find your own way back."

She sucked in a breath as I relinquished her to the ocean. For a moment, she frowned, then shook her head with a scowl.

I chuckled. "Is that disappointment, silent one?"

Her scowl turned into a snort.

"Despite what you think, you already look at me differently. You might hate the thought of what I'll one day do to you. You might fear the thought of my cock inside you and my body smothering yours, but a small part of you *wants* me to do it."

She jolted; a small splash from her fingers decorated the blackness.

I cocked my head. "Why is that? So you can stop wondering who I am and label me the same as your previous master? Or..." I rubbed my lips in promise. "Is it because you're sick of pain and want pleasure instead?"

She scoffed, her arms spreading wide to swim away.

I should shut my mouth and let her go, but I liked making her uncomfortable. Words wouldn't leave scars, but they could slice open old ones. "Beware of what you wish for, Pim." I lowered my voice, thick and heavy over the waves. "Next time I kiss you, you'll be wet and feel pleasure you've long since been denied. You'll come. I won't tolerate otherwise."

Her head tilted up in defiance coupled with the tentative hope that I could achieve what I'd promised. That when I took her, it wouldn't be rape but entirely consensual and mutually enjoyed.

Ducking underwater, she vanished.

I didn't panic, counting the wet thuds of my heart in the eardrum created by the sea. A few moments later her head broke the surface by the Phantom.

Grabbing the bottom ladder rung, she hauled herself from the depths and shimmied up the side of my yacht—broken hand and all.

Fuck, what a woman.

Her naked ass as she climbed was as perfect and inviting as the moon.

Pimlico

WHAT THE HELL is he doing?
What the hell am I doing?
What the hell happened to me last night?
First, I'd jumped off the damn yacht.
Second, I didn't shut down when he gathered me against his wet, naked body.
Third, I didn't blush when he spoke about sex and coming.
And fourth...and this was the worst one...
Fourth, when he'd pulled me close as if to kiss me, I'd *wanted* him to. For a split second, I forgot how much I hated sex and remembered how good he'd made me feel at the white mansion.
I wanted to feel that again.
I wanted to feel that way all the time because then I wouldn't have to feel everything else. Every bruise. Every bone. I could...forget.
But then he'd pulled away and growled rules and regulations—warning me I wasn't a slave he wanted, yet he wanted the woman I could become.
Only...I don't know who that is.

All I knew was that while in his care, I'd had the gift of sunshine and travel and wind. I'd wished upon stars not hidden behind glass, and my skin became honey-kissed from being outside rather than pasty, sickly white.

I wasn't stupid.

Every gift would have to be paid back. I just expected him to demand payment now—while I was still subservient and very aware of my place as a pleasure toy. Why would he want me to be any different?

If he let me continue gluing my shattered pieces together, I'd be like normal women.

I'd have opinions and rules of my own. I might not *let* him sleep with me. Was that what he wanted? The challenge? The chase? A girl to fight him rather than a slave to submit?

But why?

If he wanted a relationship, why hadn't he met someone in a bar, or however free people met these days? Why me? Why piss off my dead owner for one night with me—with the intention of fucking me with force, only to let me sleep unmolested then bring me back to life?

It doesn't make any sense!

I clutched my head.

Stop it. Focus on the present, remember. The future does not matter. It can't *matter. Not when you have no control over it.*

Breathing hard, my fingers slipped from my skull to my lap.

Whatever Elder's end game was, I had to admit, he'd started something between us that terrified me. Whenever he was around, my insides twisted and liquefied. Mostly from intense awareness in case he snapped, but partly due to that damn kiss between us.

What had he done? How did he switch the frigid ice in my blood to a cosy fire?

I didn't know, and as much as I tugged on teenage memories of chatting with girlfriends about which pop stars got us wet and what fantasies made us hot, I still struggled with hating sex.

I shouldn't want sex.

I *didn't* want sex.

But Elder…he was different.

I want him.

Not in the physical sense, but his disappearance the past few days had shown me I wanted to be near him. He terrified me, yes. But he terrified other people too, and while he was around, I was safe.

Aren't I?

Am *I safe?*

Oh, my God. Stop.

Maybe I should've kissed him last night?

Perhaps, I should've closed the distance between us and took what he wouldn't.

But why would you do that?

Because I'd treated him with suspicion and rage? I didn't trust him or his word but it didn't mean I shouldn't apologise.

So your kiss would've been a charity?

Yes.

No.

Ugh, I don't know.

It would've been a token of my gratitude. A kiss—no matter how chaste or half-hearted—was an agreement that I trusted him enough to get close, press my mouth to his, and let him hold me.

He could so easily have pulled my hair, forced me to speak—drowned me, for all he cared.

But he didn't.

He'd held me safe with no pressure, even though his erection pressed against my belly, hard and throbbing with things I wasn't strong enough to survive.

Unable to withstand my colliding thoughts, I whipped out the notepad and pen.

Dear No One,

Is this my life now? Riddled with questions and doubt?
I thought the moment I was away from Alrik, things would be easier, not harder—

A loud clunking noise wrenched my head up.

My heart donned her sneakers and took off sprinting. I dropped the pen as a lifetime of worry and self-preservation kicked in, expecting the worst. Whatever progress Elder had made with me was deleted with that one sharp bang.

Alrik's face sprang into my head, laughing and cruel.

It took all my willpower to stay seated on my bed and not hurl myself to the floor and my knees.

It came again—*clunk, clunk, clunk.*

Clutching the sheet, doing my best not to slip into a panic attack, I glanced around the room. There was no tyrant ready to beat me, no werewolf in the shadows.

Wait…

I tilted my head.

I recognise that noise.

A chain.

The metal links clinked together in an awful remembered time when something similar was used to string me up. Only, this wasn't a small chain but massive and lots of it.

The anchor maybe?

Climbing out of bed, I darted to the door only to notice I was naked (like normal) and not suitable for gallivanting around in investigation. Jogging back to the haven I'd just climbed from, I grabbed the sheet, not caring my unfinished note to No One scattered on the floor, and wrapped it around me.

Racing back to the exit, ensuring my temporary clothing covered the right places and didn't flutter open, I charged down the corridor and up the flight of stairs rather than take the lift.

I'd been on Elder's ship for over a week. In that time, I'd battled against recovery then given into it. Once I rested and ate correctly, my body had taken full advantage. The bruises were still there, only now more green moss rather than purple thunderstorm. My broken hand was still bound with a plastic cast and bandage that I'd replaced after my swim last night. However, I hadn't tethered my ribs again, and a minor twinge let me know I probably should have.

My muscles had regained enough mobility to propel me upward—not just skin and bone anymore—but tentatively filling out as if afraid the slight curves would be punished for showing health.

I panted and puffed by the time I climbed onto the top deck and squinted in glorious early morning sunshine, but I didn't collapse in a broken heap.

I was getting stronger every day.

Thanks to him.

As if thinking about him, Elder materialized, standing on the deck with a cup of coffee in his hands. He wore faded jeans with a white t-shirt and casual linen blazer slung over his shoulders.

My gaze drifted down to his feet where masculine toes were free thanks to thin black flip-flops.

He didn't notice me. Or then again, maybe he did but enjoyed me staring at him as much as I enjoyed doing it.

What time had he woken to be showered and dressed and so damn immaculate?

Striding forward, my sheet billowed behind me, doing its best to snap and vanish in the warm breeze.

Stopping beside him, he glanced in my direction. "Morning."

I merely widened my eyes and gawked at the view. He was no longer the centre of my attention. The open sea had miraculously changed from open horizon to busy, dusty port.

"Morocco," Elder said, offering me his coffee.

I held up my hand, automatically refusing his gift. My tongue was feeling much better, but I didn't want to undo that healing with scalding coffee.

He smirked. "You're getting more comfortable with me, Pimlico."

I gulped. *He's right.* I hadn't thought twice about reacting. Breathing through my cymbal smashing heartbeat, I ignored him as the sun glittered on trucks and cranes and the mania of a working harbour.

He chuckled quietly. "First, you're disappointed I didn't kiss you last night, and now, your body language speaks before you can censor it." Raising the mug to his lips, he deliberately licked them before sealing them around the porcelain. His throat contracted as he swallowed a mouthful of caffeine. "If I didn't know any better, I'd say you're beginning to trust my promise."

I don't know what you're talking about.

I kept my eyes glued on a crane hauling a container into the sky.

It didn't stop him from muttering, "My promise that I won't hurt you."

I didn't know if he'd ever hurt me, but with fresh energy came clear-headedness and confidence to face whatever came next. My anger had given me a backbone, but his peace had given me sanity.

I turned to face him. I didn't know why. To finish what we started last night? To surprise him that maybe I *was* disappointed and ready to play his game.

Elder's gaze locked onto my mouth and every electrical spark between us fizzled with fireworks. I stopped breathing as my stomach became master of my body, clenching in answer to the dark question on his face.

I didn't know what I wanted anymore. I didn't know what he was doing to me.

Either kiss me or stop—

A handsome older man interrupted our moment, his eyes crinkling against the sun's brightness. "The anchor is in position. She's all put to bed, sir."

Our connection severed like taut twine cut with scissors. I sucked in my first inhale in so many heartbeats.

Elder cleared his throat, tossing the remaining coffee

overboard, an arc of brown liquid splashing in the small gap between the dock and the ship. He showed no sign of being affected by whatever had happened.

A large gangway cracked open the shell of the Phantom a few decks below us, extending to the mainland, ready to disembark.

Elder said, "Excellent. Thank you, Jolfer."

"We'll wait here until we hear from you. We have mooring rights for seventy-two hours."

"We won't need that long." Elder placed the coffee mug on a bolted-down table by the railing. "Tell Selix to drive out and meet us by the west warehouse."

"Us, sir?" Jolfer's forehead furrowed. "You're not going alone?"

Elder turned to face me, his eyes black and guarded. "Not this time." He held out his hand. "Pimlico this is your first choice of many."

I froze.

"Be my guest. Explore an exotic city. Come meet a member of the royal family and begin to live a little. Or stay. Simple."

I jolted back a step.

Me?

Allowed to wander with strangers, inhale aromatic flavours, and...meet royalty?

I didn't understand.

Wasn't I his possession? Shouldn't he keep me hidden on his ship, far away from the prying eyes of people who might see what I was and rescue me?

Rescue you from what?

Him, of course.

The thought of running the moment my feet touched land filled my heart with helium. I could vanish in this helter-skelter city and be gone.

Elder laughed, his hair gleaming like a crow's wing in the sun. "If you come with me, fair warning. I won't put a leash on you; you'll be treated like a human being who is there of her own accord. But if you run...I won't stop you."

I sucked in a breath.

What?

"I won't stop you because I don't have time to chase an unappreciative brat." He stepped forward. "You know enough to decide if you want to stay with the devil you know or sprint to one you don't. Realistically, it would be better for me if you *did* run. You'd be off my ship and out of my life, and I could go back to the way things were."

His eyes shone with a fury I rarely saw. "I miss my regimented existence, silent one. Don't think you're the only one struggling with this arrangement."

If you're struggling why take me in the first place?

Elder rubbed his mouth with the same fingers that'd made me origami-gifts and stroked me in the sea. "For now, you're my responsibility. And it's up to you to decide. First, you make the choice to come with me. Yes or no. Then, if that choice is yes, you make another choice."

His fingers looped sensually around my elbow, dragging me forward a step in a purely dominating move. "You come, and you agree to return. Running will only get you killed—especially in this country. You're a white female with no money, passport, or voice. Do you honestly think you'll find safety?"

My chin came up.

I might.

Not all men are monsters.

He pursed his lips. "Are you willing to risk what I'm offering with the hope that someone out there will take pity on you, buy you a plane ticket, track down your mother, and send you home?"

My body froze as he stepped closer until his flip-flops brushed my bare feet. "People want to be good, silent one, but they're lazy. The novelty of helping you would wear off quickly and then where would you be? Jumping at shadows and running for the rest of your life."

My heart became a landmine, just waiting for one more push to explode.

"I'm willing to break your past and give you a future you deserve, not the world you were stolen from." He let me go. "Remember that if you ever get the urge to leave."

Turning around, he stalked toward the lift. "Inform the chef I'll return for dinner, Jolfer." He didn't give me a backward glance.

His words rang like a gong inside my ears. I knew he'd read my notes to No One but having him talk about my mother...that hurt to the point of destruction.

Would Elder find her for me if I asked him?

I hadn't even contemplated that he would want me gone eventually. I was the one who wanted to leave. The one who wanted this to be...*temporary*.

It messed with my mind to have him admit the same.

Elder wrenched to a halt a few metres away, snapping his fingers in impatience. "Yes or no, Pim. Decide, right now."

Was there any correct answer? Was I doomed if I did and doomed if I didn't? Either way, the thought of a day in Morocco after a lifetime of England and then white-captivity was no choice at all.

Striding forward, the sheet rippled around my legs.

Elder smiled as I slowed beside him. "We'll see if you made the right choice soon enough." His strong arm wrapped around me, the hardness of his bicep pressing against my spine. With the tiniest pressure, he corralled me forward into the glassed area where the lift waited.

His fingers branded me through the fine cotton. My heart suffered its final push, and the landmine exploded with shrapnel. The pieces fed into my bloodstream making every breath, twitch, and awareness of Elder Prest agonising.

Whenever he touched me, it was more than just a touch. It was possession. In every sense of the word. But it was never a threat. And I couldn't unscramble how he could be one without the other.

Pressing the button to summon the elevator, he murmured, "I haven't made a fuss of your lack of wardrobe while on Phantom. However, since you're accompanying me on business, it's time you grew accustomed to wearing clothes."

I blanched at the thought of tight clinging material in the Moroccan heat. He'd switched my life upside down—torn everything I'd known into shreds. The air conditioners that'd dried out my skin and kept me chilled no longer existed on his yacht. The heat was dispersed by natural breezes with open balconies and portals.

I'd never stopped to think about why that was.

And just how much Elder had studied me. How did he make my knees tremble when he was close? How did he take a normal touch and turn it so weighty and hot and...*dare I admit*, delicious and not disgusting?

I tried to read him as he stared into my face, both of us seeking answers to whatever riddles the other caused.

Straightening my spine, I hugged the sheet tighter in delayed answer to his dressing command.

His eyes lingered on my collarbone, dipping to the small amount of visible cleavage. "Do you want to come?"

I narrowed my eyes.

The way his voice feathered over the word *come* made it a sexual not innocent question.

He already knew I'd go with him. That despite myself, I was excited to see new things and be around people and adventures.

He didn't need an answer to his question. Especially the sexual connotation.

He only wanted me to respond.

Fine.

Cocking my chin, I sucked on my bottom lip. Two could play at this game.

I think.

His muscles locked as his eyes became obsessed with my

mouth.

The power he granted as lust filled his gaze allowed me to step outside my self-imposed rules and nod.

Just once.

Yes, I want to.

He never looked away from the glisten left by my tongue on my lip. "See, replying wasn't so hard, was it?"

Hard physically? No. Hard psychologically? Yes. A thousand times yes, especially when he looked at me as if he was no longer a man but a ravenous beast with an appetite for mute prisoners...

"I like it when you respond." His voice was ash and rubble. He swallowed hard. "Let's try another question. Do you want to come? Or do you want to *come?*"

That isn't a yes or no answer.

But I'd keep playing. I'd pretend I was mentally strong enough to flirt, even if the tangled heat he caused couldn't retrain my brain from withdrawing in horror at the thought of his fingers on my breasts, his hands dropping down my body, his cock pushing inside my—

I gulped, squeezing my eyes against the lewd picture in my head.

I thought I was strong enough.

I'm not.

Not yet.

Elder sighed heavily as I stiffened in his hold. "For a second, I saw someone I wanted—someone capable of withstanding what I need." He let me go as the lift chimed and opened wide. "Pity she's gone again."

His words were visible things. Four words, four fingers swatted across my cheek.

He'd told me I was weak before. He told me I was broken. But that was to earn a reaction from me. This...it was just a statement of truth.

It ripped out my heart and threw it overboard as chum.

"Are you coming?" Elder stepped into the elevator,

holding the doors as they tried to close. "Time to dress."

Whatever heat he'd sparked simmered into smarting discord. I held my chin high and stalked into the lift.

The doors hissed closed, trapping every unsaid animosity and desire tight around us.

Elder exhaled through his nose, his gaze bouncing from the mirrored door to mine.

Don't say anything.
Let me go to my room without another figurative slap in the face.

My request went unanswered. He lowered his jaw, watching me beneath his brow. The fact the mirror was a third party, linking our eyes while standing side by side didn't stop the spiralling heat from rekindling and crackling all over again.

He breathed, "Last night was...interesting."

I swallowed as his gaze dropped to the sheerness of my sheet. "It erased a few of your walls. We should do it again sometime."

A strange intoxication filled my veins until I swore my blood had turned to wine, filtering through my heart, making it drunk.

My knees locked as he bit his lip, the mirror showing every etch of his face, every shadow of his throat and jaw.

How much longer would I have to stand in this electrifying torture chamber with him?

My nostrils flared as his hand moved to capture a corner of the sheet. He never turned to face me, but his face darkened. "Don't hate me for what I said before. I didn't mean to hurt you."

I bowed my head. Not out of respect or acceptance of his so-called apology but because I couldn't look at him anymore.

I couldn't stare into ebony eyes and try to read what he kept hidden. It gave me a headache.

Agreeing to go to Morocco is a mistake.

"Look at me, Pimlico." His fingers tugged the sheet, forcing my fists to tighten to keep it in place.

My face pointed at the sky with fake bravado, but I

refused to meet his eyes.

"Christ," he muttered under his breath.

I shook with adrenaline but not fear. I'd been in his company long enough now not to expect a fist, but I couldn't read him. I couldn't pre-empt or stall whatever it was he was about to do.

What is he going to do?

His grip on the sheet turned aggressive. Yanking hard, he caught me by surprise, spinning me on my feet like a carousel. The white cotton escaped my broken hand while I held on with my other as tight as I could.

But it was no use.

Half-naked with the sheet draped over one shoulder, I crashed into Elder's arms only for him to turn around and slam me against the mirrored wall.

My spine screamed as the bite of coldness activated the humming sensitivity in my body. I gasped as his face twisted into a tortured mask.

He breathed hard and harsh, my inhales and exhales in total sync with his as our eyes locked in shock.

"Goddammit."

Goosebumps broke all over me as his hands suddenly landed on my shoulders, kneading me like a cat. His nose brushed mine as he bowed closer. "What is it about you that I can't ignore? Why do you have this power over me?"

I daren't move. Even though I couldn't.

I didn't know what he meant. The one with the power was him. Only him.

He bit his lip again as his fingers trailed from my shoulders to the hem of the sheet covering my left breast. My right was exposed, totally vulnerable to the brush of his chest just like our midnight swim.

I pursed my lips, fighting his control over the rest of my ill-conceived dress.

"Let go, Pim." Ever so gentle but with a ruthless, lethal command, he tugged.

I fought, but he was stronger.

My fingers hurt as the rest of the cotton fell away, leaving me naked.

I should be glad. I preferred this state. Normally, I felt nothing when the air caressed my flesh. Nothing but freedom from suffocation. Only this time...this time with his hungry eyes and the pinot noir replacing my blood, I was too hot, too alive, too damn conscious of everything a body could do and everything mine had been forced to endure.

My bruises ached.

My nipples pebbled.

My bones throbbed.

But it was nothing compared to my heart. She enlisted that damn traitorous emotion I thought had died the day I was sold.

Lust.

Damn rotten lust that I wasn't acquainted with and would never, ever tolerate. It was a sick, *sick* emotion. It caused men to buy young girls and break them. It turned rationality into insanity. It ended the lives of so many.

Stark fear sprang like a hare as his large hand cupped my hipbone, dragging me forward until his cock bruised my belly.

He groaned long and low.

I closed my eyes, waiting for the snap I knew would come. He'd spoken of giving me time—fixing me not raping me.

I'd begun to trust his promises.

I was stupid.

This was payment for all he'd done for me. I would shut up, shut down, and deal with it. I could handle it. I'd handled worse.

"Look at me," he ordered.

I merely squeezed my eyes tighter and cocked my chin. I kicked the pooled sheet off my feet, balling my hands.

"Fuck, you're too brave for your own good." His fingers curled around my chin, holding me tight, pressing my skull against the mirrors behind me. "Do you have any idea what you do to me standing there so regal and unbroken when your body tells a completely different story?"

I clamped my lips together, ignoring the fresh throb in my tongue.

His mouth skated over mine in a barely there kiss, his breath hot and angry. "I've been able to restrain myself up till now, but every second with you, it gets harder and harder."

With a feral growl, he pushed away, pressing himself against the other side as the doors chimed merrily, announcing our arrival.

The lift swung open.

The corridor was empty.

Elder stepped out. "Get dressed. Meet me on deck seven in half an hour." Before I could collapse under the colossal weight of just happened, the doors swung closed and trapped me.

Morocco suddenly wasn't the playground I'd hoped to play in—it was more of an executioner's holding pen.

For the first time, I craved white because white kept me focused on who I truly was.

I'd begun to forget.

Elder had successfully just reminded me.

I won't forget again.

ELDER

YOU FUCKED UP.
You fucked up.
You fucked up.
The ceaseless mantra echoed in my head with every step.

I didn't know why I'd slipped. Why that moment was the moment Pim drove me insane enough to contemplate taking her in the lift. It went against everything I thought I wanted. But fuck me, having her body wedged against mine had been far too bloody tempting.

I had blue balls from trying to be the perfect host. I layered frustration upon frustration trying to be her councillor, protector, and friend.

Who was I kidding?

I could never be her friend.

I couldn't even be alone with her without doubting I'd have the power not to touch her.

Marching faster, dust kicked up around my dress shoes (I'd traded my flip-flops) as the sun did its best to turn us into jerky. Pim scurried beside me, never looking at me but exquisitely aware of every move I made.

I didn't think she even knew she did it. Knew how her body flowed in accordance to how fast I travelled, how it paused if I slowed, how it swayed to the side if I lifted an arm. It was as if strings connected her to me, and I had full control over making her dance.

Had she always been so in tune to others or had her captivity given her a sixth sense? An innate ability to duck an incoming blow or pre-empt a threatening kick?

Either way, she distracted me, which was not a good thing. I was here to work.

I should've left her on the fucking boat.

In the time I'd given her to dress, I'd done my best to get myself under control. It didn't work. And when I'd met her on deck seven where the ramp rested to reach the dock, I had a headache and was in a sour mood.

It hadn't improved when Pim arrived in yet another dress far too big for her. The baby blue material hung with navy panels on the contours of her hips—the same hips I'd clutched in the elevator.

On a curvy woman, the darker fabric would make her curves pop into an hourglass figure. On Pim, she just looked like a model that'd stepped off a runway and had forgotten to eat in decades. At least, she'd had the good sense to bring a large white hat that flopped over one side of her face, keeping her protected from the sun.

It also protected her from me.

She kept me constantly in her awareness but never let me catch her eye. She'd returned to the girl I'd met at Alrik's—the one with a shawl of icy protection beneath the guise of submission. The one who intrigued me so damn much that I'd practically begged for a night with her.

This woman lived with me on my yacht. We slept a deck apart, and she wanted nothing to do with me. Why the fuck did I continue to torture myself? I should get rid of her before I did something I regretted.

The idea of removing her from my life (before it was too late) soothed my mind enough to find peace and concentrate. I ignored my silent guest and paid attention to the city of spices instead. It helped a little, concentrating on other people who didn't have nearly as much power over me as she did.

Morocco was exactly as I remembered.

Hot, dusty, archaic in its organised chaos.

My thoughts normally found sanctuary here away from its own internal jumble, but that was before I made the idiotic decision to steal Pimlico.

The entire drive to the arranged restaurant where we were to meet His Highness, Simo Riyad, she'd peered out the car window, studiously ignoring me.

Did she remember sprawling on my lap in that very vehicle as she choked on her blood? Did she remember me hugging her close, whispering I wouldn't let her die and she was mine now?

If she did…there was no sign.

Thank God we weren't in the car anymore because I might've done something I regretted.

Just to add to all the rest.

Selix strolled in front of us, protecting me as he was paid to do. We followed a little alleyway to a quaint beachfront restaurant where bodyguards rested in shadow, leaving the royal family to eat in safety.

Entering the airy space with its windowless walls and earthen design, I slipped into Elder Prest—boat builder, millionaire, and ruthless businessman.

The moment Simo Riyad spotted us, he stood and waved.

Selix subtly put his hand on his torso where his concealed weapon rested before branching to the left, letting me know he had my back but wouldn't interfere with business.

He caught my gaze, raising his eyebrow at Pimlico.

Did I want him to take her or did I want her near me?

I'd been trying to decide that since we left Phantom.

I was screwed either way.

If Selix took her, I'd wonder if she'd call my bluff and run—if she'd vanish before I had a chance to interrogate and sample her. But if she sat beside me, questions would come and what answers could I give?

Who the fuck cares?

They're business associates, not confidants. They don't need to know.

Straightening my shoulders, I shook my head and took Pimlico's elbow, guiding her away from Selix and toward the table where Simo, his wife, and two young children sat prim and proper.

Pim stiffened under my direction but didn't pull away.

Drawing up to the table, Simo's wife smiled demurely, her attention flicking from me to Pim and back again. The kids smiled too—perfect manners for royal offspring. All of them had mocha skin and rich dark hair, reminding me of a culture different to the Western world where I'd grown up, even though I had ¼ exotic blood running in my veins.

"Ah, we finally meet." Simo stood, holding out his hand to shake. His turban hid most of his head, and his cobalt three-piece suit was too stuffy for the sticky heat.

"It's been a long time coming, Your Highness." I placed mine in his, glad to finally meet the man who, on paper, I genuinely liked. Compared to the other assholes I dealt with, he was an innocent puppy dog.

However, no one truly knew another—even when living together.

I threw a scowl at Pim.

Our hands unclasped as His Highness grinned. "Please, call me Simo. And in turn, I hope to call you Elder? Or do you prefer Mr. Prest?"

I grinned, slipping back into the world I controlled. "Elder is fine."

Pim flinched beside me.

Simo glanced at her before giving me his full attention again. "In that case, it is a pleasure to meet you, Elder. I hold much regard for a man who makes such exquisite things." He motioned for me to take the seat next to him, clicking his fingers at a hidden guard to bring another chair for Pimlico. "And who is this stunning creature?" He held out his hand to

Pim. "I'm so glad you brought your wife too, Elder. Mine was rather insistent on joining me. I hope you don't mind."

I unbuttoned my blazer in preparation of sitting. "Not at all, such beauty should be shared." I threw a respectful smile at his pretty partner. "Although, please excuse the confusion. This is not my wife. She is merely my travel companion, for the time being."

Pim caught my eye, her lips thinning.

Not looking away, I murmured, "Her name is Pimlico."

Her throat worked as she swallowed. A tight lasso of her energy and mine lashed us together. Would the unwanted connection between us ever go away?

Simo leaned forward and captured Pim's unbroken hand.

I stiffened with possessiveness, watching what she would do. She barely tolerated anyone touching her—let alone a strange man.

She shocked me stupid as she tipped her nose at me and dropped into an effortless curtsy for his Royal Highness. His lips grazed the back of her knuckles.

What the fuck?

What sort of past had she lived to be more comfortable with men with titles than she was with the man who'd saved her?

"You are most welcome, my dear." Simo breathed into the chaste kiss.

Pim tucked her chin, a demure smile on her face, taking her hand back once the introduction was complete.

My heart grabbed drumsticks and pounded on my ribcage. What the hell was that?

Simo motioned to his wife. "This is my beloved Dina." He beamed with husband pride. "I'm sure she would be grateful for female company and conversation."

Pim's eyes met the woman's.

I held my breath, wondering if this was the moment she spoke. She'd slapped me in the face by giving respect to a man she'd only just met, perhaps she'd claw out my heart by speaking to a woman she didn't know.

To hear her voice was a tantalizing thought, even if it would fuck me off. How dare she give that gift to complete strangers rather than me?

When I'd told her she could come with me, I hadn't contemplated the idea she would talk. That her tongue would be healed enough to spill my secrets and inform those who should never know that I'd stolen her. That it was fully within my power to free her, but I wouldn't until I got what I wanted.

Instead of airing our sinful laundry, she glanced at me then dropped her gaze.

The drumsticks stopped playing death metal against my ribs—for the time being.

This meeting was already too long, and we'd only just begun.

Taking a collected breath, I smiled at Simo and his family, answering on Pim's behalf. "I'm afraid she doesn't speak. She's mute."

Not quite, but it was easier than the truth. Far simpler than to explain her half-severed tongue and the bruises only just beginning to fade beneath her dress.

Pim didn't give any outward reaction to my delivery of her 'condition.' If anything, she looked mildly relieved that she could be a voyeur but not participate.

Her eyes weren't passive, though. She might be silent, but she wasn't stupid. Her attention flickered between His Highness and his wife, drawing conclusions far too astute for a stolen slave.

Watching her watch them gave me a hint of how hard she would be to break. How everything I did, every vowel I uttered and every syllable I whispered was armament in her weaponry against me.

Christ, will I ever get what I want?

Dina nodded at Pim, woman to woman. "I think that's impressive—not to talk, I mean." Her voice was sweet and respectful. "Men talk so much these days. I often feel like a mute myself."

Pim gave her a rare smile, letting it reach her eyes and transforming her from sad wraith to brilliant beauty.

Once again, she stole a heartbeat. I glowered at her for such sorcery.

Not once had she looked at me that way.

Not once had she deemed me worthy of such a gift.

My shoulders tensed as anger percolated like rich coffee in my blood. She wanted to punish me? Fucking fine. *I'm willing to change the rules of this game.*

"Should we get down to business?" Simo asked.

I nodded as two waitresses brought over a tray of local beverages and finger food.

Forcing my mind away from Pim and ideas of how to earn a smile like the one she'd just bestowed, I rubbed at the unwanted tightness in my chest, pulled out my phone, and got to work.

* * * * *

Three hours and multiple revisions to the yacht schematics later, we were done. My back ached from reaching across the table to reveal updated plans. Luckily, my phone had a self-designed software that made it easy to tweak frivolous requests while important things like water displacement and ballast were all mathematically checked in the background.

Pimlico obviously hadn't said a word during the meeting, but she'd struck up a strange friendship with Dina.

While Simo and I muttered about incandescent bulbs versus the merit of LED and argued over what wood would be best in the library, Pim never took her eyes off Dina or her children.

The kids, sensing a willing victim, kept plying Pim with curried couscous on fresh pita, presented with fingers covered in sauce.

Not once did Pim refuse their offering, but she did struggle to eat. Shouldn't her tongue be mostly healed by now? I'd already set a reminder to ask Michaels when we returned home.

Home.

What an odd concept. After this meeting, I would return home with a girl in tow who was still a total stranger.

As the last round of drinks was delivered, Pim's gaze trailed over her shoulder, looking for a washroom.

Dina noticed. "They're toward the back."

Pim smiled, standing gracefully. Dina and Simo's eyes tracked over her, noticing things they hadn't when we'd first arrived—the fading bruises, the bandage on her hand, the skinniness of her arms and chest.

My hands fisted. Would they think I'd done that? That I was a psychopath who kept girls as pets?

Dina narrowed her eyes, judging my relationship with Pim from the small distance between us.

Pissed off with her scrutiny, I cocked my head at Selix to escort Pim to the facilities—not to prevent her from running, but to guard her. In her notes to No One, she said she was sold at a shabby hotel with a masquerade ball.

But how was she originally kidnapped? Was the tale true that she was at a charity function with her mother or had she been stolen by less refined means?

Selix stepped forward to collect her, but Dina stood. "You know, I might go too."

She and Pim shared a smile.

What is it with women and joint bathroom visits?

Selix caught my eye, asking if he should still follow.

I nodded subtly. He could protect from outside the bathroom while the two women protected each other inside.

Dina moved toward Pim then blew her husband a kiss.

Simo grinned before turning his attention to the latest amendment to his yacht. Meanwhile, I couldn't tear my fucking eyes off Pim as she padded across the restaurant in her floaty dress and sandals.

It was no secret I found Pim bloody stunning. Her nose, her eyes, her chin, her strength—she equalled a beautiful woman. Having the luxury of gawking at her ass and the flamingo-like curve of her spine made me hard.

"Women, huh?" Simo chuckled. "They cause the worst pain and the best pleasure."

I gave half a smile. "I wouldn't know."

"Oh?"

"I'm only taking care of her from an unfortunate incident."

Simo took a sip of his wine. "I must admit, I was doing my best not to ask who marked her."

I snorted, taking his direction and throwing a mouthful of guava juice down my throat. Wine was not an option. Alcohol had the opposite effect on me than cannabis. "Would you continue to deal with me if I said I was the one?"

"No." His face locked into place. "But I don't believe you did."

"Why?" My eyebrows rose, asking a dangerous question. "I already said we aren't lovers, and you most likely have suspicions of my intentions with her."

Why am I having this conversation with a royal?

It wasn't possible I wanted to clear my name rather than be sullied by his opinion. It didn't matter to me.

Simo patted his son's head who currently had crayon all over the tablecloth. "A man who glowers at a woman the way you do her…she's the one hurting you. Not the other way around."

Words flew from my head. For the first time in forever, I was speechless.

Simo continued. "I believe there are many kinds of men. My second cousin, the king, is one type—a possession to his beloved country. I am another type—a possession to the woman I married. And then, there is you." He looked up, stealing the crayon from his son.

I waited for him to continue, but he didn't.

Clearing my throat, I asked, "And what kind am I?"

He grinned wisely. "You, my friend, are homeless. You are

neither owned by a country or a woman. It is a place not many men can survive in for long."

Fuck.

Fuck.

Fuck.

My heart fell into my stomach, hissing with acid. Homeless. Familyless. Even Selix—after our years on the streets together—didn't know the truth about me. How had this royal looked through my façade and understood?

He waved his hand as if he hadn't just torn apart my fucking life. "I have a question if I may. It doesn't relate to boat building." His face softened. "However, after the personal conversation we just had, I don't think it's too inappropriate to ask."

I ran a hand through my hair. I'd been in control of this meeting, and now, I was on the back foot. That had never happened to me. Ever. Part of me wanted to tell him to shove his question up his ass, but my lips moved with permission. "Ask."

"Great." He opened his arms as his daughter grew tired and climbed onto his lap. "I've heard rumours about you."

My back instantly hardened.

There were too many rumours to know which one he'd heard. Some, I'd started. Some, I wanted to end. Most of them were terrible—designed to keep me feared and free.

"Oh?"

"I heard you have a gift."

I choked on another mouthful of guava. "Excuse me?"

"A gift. It's why you build impeccable yachts. It's why you're so wealthy. It's why you have many talents, I am sure."

"And what gift would that be?"

His eyes sparkled with curiosity. "Some call it a curse."

Shit.

"By the way you stiffened, I'm guessing you might call it a curse, too."

I smiled tightly. "I don't know what you mean."

"I think you do." Stroking his daughter's black hair, he whispered, "Funny how our minds fixate on things, isn't it?"

Ice fell over me like a blizzard. "What are you saying?"

He chuckled. "Depends. Show me your hands."

"What?"

"You heard me. Show me your hands." Simo looked pointedly at where I clutched my glass.

I searched for a reason to say no but couldn't find one. Slowly, I unwound my fingers and presented them palm up. I didn't breathe as Simo reached across and stroked the pads of my fingers of my left hand. "You play."

I coughed.

This meeting was over. What the fuck was he doing?

Simo held out his own left hand. "Go ahead. If it will make you feel easier." My legs bunched to walk out of the restaurant, but my fingers disobeyed me, creeping across to touch this man in the same way he'd touched me.

Calluses and thickened skin, just like mine.

"The cello?" My voice barely carried.

He nodded. "I've researched you, Elder. I hear you were a prodigy."

How the fuck did he hear that?

Memories of a happier time with music, surrounded by my mother, father, and brother—memories that riddled me with bullets and made me bleed—tried to enter my mind.

I gritted my teeth, pushing them back. "Once. That's over now."

"Yet you still play." He leaned back, cuddling his daughter. "You know, Elder, in my country, we don't label things like the western world. If one has the tendency to focus until perfection is created, we praise rather than worry. I think all great virtuosos have what you have, and you should not run from it."

"What *I* have?"

"Sorry, it's not what you have but what you *are*." Changing the subject, Simo smiled. "I wasn't going to tell you this as it has no reflection on our business together. However, I think, after learning what sort of man you are behind your reputations, it can't hurt."

Once again, he put me on the back foot.

I fucking hated it.

My brain scrambled to catch up from talking to a fellow cellist, finding out he understood what lurked inside me—now, he wanted to expose yet more revelations?

Liquor suddenly held allure as did the pull of a joint.

Doing my best to keep my voice calm and disinterested, I drawled, "Tell me what?"

His gaze darted to the bathroom, obviously wanting to finish this heart to heart before the women returned. "I might not be the king, but I have access to everything my second cousin does—including the best private investigators. When my wife and I decided to purchase a yacht, we were meticulous in our research. Your company and product are second to none, but I would never have done business with you based on your reputation and dealings with men who are corrupt beyond comprehension."

I smiled, but it wasn't the cold boastful smile I'd perfected when dealing with criminals—it bordered the man I'd been. "Normally, that's why business seeks me out."

"I figured as much." He lowered his voice. "But that's what turned us away. The royal family can't be seen to be dealing with murderers and thieves."

I hid my scowl.

What would you say if you knew I was a thief?

"So what changed your mind?" I asked.

"Your past."

"My past?" My voice snapped. "What about my past?"

Rubbing his callused fingers together, he said, "We are about the same age. I started playing the cello when I was eight, and the music community was small. The world is not a large place when the love of something draws us together."

Once again, memories that had no right to hurt me tried to swarm.

My mother bought me my first cello lesson when I was four. I'd cried when it was over because I never wanted it to end. The next week, my father borrowed money from our neighbours to buy a second-hand cello, so I could play and play and never fucking stop.

The strings. The frets. The *music*.

Shit, the notes I could create—it gave me purpose. I'd never been so drawn or so addicted. That was the beginning of the end for me. I'd cursed my entire family because of it.

Simo's voice blew away the recollection. "As I worked through my levels, a name kept being mentioned. A boy who played until his fingers bled. A boy who would strum for two days straight until he'd mastered a song he'd only just heard on the radio rather than sheet music given by a teacher."

I shot upright. "I've heard enough."

Simo didn't stop. "My parents would use him as an example if I grew bored of practice. They would say 'why can't you be more like him?' Whether he knew it or not, he became widely recognised for being the best. Until his 'death,' of course."

I bared my teeth like a cornered animal.

Motherfucking shit.

I paced away from the table, glaring at him. "Quit while you're ahead. I'm done talking about this."

His shoulders tensed as if to blurt everything I'd tried to keep hidden, everything I'd covered up, but footsteps sounded behind me, signalling our time together was over.

Thank Christ.

Relaxing, he smiled. "I don't know what happened or why that prodigy vanished, but I do know your true name, Elder Prest. I know the real man beneath the rumours. *That* is the man I hired to build my yacht. A man who has been called obsessive, a perfectionist. A man who can't let something go until he rules it. I hired you because I want to keep my family safe, and no one will do a better job because you have no choice but to deliver excellence."

He kissed his daughter's head, standing upright with her small body in his arms. "That is the man worthy of being possessed by either country or woman—not someone who should be alone."

His voice rang in my head.

He knows my true name?

I hadn't let myself remember for so long. As far as I was concerned, I *had* no other name. I had no other life—no other existence before this one.

My skin crawled to leave.

Dina appeared, heading to her husband and children. "The discussions are over so soon?"

"Yes." I didn't look at her, scooping my phone and notepad off the table and tucking them into my trouser pockets. "I've heard everything I need to hear." I glowered at Simo.

He looked back with a respectful nod rather than taunting glint. He hadn't told me he knew who I was to intimidate me. I didn't know why he had. But stupidly, I trusted him not to blab.

If I didn't trust him, he wouldn't be walking out of this restaurant. Bodyguards or royal blood be damned.

Pim drifted to my side, her gaze locked on my face. She tilted her head, sucking on her bottom lip as if she understood the turbulent anger corroding me.

She could fucking look.

But until she told me her secrets, she wouldn't be earning mine.

Simo hoisted his daughter to his hip, holding out his hand. "It was nice talking to you, Elder. We should share our love of music again sometime."

I snorted, unwillingly shaking his palm. "There won't be a next time."

"Perhaps." He smiled. "But you will email over the new blueprints once the amendments have been drawn up?"

I straightened my back. "After everything you just revealed

about me, do you doubt it?"

The little boy, jealous of his sister in his father's arms, wrapped his arms around Dina's leg, blinking sleepily.

Simo chuckled. "You are right, my friend. You will because I know who you are."

Pim sucked in a breath beside me. No doubt reading into Simo's sentence incorrectly. She thought she knew me. She thought all I wanted was to fuck her and dispose of her.

That's what you want her to believe.

And it was what she would *continue* to believe.

Because it's the goddamn truth.

Bowing slightly at Dina, I murmured, "Pleasure meeting you. I promise your yacht will have everything you require and more."

"Thank you, Elder." She hugged her son's head to her thigh. "If you're ever in Morocco again, please let us know, and we'll arrange a tour of our wonderful city."

"You're very kind." Bracing myself, I grabbed Pim's elbow and steered her away from the table. "We'll remain in touch via email. Until then, have a good afternoon."

"Goodbye, Elder." The Royal Highness and his family exited through the back of the restaurant away from the public eye.

Selix fell in step with me and Pim. She had no choice but to move as I guided her to the exit. Restaurant shadows steadily brightened as we traded fan-disturbed air for hot, sticky noon.

The doorway wasn't wide enough for both of us to pass. I pushed her ahead of me, clenching my jaw against the mottled bruises still decorating the top of her shoulders. The beads of her spine were too pronounced beneath her dress, still too stark and crying of an unhappy tale.

My hands balled in rage. After the meeting from hell and knowledge that someone other than me and my mother knew who I truly was, I wasn't in the mood to be gentle.

I wished Alrik was still alive. I'd fucking kill him all over again for what he'd done to Pim and for my own black satisfaction.

Having his marks on her drove me insane. Seeing her malnourished and unhappy while belonging to me made me criticize the very reason why I'd got involved with her in the first place.

I need to do better.

I was someone who cared about perfection.

When had I forgotten that and twisted perfection into an obsession I could no longer handle?

I needed her healthier, happier if I was to earn whatever it was I wanted. The hard part was I still didn't know what I wanted. Or why I kept up this farce when she only complicated my life.

Pim raised her head to the cloudless sky, letting the sun decorate her face. She inhaled the scents of dust and dung from camels tethered nearby.

For a fleeting second, I saw the girl she'd been before she'd been sold.

I saw how she could look if I fucking let her go and—

No, she would never be that innocent or happy again—no matter if she was with me or the mother I couldn't track down. Such hardship and evil she'd endured marked someone forever. Sure, she'd find pockets of happiness tucked in the overalls of life, but most of the time, those memories would steal her back, reminding her time and time again what she could never run from.

I knew because that was my life. And it fucking sucked.

Her head tilted until her eyes met mine. The rare freedom on her face vanished, smothered beneath distrust and wariness. Taking a step toward the black car that'd brought us here, Selix dashed in front to open the door for her.

I stalked behind, never removing my eyes as she gathered her long dress and slipped into the shaded leather interior.

The thought of returning to the ship so soon didn't entice me. Even that rarity pissed me off. Normally, I couldn't wait to run from crowds and chaos. However, nothing called to me to return. The only thing that did was locked in a secure box with its bow freshly strung ready to play. I hadn't created music since Pim stepped on board. Solving a different problem in my stowaway had buried the itch.

If we returned to the Phantom, Pim would vanish to her rooms. I would vanish to mine and we would be right back where we started before I dragged her outside.

No.

What do I want from you, girl? And why can't I decide how to take it?

"Get out." I marched forward, yanking the door from Selix as he moved to close it. Pim looked up in shock. "We're walking back."

"But sir—" Selix cleared his throat. "It's height of the day, the heat—"

"Don't care. It's only a few kilometres to the port. I want some exercise."

Selix wisely kept his mouth shut and didn't mention we'd exercised together just this morning in the marital arts gym a few decks below. He'd favoured crescent knives. I'd wielded a katakana sword. It had been fun.

Pim glanced from my bodyguard back to me, her eyes widening.

I held out my hand like a gentleman, battling the urge to yank her from the car and drag her to my side. If Pim was ever going to be strong enough to give me what I wanted, she had to start making decisions and take responsibilities for those decisions.

Perhaps that's what's missing? She's never been given a choice. Not by me or Alrik. Chances are not even by her own mother.

I'd given her a choice this morning to come with me.

The least I could do was give her another. "I'm walking. You're welcome to join me." I closed my hand, dropping it to my side. "Or you can drive back with Selix."

Her mouth parted, searching for a trap.

Selix stood calmly, his black top knot glistening in the hot sun.

A few seconds ticked past. Sweat tickled my back beneath my jacket. Shrugging the linen off, I threw the blazer past Pim to sprawl on the backseat. The muggy air on my white t-shirt didn't really help, but I couldn't be assed wearing more clothes than what was needed.

I suddenly had a small understanding for Pim and her aversion. If she'd been trained to accept nakedness as her uniform, how hard would it be to go back to confines of elastic and thread?

My patience stretched thin. "Are you coming or not?" Facing away from the car, I took a step toward the bustling street where street vendors hid under the shade of their cart sails and shopkeepers did their best to keep away flies and ragamuffins.

Pim bit her lip; her hands splayed on the car leather. The anxiety on her face from being forced to choose made my gut clench. "There is no right or wrong answer here, silent one. You return to the boat either with Selix or with me. I won't hurt you for choosing."

Still, she didn't decide.

"Fine. I'll make it for you. Go back to the boat with Selix. You're probably still too weak to walk that far anyway."

The moment I spoke, she leapt from the car, hiding her wince from sore knees. Keeping her head high, she came to my side as if daring me to call her weak again. I'd probably get my ass kicked by Michaels when we boarded in a few hours, berating me for dragging his patient through grungy streets, but I couldn't hide my grin as I struck off with her glued to my shadow.

"Fair enough. Let's walk."

Pimlico

WHAT WAS THIS new game?

What were the rules? How should I act, behave, or respond? There were so many unfinished games between us, I was lost on how to continue.

For fifteen minutes, I kept pace with Elder's long stride as we headed toward the dock. Cafes and shops bustling with people with families and loved ones, people who had their own burdens to bear, slowly blocked the sea view.

Had one of them been kidnapped? Did they share a story similar to mine or was I an anomaly here, just like I would be if I ever returned home?

Elder kept glancing at me, but he didn't speak, letting silence weave us together instead. If he was trying to use quietness against me, he wasn't successful.

Ever since we'd walked into that restaurant, I'd been hyper-aware of everything about him. For three hours, he sat and answered every question with fluid intelligence and grace. He wasn't just a business owner who barricaded himself in a seafaring tower and let minions do the work. He *was* the business.

My mouth had parted multiple times when technical terms and complex mathematical calculations were given in mere seconds of being asked. With his attention on Dina and her husband, I was free to watch, to listen, to understand.

Finally, I'd had enough time to use the meagre skills my mother had taught me on how to read body language and find out I'd been wrong about him.

I'd seen him as a single dimensional arrogant bastard who pursued me for his own gain with just enough decorum to be respectful to those who worked for him.

Oh my God, I was so wrong.

He wasn't just multifaceted; he was layers upon layers of hypocrisies.

The outer shell he wore—roguish and suave—had holes enough to glimpse into the veiled worlds beneath. And in those worlds were shadows holding such pain.

He thought he kept it hidden as he studied schematics and blueprints with His Highness, but I saw how he never took his eyes off the way Dina cuddled close to her husband or how the two children leaned together in sibling-bond.

He ached.

It was a physical thing.

He craved.

It was a visible thing.

I saw so much while enjoying the luxury of sitting quiet and undisturbed.

But why did he covet a family when he was a bachelor of his own devices—surrounding himself in water and horizons? Why did he look at children, not as a man who was desperate for his own, but with nostalgia—heralding the ghosts of perhaps a brother or sister he missed.

Despite myself, I thawed toward him.

But I didn't fully let go of my dislike until the second course of our luncheon. The switch inside me happened when Elder sketched a third amendment to the drawings and laughed real and carefree when the little girl swatted her brother for snapping a crayon and gave her his expensive biro to replace it.

The moment stretched a tad too long; he'd frozen, remembering a different time. He didn't shutter his eyes enough to hide the agony resounding inside.

He was no longer just Elder. My saviour and captor.

He was so, *so* much more.

And it hurt because I wanted to know how deep that more went.

It seemed I wasn't the only one.

Whatever conversation occurred while Dina and I were in the bathroom had stripped Elder down to his bare defences. He no longer had a swagger or solid footing in whatever persona he'd created. He'd suffered a trip down memory lane and somehow left pieces of himself behind when he returned to the present.

I wished I'd been there to listen—a spider in its web, catching the puzzle pieces like fat juicy flies. However, I wouldn't trade my own bathroom conversation because Dina had done for me what Simo had done for Elder.

She'd woken me up.

Giving into the lull of walking in hot sunshine and enjoying the dusty grit on my feet after too long of being pristine and undirty, I recalled the first chat with a woman in two years.

"How are you enjoying our country, Pim?" Dina escorted me into the bathroom, her eyes warm and kind. The moment the door shut, blocking us from Selix standing guard, I tensed for those eyes to leave mine and lock onto my bruises.

Self-consciousness brought my arms up, wrapping tight around my waist. Did she know what I was? Did she come to the washroom to interrogate me and somehow get Elder into trouble?

For a brief second, I wondered if she might've started as a slave to His Royal Highness, but the idea was hilarious as well as preposterous. Anyone could see the love they shared. I certainly could, and Elder definitely could.

He hadn't taken his gaze off them even when it looked as if he was sketching a quick design.

Being with a man joined only in the worst circumstances of captivity and death, it prickled my skin to be surrounded by a family who cherished each other. They were by far the richest people I'd ever met and not because they were a prince and princess (I think that's their title being cousins to the crown) but because of what they shared.

No one cherished me.

Or at least...not for the right reasons.

"I must admit, it's weird to ask questions and not earn a response." Dina placed her purse on the terracotta-coloured vanity. "Excuse me if I prattle on."

I smiled and broke yet another of my rules. I shrugged, shaking my head to put her at ease.

I hated how easy such a response was, how freeing communicating could be if I just stopped doubting everyone and began to trust again.

"I'll be right back." Dina opened a stall and disappeared.

I followed suit, and after we'd done our business, we smiled at each other in the mirror as we washed our hands in the double sink. The tepid water wasn't refreshing in such stagnant heat, but at least we were clean.

Fantasies of jumping in the ocean with Elder tonight made the bathroom splutter as if I could step through a veil of time and return to moonlight and salt rather than stay in a bathroom in the middle of the day.

"How long has it been?" Dina flicked remaining droplets off her fingers and reached for a towelette. "Since you've talked, I mean?"

I tensed.

I could lift up two fingers and give her an answer. But I wasn't ready. I shrugged again. I'd already broken that barrier. It was easy to repeat.

"Do you miss it? Being able to converse and demand answers to whatever you're thinking?"

Turning off the tap, I swallowed and moved my tongue, testing how easy or how hard it would be to give this woman my voice and just get it over with. I'd forgotten what I sounded like, and how it felt to have sound resonate through my throat.

And if I did break my cardinal rule, what would I say to her? Would I tell her about Alrik? Would I ask her to help me? Would she laugh when I said Elder had saved me but at the same time prevented me from going home? Would she take me away from Elder and if she did...how would I feel about that?

After watching him today, I was hesitant to speak badly of him.

"What am I saying!" She held up her hands. "I'm so sorry for being nosy. I don't even know if you could ever talk. I never thought it might be a thing you've dealt with since birth. Forgive my ignorance." Opening her purse, she pulled out dusky pink lipstick.

Painting her lips, she put the lid back on. "Changing the subject, let's talk about that man out there."

I froze.

What about him?

She smiled softly. "You do know he cares about you."

Frost worked on my freeze, turning me rigid.

He does?

No, you're mistaken.

He tolerates me, that's all.

She couldn't mean Elder. But there was no other man—apart from her husband. And technically, he did care. He'd saved me, killed for me, set me up with everything my body needed to heal.

She patted my hand, still locked on the tap. "You're new to one another, aren't you?"

I blinked.

"I remember those first days with Simo. It's terrifying but thrilling, don't you find?"

Terrifying, yes.

Thrilling...I hadn't thought about it.

Elder did thrill me, but it wasn't a happy thrill from passing a feared exam or surviving a crazy rollercoaster. This thrill was entirely different. I just didn't know if it was from adrenaline of wanting to run away or needing to run closer so I could understand.

"Treat that man right, and he'll do the same in return." Dina removed a comb from the side of her head and repositioned it to scoop a cascade of black hair from her face. "That's what today's society has forgotten."

Seeing her beautify an already beautiful face prompted me to stare hard at myself in the mirror. The shadows under my eyes were more grey than black, thanks to regular meals. My hair held a tentative shine as if wanting to return to glossiness but still afraid. And my collarbones still stuck out, but at least my arms weren't as gaunt.

Was I pretty?

No, not really.

But I was a survivor, and I wholeheartedly accepted the girl before me because she was the first stepping-stone back to health.

Copying Dina, I combed my fingers through my hair and rubbed my skin to rid the heat shine on my forehead and chin.

Closing her purse, Dina said, "From a fifteen-year married woman to a girl in a new relationship, let me give you one word of advice."

I sucked in a breath, my hands twisting my hair and draping the coiled mess over my shoulder.

"Treat him right because men respond to praise. If they know they've done well, they want to try harder. If they see how happy they make you, they'll do more to keep you that way. Don't belittle them and never, ever blame them for things that aren't their fault. Even the things that are their fault, give them some slack."

You make them sound like a dog.

She turned, giggling. "I didn't exactly make that point eloquently—they aren't an animal. Well, sometimes, they can be." Her eyes twinkled. "Simo is the public speaker, not me. All I mean is I see the way he looks at you and the way you look at him. There is suspicion there but interest too."

She headed toward the door. "No matter what happens, never hold grudges. Grudges are the worst things in life. No matter if that grudge is justified, it's the poison that kills entire cities."

Even if I could talk, I wouldn't have known what to say to that.

Instead, I trailed behind her and returned to the man she said cared for me.

"Are you okay?"

Elder's voice interrupted my daydreaming, wafting away Dina as if she were a whiff of incense. His exotic aftershave tantalized my nose, buying into the analogy.

I squinted at his height, vaguely making out the dragon tattoo on his chest beneath the white cotton wrapped around his torso.

He narrowed his eyes as if wondering where my mind had

gone and dying to ask. But he wouldn't. He knew by now he wouldn't get an answer.

Pointing at my legs, he grumbled, "Are you tired? Do you hurt? Should I call for the car?"

I hadn't even noticed the slight ache in my hips from walking after so long of being huddled in a ball. I didn't feel the burn of a freshly formed blister from the slightly too big gold sandals—even the throb in my knees and tongue couldn't steal what this day meant to me.

The only thing I did notice was how bright the sun was and how I'd stupidly left the hat I'd commandeered this morning in the restaurant.

Whoops.

Would he punish me for that? Would he even notice?

Today had started off terrifying with Elder stripping me in the lift. But it had ended in female company and sunshine, and he could never take that away from me. Whatever minor discomforts I suffered was nothing compared to the pricelessness of such an adventure.

However, the longer we were in public, the stronger Alrik hovered in my mind—his ghost doing its best to scare me by making me suspect the men walking close by. I jolted from raised voices and winced when shopkeepers raised their arm to tote their wares.

All mundane things but in them I saw a torturer, a scream, and abuse.

I was happy.

I was nervous.

It was a constant battle to stay in the moment.

But for the first time, I actually *wanted* to be present. Not in the future where I was safe with my mother and friends. Not in a police building about to inform the world of the QMB and begin the tirade on saving the women I'd been sold with.

I wanted to be here.

With Elder.

He huffed when I didn't respond, growling with

impatience. "Michaels gave me a report on your healing last night." He glanced away, his attention landing on a young boy running across the street with a scruffy dog on a piece of string. "He said the stitches will begin to dissolve soon. That your tongue is well on its way to normalcy."

I kept pace beside him, neither agreeing nor disagreeing. He was right, though. The swelling receded every day, and the sharpness from the stitches was already beginning to soften. Although eating couscous at lunch today had been tricky. The tiny granules had escaped into my cheeks, and I didn't have the dexterity to find them.

His voice darkened. "Once I know you're healed, there won't be any more excuses, Pim."

I know.

"I want what I deserve. I need things from you."

I know that, too.

"I've been more than fair—"

I skidded on a loose piece of gravel.

My arms flew out to catch my balance. My bruised bones bellowed against upcoming impact.

But I never fell.

One second, I was falling; the next, I was not.

As if we'd danced this dance before, Elder's hands gripped my waist, his fingers digging protectively into me, keeping me upright.

The electricity when we'd first met licked like wildfire from him to me, crackling and spitting. Everything that'd happened on his yacht up until now was deleted. We were back to square one when he'd walked into the white mansion in his stain of black and demanded one night with me.

The penny he tried to give me for my thoughts.

The way his pinkie grazed mine.

The way his lips descended and his tongue captured and that damn kiss that ruined everything. All of it drugged us until we were lost.

I shivered as things inside me sprang awake. Things that

weren't just dormant but had never had the chance to bloom. Things a woman felt, not just a girl. Desire I'd only just sampled but now ricocheted through me like a rocket.

He sucked in a breath, his fingers pressing harder. Too hard. Not hard enough. Bruises tried to enlist a panic attack. Instinct tried to make me flee. But Elder…he was the anchor keeping me steady. I didn't tremble from fear but interest. I didn't gasp from terror but attraction.

In the Moroccan sunshine, his skin turned a molten honey while his hair carried nightmares itself. His eyes, with its secrets and hidden windows, were wide and full of dazzling heat.

His head bowed as his hands dragged me forward. Without thinking, my body turned supple, bending into him as my chin tipped up.

Whatever this was, we didn't choreograph it. Something else did. Something neither of us could ignore.

His hands slipped around my back, bracing me against his body. My belly hit his waistband and my spine arched as he pressed his hardening erection into me.

I didn't think about where we were or who was watching. Nothing else existed but him and me and whatever this searing connection was.

"Fuck…" His eyes dropped to my lips.

I licked them, not in invitation but because my mouth watered for a kiss. *His* kiss. The kiss I wanted because his hands were on me in protection, not damnation. The kiss I wanted to build on the one he'd given back when my existence had been ripped apart.

One hand gripped my lower spine while the other crept up my back. He wasn't gentle; he didn't apologise for pressing bruises or gathering me so tight I couldn't breathe.

I didn't care.

For some reason, his violence was acceptable, not just accepted…wanted. Desperately wanted.

My fingers came up, clutching his biceps as he bent me deeper into him. His every muscle, his every breath and heat, fed into my body, making me wet for the first time since I could remember.

I didn't know how to describe it as my body shed its hardened exterior and swelled and liquefied. It took back what had been stolen and *lusted*. Lusted after being taught lust was so awfully wrong.

His breath scattered over my lips as he dragged me the final distance.

My eyes fluttered to half mast, entirely drunk and willing and wanting and waiting and—

"Shit." Elder stumbled, pushing me away so I wouldn't trip with him. His face etched in feral need, waging with anger at the interruption.

His head whipped to the side just in time to see the dog on the piece of string barrel down the road with the kid in tow. He must've run into us, locked unmovable in the street.

As suddenly as the moment had happened, it ended.

Elder wrenched his hands from me.

I sucked in a ragged breath, unable to control the leaping lemmings that'd replaced my blood.

What the hell was that?

And what would've happened if the dog hadn't run into us? Would we have kissed? Would we have lost ourselves in the middle of a congested country where public displays of affection were a criminal offence?

Spinning on his heel, Elder clamped both hands on his head, staring at the sun. With his back to me, I didn't catch what he said, but his curse curdled the perfumed air with untold frustration.

While away from the intensity of his stare, I wiped my lips, flinching at how sensitive they were. Dropping my hands down my front—trying to get myself under control—I shivered as my nipples tingled against the dress.

The foreign wetness remained slick on my inner thigh. Not wearing underwear made what'd happened unmistakable. A rainbow of pride filled me that even after two years of abuse, after promising I would never tolerate sex or lust, my body had found a way to heal just enough to accept a kiss.

From Elder at least.

I picked at the scabs in my mind from everything Alrik had done, hoping to see if perhaps, one day, I could tolerate more than just a kiss from a man who hopefully might earn my trust. But the minute I thought of naked bodies and entwined thrusting, a cold sweat drenched me; a panic attack snaked through my desire, turning it into rancid sickness.

I gulped at the suddenness of how something so desirable could turn into something horrific.

Elder spun around, dropping his hands. "I didn't mean—" His arm came up.

All I saw was pain. I cringed, taking a step back.

He stiffened, looking from his me to his arm. Accusation and disappointment replaced whatever attraction remained in his eyes. "I wasn't going to hit you." His nostrils flared. "Fuck, what the hell happened between us? You fell, I caught you." He pinched the bridge of his nose. "I told you I was doing my best around you, Pim, but *Christ* you felt good in my arms."

A swarm of locals cascaded around us like a swiftly flowing river around a boulder in its path.

Elder didn't notice. "You didn't fight me." His voice lowered. "You responded. You *wanted* me to kiss you. Are you going to stand there and fucking deny it?"

I looked down, rubbing my arm as prickles raced over my skin.

"You wanted me, yet now you look as if I was about to bloody rape you. You're still afraid I'll hurt you, even now?"

I couldn't fill my lungs. My heart tightened itself in a rusty metal thumbscrew, making me hiss in pain.

I'm afraid of myself.
Of what irreparable damage that bastard did to my body.

His head lowered, blocking the sun and casting heavy shade over me. The symbolism of standing in the shadows wasn't lost on me. I'd been in the shadows for years. How the hell did I think I could live in the sunshine without getting burned?

"Goddammit, you frustrate me." Glowering as if he'd expected better from me—as if he could snap his fingers and have me sing for him and kiss him and be cured by him—he dragged a hand through his hair and stormed off.

ELDER

ONE WORD.
Fuck.
Two words.
Motherfucking Christ.
Three words.
I'm fucking screwed.

Pimlico

THE DUST EDDIES left by his shoes captured my attention.

He left.

He stormed away without Selix to watch me, guards to corral me, or leashes to hold me.

The chemistry between us snapped away—partly buried by the brutal history I couldn't shake but mainly due to the freedom that suddenly opened up all around me.

I'm alone.

My heart looked up with binoculars.

I could run.

My lungs shed its sticky fear, demanding oxygen, feeding my legs in preparation of a sprint.

I could vanish.

I could hide.

I should run in the opposite direction.

My eyes locked on Elder as he continued to stalk away. He didn't look back. Did he want me to run? Was this a test? If I did run, would he chase me? And if he did chase me, how far would I get thanks to my battered body and ill health?

But that wasn't the point.

The point was to attempt to flee—to create a scene, to hopefully get the police involved.
To let people know I'm still alive and ready to go home.
Beneath the scintillating idea of running, guilt slowly bubbled.
Guilt at leaving without a thank you or explanation that it wasn't *him* I ran from but the captivity he wanted to keep me in. Regret at leaving whatever connection had budded between us.
He freed you from agony. He killed Tony and broke Alrik into pieces ready for you to deliver the finishing bullet.
I bounced on the balls of my feet.
So what?
Yes, he'd helped me. Yes, I would always be grateful. But he'd done it for his own gain, not mine. When Tony had bashed in the door with a baseball bat and Alrik pressed a gun to my temple, he'd almost let them kill me.
He'd contemplated it far longer than someone who didn't have darkness in their soul would.
Strangers milled around me, their soft conversation threading with my thoughts in a wash of deliberation.
Go.
You might not get another chance.
But then Elder turned.
His elegant body twisted to face me, his eyes latching onto mine down the street. Enough metres separated us that I could still run. I'd get a decent head start.
Go...
The command whispered with authority, surging down my leg.
Elder froze as my left foot moved backward, deciding it wanted to gamble on running, that it wanted freedom.
His lips pressed into a thin line. He didn't move, but he knew. He knew I was moments away from bolting. Instead of moving to face me fully, to prepare to chase, he merely rolled his shoulders and dug one hand into his jeans pocket.

The other, he brought up, rubbed his mouth, then splayed it open; encapsulating the busy market around us, the steaming sunshine, and the wide-open world I could disappear into.

He gave me his approval.

And then he waited to see what I would do.

My body swayed backward, taking pressure off my right foot to join my left in retreat. However, as the sandal disengaged from the hot concrete, I stumbled forward instead.

Despite every instinct yanking me down the street and into the cobblestone alley to a sanctuary I didn't know, I found myself walking to the beast I was beginning to understand.

Step after step, I waged war on my decision. Step after step, Elder's face tightened as his arm fell to his side, patiently waiting.

It took a year and a day or perhaps only a second, but I reached his side, and my mind quietened all thoughts of running as he smiled. "Why didn't you?"

I don't know.

I dropped my head to our grimey feet.

His hand came up, then paused. His shadow on the pavement resembled the bat I'd so often been struck with; I couldn't stop my body from cowering. My mind knew the chances of abuse were slimmer every moment I spent in Elder's company. But my muscles didn't speak the language of my heart and only saw a slayer ready to maim.

He hesitated with his hand outstretched between us.

Gritting my teeth, I forced myself to look up. The second my eyes met his, his hand connected with my chin, keeping my head high and at his mercy.

His jaw worked as he sorted through the words he wanted to spend. "I don't know why you didn't run. But I'll tell you now, you made the right choice." Stepping closer, his nostrils flared as my lips parted.

The attraction and almost kiss of before sprang feverish and unrequited. His fingers tightened on my jaw. "I wanted to see what you would do. If you'd run, you wouldn't have gone far. Do you believe me?" His eyes searched mine. "I lied this morning when I said I wouldn't chase after you. I'd chase until you gave up. I can't let you go yet, Pim. But today has been about choices for you, and you needed to make that for yourself. Run or come to me, the outcome would've been the same."

He bowed his head, his mouth tickling my ear. "You would've been back on the Phantom whether you liked it or not. Don't torture yourself wondering what could've happened if you *had* run. *This* is what would've happened because there is no other choice for us."

Letting me go, he growled. "The moment we met, our choices were stolen from us. Yours because I've decided to control your fate. And mine because you've decided to deny me what I want." He bared his teeth. "One of these days, I'll know who you are. You *will* answer my every question, and you *will* let me inside your mind. It's an inevitability, not a choice, Pim. You might as well get used to that."

I sucked in a breath as he let me go.

Berating me with his black gaze, he added, "In the meantime, let me return the favour. Allow me to show you who I am, so there is no doubt to what I expect."

My blood scurried faster. I didn't know how he planned to show me, but tension glimmered in the air around us, pregnant with promise.

Squirming bodies of a Chinese tour group suddenly engulfed the busy streets. They descended on the sidewalk in matching baseball hats and named lanyards.

Elder dodged to the left, forcing me to go to my right to let the two-by-two crowd slip past.

He never took his eyes off me as if expecting me to run again.

His voice kept repeating in my head, activating fear and the slightest hint of a threat. It had been a threat but unlike any I'd had before.

I'd chase until you gave up.

At the core of that was a promise to never let me go. The primal part of me liked it more than loathed it.

After tour-group-badge-twenty-two brushed by, Elder stepped toward me as I stepped toward him in perfect synchronicity. We snapped back together as if being far apart was unnatural.

It made no sense to be so aware of him when only seconds ago I'd been so close to never looking back.

His lips spread into a smirk as he held up a black wallet with a wad of Yuan currency sticking from the top. "I'll tell you a few secrets of my own, silent one. I steal because I'm good at it. I steal because I get pleasure from it. You are my possession, and once stolen, I don't relinquish what is mine—to anyone. And this—" he waggled the wallet— "is how easy I take things that don't belong to me."

My eyes widened as he opened the leather and thumbed nonchalantly through the cash.

Did he just steal that?

He didn't care he was on a street in front of hundreds of people with property that didn't belong to him. His body language didn't change. He remained aloof and uncondemnable.

His thumb and forefinger pinched a colourful bill, rubbing it in a way that made my cheeks flare. Images of his fingers rubbing my nipple sprang from nowhere; only this time, it didn't make me want to vomit.

He glanced up. "A few years ago, I would've stolen his money, thrown his identification and credit cards in the gutter, and run. I would've taken what was his because I believed I had every right to do what I needed to survive."

He moved closer, drawing to his full height. "Just like you think you're doing everything you have the right to do to survive." Tapping my nose with the wallet, he whispered, "But sometimes, what you think you have the right to do isn't the right thing at all. Sometimes, it's wrong, and others get hurt."

I ignored the condescending lesson he preached; my eyes

darted from his, desperate to lock onto the man he'd pilfered from. Stealing me was one thing. Stealing someone's hard earned cash just because he could was entirely another.

The babble of voices from the tour group wrenched me around.

Them.

He stole it from them.

Elder murmured in my ear. "Third man from the back. It was too easy. A small reach into his back pocket and goodbye holiday funds. What should we buy, Pimlico? Should we blow it on things we don't deserve or donate it to another who has nothing? I could play Robin Hood, if you're inclined."

How could he take from someone who might've saved their entire life for this trip? How could he just remove someone's property without a flicker of culpability or empathy?

You're evil.

Trying to snatch the wallet from his hand, I glowered.

Give it back to him.

He chuckled, holding the cash out of reach. "Frustrating when the other doesn't do what you want, isn't it?"

I pointed at the leather, narrowing my eyes in reproof then pointed at the tour group. I didn't stop to think I'd broken a very clear rule not to communicate. The audacity of his theft put aside my own issues in order to battle for someone else's.

It's not yours to take.

"What is ours in this world? Is anything truly ours? You were a belonging for a long time…but you're a woman. Are you for sale? Was your incarceration unacceptable or merely an inconvenience to you?"

I had enough of this twisted conversation.

Shut up and give me that.

I jumped, stretching as he held the money higher. My spine screamed as whatever shock absorbers I should have had no longer operated for such activities.

Ignoring the pain, I tried to seize the wallet again, wishing I could scream to the group to halt and check their belongings.

Is this a worthy enough cause to speak?

To smear Elder with petty theft? Or could I fix this without giving up everything I had left?

Elder narrowed his eyes before dropping his arm and pressing the bulging wallet into my hand. "I haven't stolen in a very long time. Until you, of course." He licked his bottom lip, his gaze burning with hell. "I'm a taker, Pim, but I'm done stealing from those who don't deserve it." His voice darkened. "Go give it back to him."

What?

"Go on. Before it's too late." Without another word, he stuck his far too dextrous hands into his pockets and strolled down the road.

I stood on my own amongst chaos.

A dilemma slammed into me.

The same one as before, only this time…I had money.

I had dollars.

I had time.

I had anonymity.

I could run. Right now.

I could hide. Straight away.

The cash turned heavy in my hands offering salvation as well as condemnation. Was it wrong to use someone else's money if I needed it? Who had the power to justify who deserved it most?

Taking a step to the curb to cross the road, all thoughts of doing the right thing vanished. All I could think about was disappearing so Elder with his sexual threats and men like Alrik with his fists could never touch me again.

My heart wrenched tight on an invisible collar, yanking me to a stop.

You're better than that.

Don't become the criminal to justify a crime done to you.

The wallet hissed with slurs, calling me a thief—weak to take and wrong to keep.

My shoulders slouched.

No, I couldn't do it.

I couldn't steal from another even if it meant my freedom. And Elder knew that. He'd made me face the truth by giving me yet another choice.

Choices.

I hate them!

This was the fourth in a long day of directing my life rather than having it puppeteered for me. How different would it have been if I never said yes to coming into Morocco? Could I have sun-baked on the deck and people watched as the port went about its daily bustle?

I could've avoided the almost kiss, the conversation with Dina, and the awful awakening that'd been prodded to open its blurry eyes inside me.

But I'd made those choices, and I had to live with them—just like I had to live with myself with whatever choice I made with the wallet.

Dammit.

Pirouetting, I broke into a jog, cursing the way my lungs wheezed and sweat rolled down my spine. I couldn't call out for the tour group to pause and clambered back the way we'd come, trailing after them.

Not only had Elder given me the choice to steal or not steal and then the task of chasing after a wronged man with his robbed dollars, but he now forced me to break my silence for the second time in a matter of minutes.

Not trusting my tongue to form cohesive words, I swallowed hard, gathered my courage, and tapped the third man from the end on his shoulder.

He turned around, blinking with his camera in his hands ready to capture another picturesque memory of Morocco.

I held up his wallet.

Immediately, rage filled his face. His eyes narrowed, his tanned skin pinking with anger. He shouted at me in a language I couldn't understand. Snatching his money, he waved at his friends, blabbering in animation.

I held up my hands, saying in unknown sign language that I'd found it in the gutter and returned to him.

A lie.

My badly orchestrated articulation didn't work.

His friends joined in, pointing fingers, getting louder with their blame. One reached for my shoulder, yelling for the tour leader to bring reinforcements.

Terror unlocked the preservation gates inside me. I did the only thing I could.

I turned and bolted.

I ran, ducking around children and animals, weaving around women with shopping bags and men selling their wares. My knees bleated like massacred livestock; my tongue twinged from bouncing in my mouth.

But I didn't stop.

Part of the tour group gave chase. Their foreign voices angry and whipping my back with memories of being punished. Of blood dripping, of tears falling, of silent screams shredding my throat.

My past blended with my present, and I didn't just run from them; I ran from *him*.

Alrik.

My heart yelped, grabbing bellows to force more oxygen into my almost crippled limbs. Stumbling, I never gave up until I skidded to a stop beside Elder.

He didn't flinch, merely glanced at me as if I'd been there all along.

I was safe with him, but the chasing stampede continued. I looked over my shoulder, fear once again ransacking my stomach.

Elder stopped and spun in place, dragging me behind him with a firm grip.

The men locked their knees, turning their jog into a standstill. They glanced from me to Elder who stiffened with frost then crossed his arms in predatory invitation.

For a second, they sized him up, their desire to punish me

willing to earn a few bruises in a fight. But as Elder took a heavy step in their direction, they decided it wasn't worth it and turned around.

A few pissed off glances sailed over their shoulders, interlaced with angry grumbles.

As the distance between them and us widened, I gave into the residual pain and hugged myself, breathing hard.

Elder interrupted my recovery with a harsh snip. "How does it feel to be punished for doing the right thing?"

I threw him a withering look.

He gave me a raised eyebrow.

I glowered at him the entire way back to the Phantom.

ELDER

"SIR? YOU WANTED the car again?"

I looked up from my email as Selix entered my office.

After returning to Phantom yesterday, I'd left Pimlico to her own devices. I had too much work to do to spend yet more energy on her.

I'd forced her to take responsibility for herself and her choices. I wouldn't say my method of teaching had backfired, but she hadn't forgiven me for stealing or for making her give it back.

As we'd boarded the yacht and gone our separate ways, her temper crackled so fierce it lashed my skin long after I'd said goodbye.

I'd witnessed her wrath hidden beneath servitude at Alrik's, but this was the first time I'd seen it uncoil and silently rage against my actions. She wanted a fight—her tone of glances and language of harsh sniffs said as much.

And as much as I'd like to argue with her, to engage in a battle of wills—to prove once and for all she couldn't fucking win, I couldn't.

I had to keep my distance because, *fuck me*, that almost kiss.

That moment of sheer insanity in the middle of a dirty street.

The moment I caught her, I'd grown hard. The closer I'd dragged her, the harder I got. And the longer we played whatever bloody game we played, the more I craved a release.

She'd decimated the rickety foundation I'd created after losing everything. She had the power to make me lust far more than a master should his slave.

She's never been a slave.

That was true. But now was not the time to admit it.

She wouldn't push me so much if she knew how graphic my thoughts had become. How salacious and explicit.

I'd seen her naked often enough that my fantasies had become far too realistic. I'd done things to her that I could never do thanks to her history carving great scars into her.

I kept my distance for both our sakes.

"Yes." I closed my laptop. "His Royal Highness has been called away to a diplomatic meeting. He would like the original blueprints delivered in A5 before he leaves."

So much for never meeting him again.

I doubted I'd ever be comfortable now he knew my true identity.

"I can drop them off." Selix straightened his black blazer. "It's no hardship."

I shook my head. "I promised I'd do it personally. I'd planned on heading into the city again before we departed anyway." Standing, I moved to the cabinet where the copies of the current yachts under construction rested in tight scrolls. Selecting the right one, I tapped it against my palm. "Tell Pim to meet me by the ramp. Yesterday, she did well—despite a few mishaps. Today, I'll reward her."

Selix smiled tightly. "Fine. See you on the dock in five."

* * * * *

"These plans don't have the amendments we discussed but the minute they're completed, I'll email." I passed Simo the silky pages of his soon-to-be-waterproof creation.

Like yesterday, he wore a three-piece suit with a crisp white turban on his head. Unlike yesterday, his wife and children weren't present.

He glanced around the park where we'd arranged to meet—half-way for me from the Phantom and half-way for him from his house before heading to the airport. Even for a sea lover like me, the park was perfect in its natural simplicity.

Simo sighed. "It's times like this I don't want to leave my home country."

I focused on the quaint quietness around us. Bird song and the occasional squeal of children playing tag in the rose bushes. It did have a sense of peace, but it was too still beneath my feet, too quiet without the dull roar of engines and ocean squalls.

But I smiled and agreed. "Your home is beautiful. I understand why."

Simo grinned. "And your home? Do you miss it?"

I stiffened; very aware he could bring up my true identity and blab to Pim who stood beside me.

She watched silently but not stupidly. Her gaze stole every twitch and motion, storing for future reference. She never stopped judging, trying to slip beneath my walls and loot my secrets. Her silence was deadly in that respect. How had Alrik never sensed the sleeping assassin inside her? The power hidden beneath survival just waiting to put everything she'd gleaned into practice?

"I have a home." My hands clenched by my sides. "And soon, you will have one too and see how much better it is to float wherever the tide takes you rather than be locked to one continent."

Simo grinned. "An adventure every day."

I chuckled, indulging him. "Exactly. Your children will have a childhood every kid would kill for, and your wife will be able to travel with you on your engagements."

Simo's body softened at the mention of his family.

What would it be like to have such strong emotions? To

hand over your entire heart, never fearing it would be rejected? I'd known what that was like once upon a time. It'd been such a long time ago, I'd forgotten. Shared affection was as mythical to me now as breathing beneath the waves like a fish.

"Speaking of engagements, I really must be going." Simo tapped his temple with the blueprint scroll. "Once again, thank you for meeting me here. I'll look forward to catching up soon." He held out his hand.

I shook his. "Safe travels, Your Highness." Stepping back, Pim moved with me, her dainty feet aligning with mine to avoid the four bodyguards shadowing Simo.

Her soft scent enticed my nose. My senses once again intensified as my lower belly tightened with desire.

The more she pissed me off and defied me, the more I wanted her.

The more I pulled away and tried to guard myself, the more I wanted to trade her truth for mine.

Our connection made no sense. We'd never talked. We'd shared a single kiss and a string of profound relapses in judgment.

She blistered my mind with a new curse—taking my previous obsession for perfection and twisting it, so every breath and heartbeat increased this stupid crush to delusional proportions.

I knew I was being ridiculous.

I just didn't have the cure to stop it.

I'm Pim-sick and it's not a good illness to have.

We didn't move as Simo crossed the park and slid into a black limousine. His driver pulled away in a thunder of expensive horsepower.

Selix asked, "Are you ready to return?"

I glanced around the park—at the dappled sunshine on the short dry grass and the rustling thirsty trees. I could stay a while in a place like this, but Pim was jumpy, and I meant what I said about giving her a reward.

I'd caused her jumpiness.

I could erase it if I ignored my own dilemma and focused on her.

Unable to glance at Pim, in case I backed her against a tree and gave the world a big fuck you by molesting her in public, I muttered, "Not yet. Lunch is in order."

Pim shifted beside me, no doubt wondering if I had another business meeting.

Gritting my teeth, I turned to her, focusing on how skinny she was and how it was my job to feed her. Lunch was about nutrition, that was all. It wasn't a date or had any romantic connotations. The moment she'd eaten, I'd escort her back to the yacht and take my medicine, so I could ignore my one-tracked brain.

Her eyes kissed mine, content to let me rule for once with no competition.

Maybe today she would finally talk.

If she's forgiven me, of course.

She hadn't been impressed with my pickpocketing skills yesterday. My lips curled at how easy stealing that wallet had been. It had taken no thought at all. If I was honest, I missed the rush, the power. What would she say if she knew all of this—my life, my wealth, my company—came down to a single robbery that'd changed my world forever?

Would she understand why I kept what I stole? Or would she hate me for being so fucking selfish?

Not that it mattered. Whatever she'd felt for me when we'd almost kissed was drowned out by her strong barometer of right and wrong.

"I heard of a good restaurant half an hour from here," Selix said. "If that sounds of interest, I'll look up directions."

"By foot or car?"

Selix frowned. "Car, of course." His lips curled a little as if walking was for paupers, not businessmen.

Pim shuffled, the smoky grey dress hanging off her with no sexuality, which somehow only amplified hers. Her pretty face half-hidden by a sash of dark brown hair.

"I'm in the mood to walk again." I pushed off, not looking back to see if Pim followed. "Leave the car. We'll send a crew member to collect it. You'll come with us."

It went without saying after the Chinese tour group incident and potential fight over the returned wallet, it was prudent to have Selix close by in case I did anything else idiotic.

"Of course." Selix fell into step with me. "Do you wish to dine alone? I can return the girl and escort you once she's safe?"

She's not going anywhere without me. Pim would eat with me whether she wanted to or not. But just like yesterday, I would give her the illusion of choice and see how she fared.

"If she wants to join me, let her." I turned to face her with a deliberate cold smile. "After all, it's her life and decision."

She scowled as the grey dress licked around her legs. Her skin already pink from the sun.

It seemed she'd already made her choice as she stepped forward with her chin high and gold sandals glinting in preparation for a hike. Michaels had warned me last night that making her do too much exercise could ruin her current healing.

I shouldn't have brought her. I did the opposite of the right thing.

But I wouldn't send her away.

Not today.

I gave her a curt nod, and we all moved forward in uniform—a perfect triangle of travel. Me at the apex with Selix on my left and Pim on my right a few steps behind. Talking wasn't on my agenda and neither was it on Pim's. I'd thrown on a linen shirt this morning with black slacks, and already sweat stuck the material to my skin. I pitied Selix in his black suit walking in this intense heat, but that was why his salary was so damn good.

I paid for his discomfort and pain to keep me safe.

Leaving the park and entering the busy streets of Morocco, Pim's tiny feet barely made a sound on the gravelled walkway. This time, we were on the other side of town where undisciplined children and the occasional squawking chicken congested the roads. Despite the lack of resident wealth, high-fashion glass-fronted stores glittered for tourists—two worlds so far apart but sandwiched together so tightly.

Like Pim and me?

I didn't know the answer because I didn't know if Pim came from money or poverty.

Yet another question to add to the pyramid of all the others.

Selix kept his distance, dropping back a little more as Pim drew up to my side. We walked that way for a while, falling into a rhythm.

Half-way to the yacht, I still hadn't seen a restaurant that didn't look either unsanitary or too crowded. Every few hundred metres, I slowed enough for Pim to catch up. Whatever aches she suffered slowed her considerably more than yesterday.

I hated that I'd been the cause of some of her sprains and pain. But her presence didn't relax me, so it was only fair we were both uncomfortable.

Even the manic world of Morocco couldn't distract me from being all too aware of her soft breathing and sweat-gleaming skin. If the sun caught her shoulders just right, it painted her in a golden glow, hiding the remnants of bruises, making her seem ready for harsher manipulation to talk.

Her time is running out—

"Hey, Prest!"

Shit.

I pulled to a stop, looking through the crowds for whoever had recognised me. Pim stiffened, drawing to a halt.

A man I vaguely recognised appeared in a rumpled maroon suit and black shirt. Glossy gel lacquered his dark blond hair, making him seem sleazy despite the expensive tailoring.

His hand speared out as he grinned. "Been wondering if

I'd ever bump into you again." He pumped my palm as if I was his long lost brother.

Who the fuck is this?

"Do I know you?"

The guy wrinkled his nose. His unkempt beard caught the light as his gaze flicked from me to Pim and back again. "Hong Kong, four years ago? We were at the same dinner party." He waggled his eyebrows. "Remember?"

My brain kicked into gear, sorting through memories I no longer had any urge to recall. And there, sulking at the very bottom covered in shame and guilt, was the dinner party in question.

I clenched my jaw. "Ah yes, Darren?"

"Dafford." The guy grinned. "Dafford Cartwright." His attention slipped back to Pim.

Livid acrimony and disgust filled me. A growl built from nowhere. I knew why he watched her—why he looked at her with carnivorous eyes and not that of a normal man.

That dinner party hadn't just been a dinner. It had been a meal, yes. But on the tears and fears of women. Strippers had been hired to entertain, but they hadn't signed up for the bonus activities the men decided were in order.

Force had been used.

I hadn't done what they had, but I hadn't tried to stop it either. I was there to step into the underworld. What was the point in showing my hand to the devils I was trying to play with by stopping their fun?

"New tricks, huh?" Dafford grinned. "How much did you spend?"

My back snapped straight. "How much?"

"Oh, come on." He lowered his voice, stepping closer. "I know a possession when I see one." He slapped me on the back. "Good pickings. Pretty enough."

I struggled not to tear his motherfucking arm off.

My jaw locked, preventing me from tearing his ears a new asshole and rendering him deaf.

"Had one of my own for a few years until…well." He shrugged. "Things happen, I guess."

Pim sucked in a tattered gasp, understanding his vague insinuation of abusing a life and then fucking *shrugging* when that life was snuffed out. Brimstone boiled in her blood, tainting the air between us as if any second she'd launch at him, regardless she was still weak.

If she did, we'd have a full on brawl, most likely ending in death.

His death.

I took a subtle step toward her, pressing my side against hers. I assured myself it was for her benefit, when in reality…it was probably for mine.

She trembled. Her heat scorching through my shirt, my skin, past my tattoo and right into my bloody heart.

Her face lost all kindness or inquisitive awareness of the city. She stood taller, tighter, slamming doors to each partition that I'd finally cracked open, throwing locks home and shutting down into ice.

She glowered at Dafford as if he were Alrik reincarnated from the dead.

Dafford grinned at her silence, misreading her for meekness rather than trembling with vehemence. "Where did you buy her from?"

I swallowed hard against my ever-growing hate. "I didn't."

"You didn't?" His eyes glittered. "Hand-me-down?" He raked his attention over her.

I wanted to fucking stab out his eyeballs. I buffed my nails on my shirt, doing my best to remain above his cheap filth. "I suggest you shut the fuck up."

How *dare* he look at her? I never wanted another fucking bastard looking at her that way again.

His eye twitched. "Aww, I get it. Sensitive subject in public." He lowered his voice. "She's well trained, though, judging by her condition. But you could work on her making eye contact. That's a bit rude."

I ignored most of his sentence, temper hissing through my nose.

Well trained? What fucking condition? "You're basing your conclusion on her behaviour by her bruises, am I correct?"

He laughed. "Yeah, they're the signature of good control. Don't you think?"

My hands clenched until my knuckles popped.

Selix crept up behind me. His solid power was comforting even if I didn't need his help to kill a turd like this. He shifted slightly, moving to shadow Pim, placing himself unasked to protect the girl I'd stolen—the woman he couldn't understand why I was fascinated with but wouldn't say a word because he knew I didn't need logic to do things.

Just as I didn't need any more encouragement to hurt this prick.

Pim trembled against me as Dafford leered at her. "Pick her up from Morocco? That's why I'm here actually. Heard there's a travelling company called the QMB that finds locals and prepares them in an auction. Heading there in two days." He sighed dramatically. "Pity I don't already have a replacement. We could've shared for the night."

Cunt.

"I don't share."

Pim's feet scuffed the pavement. I didn't know if she was preparing to attack or sprint far away. Either way, I was done listening to such garbage.

Already, our little tête-à-tête had garnered attention from locals. We were a novelty. With such attention, I didn't want to cause a scene. Then again, I knew a thousand different ways to kill—seen and unseen.

Selix cleared his throat, a code for us to move or act but not to dally any longer.

I wanted to flat out murder Dafford.

But I had enough self-restraint to suck in a breath and convince myself he wasn't fucking worth it.

Straightening my back, I growled. "Well, as entertaining as

this *chat* has been, we've got to go." I gave Dafford a tight smile, keeping my temper and every other demon I battled locked tight.

I gave him a lifeline even though he didn't bloody deserve it.

He didn't take it.

Reaching out, he had the motherfucking audacity to touch Pimlico's shoulder. She flinched, whiteness coating her face as she bared her teeth.

He gripped her hard in reproach. "No way to respond to a master touching you, girl."

And yep, I'd known this would happen.

I'd known the minute I stole her that Pim would be the cause of my unravelling, my undoing, my self-control.

Yanking her forward, he snarled, "Tell you what, Prest. If she's a hand-me-down, you're not doing a good job keeping up her training. I'll buy her off you, right here, right now. Name your price."

Pim's eyes doubled in size but instead of looking to me for help, she twisted and fought on her own. Always on her own. Never leaning, never seeking.

I'd been waiting for this opportunity. To offload her. To make her someone else's problem. I didn't have the willpower or the strength to live with her and not hurt her.

But to sell her knowing her fate?

Sell her after getting to know her in the small silent snippets she'd given.

Fuck no.

Dafford laughed, still holding what was mine. "Come on, man, I hate this place. If I can leave sooner, I will. Tell you what, I'll buy this one and you take my ticket to the auction and pick up a newer model." His face romped with evil. "I've always liked the unbroken ones. More fun that way."

It didn't take a thought. Nothing did when I reached such a dangerous calm. My arm shot out, my hand wrapped around his throat, and I squeezed.

Pimlico stood there, frozen as I squeezed and motherfucking *squeezed*.

Selix moved to the side, blocking my violence from those gawking as best he could.

It would be so easy to kill him.

To stop him hurting others and repair a little of my damaged karma, but this was too public, and I wouldn't go to jail for him.

Letting Dafford go, he slammed to his knees, gasping for breath, holding his bruised neck. "You fucking—"

I stepped closer, crowding him. "Finish that sentence, and I finish you. Get out of town. If I hear you went to the auction, I'll find you and kill you. No more girls. Do you understand?"

He sneered. "Always did think you were a pussy. Bet she's not even yours." He glared at Pim. "Bet you haven't even fucked her."

I couldn't stop my leg as it shot forward and connected solid and true on his chest.

He wheezed, doubling over.

"She is mine. And she's not for sale. If we cross paths again, asshole, you know what will happen."

Grabbing Pim's arm, I dragged her with me as I stormed away.

I needed to leave before I reneged and decided his death was worth more than my future tasks. I had too much to do before my journey was at an end—too many apologies to utter, too many wrongs to right.

Walking away was the only thing to do but fuck it pissed me off.

Selix kept up closer than before, his gaze hopping over the gathered crowd. Men in tatty work clothes, women with blinking children. The public's disapproval was readable, trying to conclude if I was the bad guy or if the man on his knees was.

Who to stop, who to question?

Luckily, deliberation was our friend, and after a few glowers, the welldoers decided to leave well alone.

We continued down the road with no harassment.

Pim trotted beside me as my stride lengthened.

My thoughts were on home—of getting on the water regardless if we weren't due to leave for another night. I wanted the empty horizon. I wanted freedom from the slime inhabiting the earth.

Ducking through a pop-up market selling bright fabrics and pungent curries, Pim stumbled on a crumpled water bottle. Her weight landed squarely in my hand where I held her, reminding me she wasn't physically fit to tear through the streets with no pause.

Letting her go, I jerked both hands through my hair. "Sorry." The shakes began—the energy my body conjured to pummel that bastard into smithereens had no violent outlet so it hijacked my nervous system.

If we weren't so close to the port, I'd order Selix to run back and grab the car, but the welcoming sight of water glittered up ahead. The urge to sprint consumed me.

Pim's gaze fell on a shopping cart full of bronze figurines and touristy paraphernalia.

The haunted look was back in her eyes. The memory of what she'd been and what could happen again hounding her.

Screw lunch and mingling with likeminded diners. My appetite was nil. I was sure Pim felt the same.

Her fingers hovered over a small bronze lantern the size of her thumb.

The wrinkled shopkeeper smiled with capped teeth and a teal veil over her head. "It's the genie lamp. Touch it. Rub it. Tell it your secrets."

Pim gave me a hesitant look as if she'd been caught breaking a rule. She snatched her hand away, backing from the stall.

The shopkeeper, sensing a losing sale, held up the figurine, plucking a small wooden bound notebook below it. "This is the wishing book that comes with it. You write in your wishes and rub the lamp, and it comes true." She leaned across her wares.

"Here, take it. All your dreams for only ten dollars."

Pimlico stepped away, keeping her head down and body wrapped low. The straightness of her spine from the past week or so together rolled, curving down and down into the question mark of her existence. I'd somehow managed to give her answers enough to trust life and not seek death. And that fucking cocksucker had undone my hard work. I hated that she'd come face-to-face with a man who would pay an exuberant amount of money to do exactly what Alrik had done. That her faith in humanity was once again shattered because where good lived evil did too, and sometimes, it cast a shadow over everything.

I couldn't let that bastard undo everything I'd achieved.

She was mine.

She owed me.

Her time was almost up on repaying.

Pulling out a fifty US dollar, I shoved it at the shopkeeper then scooped up the notebook and genie lamp. "Keep the change."

The bronze token was surprisingly heavy as I strode to Pim and captured her elbow. Taking a deep breath, I ignored the heat between us, banked like a small furnace waiting for more fuel.

"Whatever happened today doesn't matter. It's your choice to relive or forget. I can't do that for you." Pressing the gift into her hands, I added, "However, perhaps I'll be your genie. Write down your wishes, silent one. Tell me what I can do to make it right."

"Who knows what will come true."

Pimlico

LIFE DIDN'T SUDDENLY change, even though my heart had.

It'd slammed back the steel lock, flooded the moat, and cranked up the drawbridge after tentatively tiptoeing into the world Elder promised I would be safe in.

For a moment, I was able to notice what others did—the sun, the wind, the shopping, the scents of a hustling city.

But then I'd been slapped in the face by rancid cruelty once again.

He wanted to buy me.
He wanted to hurt me like Alrik, Tony, and Monty.
He has tickets to the same auction I was sold at.
Bastard!

Would I never be free to just be me? To be a girl walking down a street without worry of being kidnapped and sold?

Clutching the bronze genie lamp, I glanced at the wooden book that accompanied it. A wishing book.

Don't I already write wishes to No One?

I sat cross-legged on my bed (even though it hurt my hips) and stroked the notepad to my imaginary friend while eyeing up the wood-bound gift Elder had purchased.

You don't write wishes, you write confessions. There's a difference.

Ever since the awful incident where Elder almost killed yet another man to keep me safe, then brushed off the confrontation and bought me this innocuous figurine, we hadn't spoken. He'd marched me back to the Phantom with both him and Selix glowering at every shopper and peering into every shadow.

By the time we boarded, my nerves resembled chewed up spaghetti and Elder was no better. A grunted goodbye was all I earned before he vanished to his quarters, leaving me to dwindle off to mine.

For the past hour, I'd sat clicking my pen's nib open and closed, open and closed, trying to decide if I should write a secret to No One or indulge in a wish to Elder.

Guilt sat heavy at the thought of using Elder's gift over a lifetime of spilling my soul to No One. But it didn't stop me from cracking open the wishing book. No One had been there for me in my darkest moments. Perhaps it was time to let Elder be there in my future.

He was going to kill him.

My heart wrapped itself up in warm blankets before I recalled his face when the offer of ownership was first discussed.

He'd contemplated giving me up.

He'd been both saint and sinner and I hated that. I needed him to be either good or bad, commendable or corrupt. How could I decide what I felt toward him if he was human? Humans weren't perfect. But I expected Elder to be.

My pen came down, a whisper of a wish formed, but a loud clanking noise interrupted.

My head wrenched up, my nerves still shredded into strings thanks to that asshole in Morocco.

It's the anchor.

My heart didn't listen, whizz-banging in terror.

We're leaving.

Abandoning the wishing book on the bed, I traded the pen for my genie lamp and headed across the suite. By the time I made it to the door and down the corridor to herald the lift, the clunking anchor chain had spindled, and the noise stopped.

A more familiar rumble followed—the cranking of massive engines waking from mechanical slumber to chug us far away. Away from men with penny-bulging pockets to buy a life to torment.

Thank God.

Stepping into the lift, I glowered as the mirrored walls reflected not me but the scene of Elder stripping me yesterday. Instead of the heated fear from him caressing me, my skin crawled.

Had that been a test?

Had he pushed me to see if I was ready? For all his talk of not touching me...had he run out of patience?

When that man asked for my price tag—

My insides hurt, remembering yet again the way Elder sighed before exploding. For a second, his body language relaxed in relief.

He lingered over the chance to be rid of me.

And why shouldn't he? I was a thorn in his unblemished kingdom, pricking holes into whatever peace he valued.

He *should* get rid of me.

I wanted to get rid of me most of the time. Just because I was stuck fighting my way back to health, bound to fixing every fault before I could live again...it didn't mean Elder was obligated.

He can do what he wants with me. I'm completely at his mercy.

More nerves quaked at how flimsy my existence was as I stepped off the elevator onto the top deck and padded barefoot on the polished, silky wood. My fingers never let go of my genie lamp. Elder had bought me clothes and kept me fed, but it was the first thing I'd been given that was frivolous and unnecessary to survival—apart from my origami gifts.

It's mine.

An intense need to keep it close enveloped me. It was such a new possession, but I was in love with it as much as I'd been with my Minnie Mouse watch my dad had given and my murderer had stolen.

Squinting in the russet aging sun, I spotted him.

He stood at the front of the yacht. The telltale sweet smoke wisped around his head as he faced out to sea. His back remained taut and tense, his shoulders locked in stress. He didn't look around as I moved toward the side, drinking in the departing scene of Morocco at sunset.

The dusty city changed from every-day colours to drenched in orange and sienna. People moved like ants in the distance, and even now, a faint smell of curry and exotic spices carried on the breeze.

I kept Elder locked in my peripheral, watching but pretending otherwise. I wanted to judge him—to read his thoughts, to understand my stability in his life. Was he rethinking keeping me? After saying no to Dafford, did he think about the possibility of selling me to another who he approved of?

Navigating the harbour, the captain slowly opened up the engines, speeding us farther and farther from the man who'd reminded me that the world was no longer a safe place, no matter where I lived.

England, America, Morocco—each was tainted by evil running unrepentant over good. How did anyone stay decent when self-obsession and lawlessness seemed to favour the bold?

Was that what happened to Elder?

Had he once been a normal son, brother, and friend—then lost sight of his goodness and embraced bad instead?

I never moved from my spot on the railing, my fingers warming the genie lamp. Other vessels and tanker ships were our neighbours as we steadily made our way out to sea. As Morocco slowly turned from large cosmopolitan to toy city, I made my first wish.

I wish to no longer have a dollar value that people can bargain and buy.

The universe offered no answer, and I placed my elbows on the railing, letting the water world put me in a trance.

* * * * *

An hour or so later, stars blanketed the sky and my stomach rumbled for food. Elder's weed cigarette had long since been smoked and he stalked past my resting spot without a word.

My skin tickled with rejection. He'd seen me but hadn't stopped.

Why?

What did he mean about being my genie? Did he think he could grant me happiness again? Could he somehow remove the torture and pain associated with sex and leave me normal—so I might run toward rather than away from the electricity between us?

Trapped by yet more questions, I headed below and entered my suite. There, I found dinner waiting for me on my dining table—pan-fried fish with couscous and a tagine full of roasted vegetables.

Something inedible also waited, tucked carefully next to aromatic food: a folded masterpiece in the shape of an exquisite dollar rose.

An origami creation denoting my worth to the printed value of one hundred pennies.

The contorted money flipped my stomach and made me sad at the same time.

Whatever had happened between us yesterday—the almost kiss, pickpocketing, and meeting the prince and princess—today had ruined it.

Knowing without being told I would be undisturbed for the rest of the night, I pushed the dress off my shoulders, stepped from the puddle, and sat down to my meal with my dollar rose.

Alone.

* * * * *

Three days passed.

They were the worst since Elder had saved me.

Not because he was cruel or violent, not even because he avoided me and only graced me with tight glances and surly commands to eat, rest, and get out of his way so he could work in peace.

But because he pulled away from me.

So much for his comment about being my genie.

No matter how much I rubbed that little lamp, I received no magical smoke or mystical being ready to listen and deliver.

He no longer made an effort to ask me questions. He didn't command me to bring the wooden notebook to him and write replies to things he wanted to know.

He just stopped caring.

As if…as if…the thought of doing yet more for me, when he'd seen how totally ruined my mind was, was no longer feasible but stupid—a total waste of time.

He'd been slapped with alternatives. I wasn't what he wanted. I could no longer be his crucifix to bear. He might get off on bringing me back from the dead, but he'd never get me to sleep with him willingly. He'd never hear the secrets he wanted to hear.

Even the sizzling chemistry whenever we were near didn't have the same pop and crackle.

His eyes were void of lust. Even though I hated those four letters and the word they depicted, lust was what hummed quietly between us—it was what gave us the glue to keep dancing this strange dance.

But now…nothing.

And I knew why.

He's going to sell me.

That's why he's waiting. That was why we'd left port—to travel to another city with better prospects for a deal.

That man had mentioned Hong Kong with connotations of women being used.

Is that where he's taking me?

Elder had fattened me up, increased my strength, and repaired my bodily flaws not for him, but for another. Someone like Alrik who would continue my existence in hell.

I struggled to breathe.

My awful, awful suspicions were confirmed when Michaels came to remove the bandage around my hand and checked on my tongue the third day at sea.

I was on the mend. A healed trinket for sale whenever Elder chose.

"Your stitches are gone." Michaels grinned as if this was good not disastrous. "How do you feel?"

Answering his questions had become easy. Besides, I was distracted by uglier things.

My body moved without thought. I shrugged. I wouldn't tell him I physically felt better but mentally I'd stepped ten paces back. I'd locked myself in a doubt-filled cell I couldn't escape from.

"You can test it out, you know. It won't fall off if you speak." He tilted his head, patience painting his softly freckled face.

My tongue was no longer swollen. Tender and sore with certain movements but miraculous in how it'd reduced in injury. Being able to lick an ice cream or curl it to blow on hot soup was a blessing.

Alrik hadn't stolen my power of speech, after all.

Not that I would know. I hadn't attempted to use it.

I was afraid.

Petrified.

If I spoke now, how could I go back to being silent when all of this was gone and the Phantom dropped me in Elder's wake never to be free again?

I bowed my head, not looking at Michaels even though he breathed heavily with frustration.

He patted my healed hand, his eyes dancing over the fading bruises still lingering on my chest. Once again, I sat naked with just a sheet covering me. He'd grown used to my dislike of clothes; he made me feel accepted in a way Elder did not.

If I was ever going to speak, it would be to Michaels. To this man who understood the struggle I lived with, the struggle *inside* not outside.

But that first word would be so precious. I couldn't just give it away. *Give it to Elder to repay him for his generosity, regardless of his end intentions.*

I bit my lip at the thought. Would that stop him from getting rid of me?

Was it worth the cost?

Yes.

No.

Yes.

I don't know.

Around and around on the merry-go-round of my topsy-turvy thoughts.

The conundrum kept me silent. The fear that he would sell me kept me mute.

"You know where I am if you're ever ready to talk." Standing, Michaels collected his bag and headed to the door. "You know, if you won't speak to me, then perhaps it's time you spoke to him." He didn't wait for my nonverbal reply before disappearing out the door.

* * * * *

That night, after another lonely dinner, I headed into the bathroom.

If Elder *was* going to get rid of me, shouldn't I attempt to escape? Shouldn't I do everything I could to change his mind?

Why was I wasting time doing nothing? Hadn't I fought my entire life?

Why am I stopping now when freedom is closer than it's ever been?

My depression from the past seventy-two hours dispersed, incinerating under the quick blast of determination. I liked those questions. They didn't drown me but gave me a ladder to put my head above the tide and think clearly.

I'd allowed Elder to replace Alrik. I slipped into old patterns of letting him decide my fate.

Not anymore.

A terrifying, totally insane plan quickly unravelled in my head.

Could it work?

Can I do it?

My hands shook as I grabbed the genie lamp and squeezed, sending a quick wish.

I wish to change his mind by any means necessary.

Dina's advice from our bathroom chat came back. She spoke of rewarding men for their good deeds. To lavish them with praise that kept them generous and kind because they felt noticed and appreciated.

Perhaps, Elder needed to be lavished. To be told he meant a lot to me rather than barely tolerated.

Do it then…

Do what exactly?

Sit him down and blurt out a mismatch of condescending praise like I would to a puppy that'd retrieved a saliva-soaked tennis ball? Pat his head and rub his nose and pitch my voice into sickly sweet, hoping such tribute would keep me by his side?

You have better skills.

My heart gasped, remembering those skills. Those disgusting talents I'd been forced to adapt to survive.

Use them.

Bribe him…

Adrenaline filled me as I swallowed back foul memories, doing my best to envision using beaten-taught expertise to buy myself more time.

Do it.

It's the only way.

Clamping down on doubt, I jogged into the bathroom.

For a moment, I just stood there.

What am I thinking?
I shook my head. No, I couldn't do it.
You can.
I *hated* it with Alrik.
I'll hate it with Elder.
But if it kept me safe…wasn't the discomfort worth it?
Sucking in a breath, I stared at myself in the mirror.

A girl I no longer recognised stared back. I couldn't believe I contemplated doing the one act I deplored above everything, all in the name of bartering for my freedom. Taking my own life was more preferable, more acceptable.

But I lived in a commerce world. People traded things all the time. Items that didn't hold value for the current owner were priceless to another.

All it would cost me was dignity and self-worth. I'd given up such things the moment I was sold. It was the currency I'd been taught—the sum value I was willing to spend.

It would bankrupt me, but to Elder, it would carry the weight of winning.

And if he felt I'd finally accepted his terms…

It's worth a try.

Ignoring my trembles, I combed my hair until it shone glossy and thick. I pinched my cheeks until a healthy young girl stared back. I opened my mouth, touching the red line on my tongue where no black stitches remained, then sucked up every droplet of courage I had left.

Placing my hands on the marble either side of the sink, I leaned forward, braced, fidgeted, braced again, then parted my lips.

My tongue shaped and tested silent words. My vocal cords tossed off grime and grit to obey. And my lungs inflated with the knowledge that here and now, I took back a piece of myself I'd locked away.

My first word was my own.

I was the one who deserved it the most.

Looking into my moss-coloured eyes, I whispered, "Stop

being we—" Pain lacerated my throat. I stopped, coughing as tears formed and I massaged the abused larynx that was no longer on a sabbatical.

The first vibration into understandable sounds was hard and painful and croaky.

But to my ears, they were utterly sublime.

Smiling through tears, I tried again. "Stop being weak, you—" another cough, swallow, wince "—have to—to decide."

The stutter-hum of my voice sent goosebumps down my spine. I'd forgotten what I sounded like. My English accent was different to the many ethnicities Elder hired on board.

I sound like my mother.

Wetness spilled over my cheeks as I let questions flow. Where was she? Why hadn't she picked up the phone that day? Did she ever think about me?

Pushing her away, I dug my fingernails into the marble and inhaled deep. I prepared to unlock the remaining snares and bear-traps around my throat. "No one else deser—deserved your first words but y—you. Stop being a vic—" *Ouch*, that word hurt more than the others.

Turning on the tap, I poured a little water into my palm and drank. Once the burn in my throat was dampened, I finished. "Stop being a vic—victim."

My eyes narrowed in reproach even as I continued to berate myself. "You have to decide, Min—Minnie Mouse."

I coughed, swallowed, took another drink of water. My father's nickname sent more tears plopping against the sink. My voice wobbled from sadness as well as ill practice. "Run. Find a way to escape—"

Another cough stopped me short. Hot pain overwhelmed me, and as much as I wanted to continue talking, my body was not ready.

Locking eyes to the mirrored reflection, my forehead furrowed with concentration.

Escape, Tasmin. Go home…even if there is no home to return to. Do whatever it takes. Or decide if you want him to keep you. The world is not safe out there. You saw first-hand how Elder steals and that man buys pleasure. Perhaps you were never meant to live amongst normal. Perhaps there is *no more normal.*

My fingertips pressed against the mirror. *This isn't so bad, is it? Sure, he'll make you do things, sexual things, but he's proven to be human beneath his monster.*

I couldn't look deep enough inside myself to find answers. I didn't know what I wanted. But I did know I didn't want to be sold.

Not now. Not ever.

Never again.

You know what you must do then.

I nodded at my reflection, dropping my fingers from the cool mirror and swiping at the streaks of salt on my cheeks. Each breath plugged up the holes inside with ideas and fears and wishes.

Swallowing, I muttered two words before embracing my silence once again. Two words solidifying my commitment to doing whatever was necessary to keep myself alive, no matter what world I stayed alive in.

"I know."

Pushing off from the sink, I strode from the bathroom before I could change my mind.

ELDER

I HEARD HER before I saw her.

The gentle breathing of determination sneaking on silent feet.

My muscles locked.

I'd deliberately kept my distance for three days, taking my issues out on Selix in the ring and swimming in the ocean.

I was exhausted. Not just physically but mentally, too.

Pim had dragged me back to a time when things were perfect. She'd reminded me of how I was before the catastrophe and showed me just how much I'd changed. The boy in my past would've taken her anywhere she wanted the moment I'd rescued her. I would've given her money to survive and professional help to thrive. Everything I'd stolen up to that point would've been shared because I knew what it was like to have no one.

I was no longer that boy.

I was a man who'd spent the last seventy-two hours obsessing over which choice was the lesser of two evils: keep her and destroy myself, or sell her and destroy whatever was left inside her.

Freeing her was not an option—not because I hadn't been able to track down her mother—even though I'd tried again to trace her number—but because I hadn't finished what I needed to do before my past came to light and I was incarcerated for life.

I didn't know Pim's name. I didn't have an accent to go off, skin colouring to hint, habits to trace. I had no idea where she came from. She wrote to No One, but she *was* no one. Alone in the vast world of sin.

Wait...that's wrong.

My fists clenched as my world imploded, crushing me with a new thought.

She's not No One.

...I am.

For years, I'd been adrift. I'd been forgotten, shunned, unwanted. I had no one to call my own, no home, no love. No one knew my true name (apart from three people). No one knew who I was anymore—including myself.

I was the epitome of no one and nothing.

Christ, had she been writing to me the entire time?

Goosebumps snarled over my flesh that it wasn't Alrik and his desire to build an armoured yacht that'd brought me to her, but her notes to No One—all along addressed to me.

The determined footstep came again, smashing my stampeding thoughts into a singular one.

Her.

I stopped breathing.

Stepping into the moonlight, Pim moved with a white sheet haloed around her. She'd tied the ends behind her neck, creating a loose toga that turned her from human girl to Grecian goddess.

Every part of me stiffened.

Fuck.

How did she get even more beautiful in three days?

My sea-droplet covered chest warmed until I was sure I'd steam with heat. My heart, already darting wildly from my prior conclusion of being her No One, increased its tempo until I grew lightheaded with need.

Intensity arrowed down my belly, feeding my cock in a rush of lust.

My wet boxer-briefs couldn't hide my reaction as I thickened and lengthened with how gracefully and brave she moved.

What are you up to, Pim?

Why did you have to seek me out now, when I'm so fucking close to breaking every rule and claiming you?

If I was a better man, I'd command her to go—to turn around and return to her rooms, far away from me. But I wasn't a man.

I was No One and as our eyes met, I fell completely under her spell. I did my best to slow my pulse from my late night swim.

It didn't work.

My heart decided it wouldn't calm, not now she'd bewitched me with her immortal strength and fragile hope and the way her damn eyes dove into mine. Not now I felt tethered to her in a way I never thought I would again.

Tension poured into being, waking around our ankles, getting thicker the longer we stared.

Pim stood there silently judging, waiting, watching.

I should put her on the helicopter and drop her off at the nearest police station. Fuck my past. I had the Phantom. I could outrun the law for long enough.

So why did the very thought of sending her away hurt something inside that I thought was long dead?

Tell her to go back to her fucking room.

Coming to a stop in front of me, Pimlico bowed her head and clasped her hands loosely. The goddess herself prayed before me—for what I didn't know—but she looked celestial and chills ran over my skin, adding to my previous layer of goosebumps.

It was no longer about how beautiful or broken she was. My attraction for her had exceeded normal barriers; I didn't know how to deal with that.

Get away from me, Pim.
Before I do something we'll both regret.
Her chest rose and fell as if she'd heard me, her hair silky and sensual, cascading over her shoulder.

My muscles tensed as she slowly reached up, her hands disappearing beneath her hair to tug at the loose knot holding the sheet.

My chair creaked as I tensed.

The white cotton fell in a quicksilver cascade, puddling on the deck.

Christ.

Her eyes met mine, her chin tilted in regal power.

Her nakedness wasn't vulnerability. It was her strength. The one thing she'd claimed as her weapon. She stood before me bare and unyielding and fucking decimated me with how much I wanted her.

I sucked in a breath, my cock hardening to the point of agony. I should've stood up the moment she arrived. I should've slung a towel over my waist so she wouldn't be appalled with the lust I had suffered when lust had been what hurt her. But sitting on the deck chair with my legs sprawled in front of me, there was no hiding my arousal.

Her gaze dropped to my crotch, her jaw tightening. Shadows crossed her eyes, faint lines etching her mouth as if she argued some internal debate.

And then, she thudded to her knees.

She winced at the hard wood on already punished bones.

My stomach clenched to sit upright and pick her up, terrified she'd tripped.

But her hands shot forward, one landing on my chest to keep me reclined, the other grasping my waistband and pulling.

My cock leapt free from its confinements, not caring about right or wrong.

What the—

Before I could stop her, she inserted my length into her mouth.

Holy.
Fucking.
Jesus.

My mind collapsed as her hot wet mouth sucked me hard. She didn't tease. She didn't toy. Her hands slipped over me as her lips followed, sucking me deep, turning me brain dead.

Instinct roared into control. Pent-up desire unleashing and taking ownership. My hips thrust up as my hand landed on her head. Somewhere in the back of sanity, I noticed how soft her hair felt. How she bobbed over me. How fucking good her tongue worked my crown.

I didn't think about her injury.
I didn't think about her past.

All I thought about was how goddamn good she felt. What a magician she was with her tongue and fingers and mouth.

Every blood cell relocated in my cock, throbbing for more. And she gave it to me as if she understood my body more than I did.

Her tongue swiped again, dancing around the tip, dragging a ragged groan from deep inside me.

I couldn't fight.
I couldn't win.

My legs widened as she shuffled closer on her knees. Her hair blanketed my thighs as she kept my ocean-damp boxer-briefs pulled away while her other hand dropped over my stomach to cup my balls below.

She drove me *insane*.

I shivered with every touch and lick.

It'd been a age since I'd been with a woman. Been with a *willing* woman.

The word 'willing' shot into my head, tearing through my lust.

Pimlico was a woman, but was she willing?

Why was her mouth on me? Her tongue tasting me; her hand superbly working me to come?

Why was she on her knees after a lifetime of hell with another man?

Shit.

My teeth gritted as I dropped my hand from her scalp to her chin. It fucking killed me, but I summoned every decency I had left and tugged her away.

My body trembled. Pre-cum rippled as she sucked harder, refusing to move.

I pulled harder, battling so many things at once.

I wanted to throw her down and fuck her beneath the open sky. I wanted to hit her to get her far away from me so I could gather my tattered thoughts and make sense of this.

I wanted her to stop.

"Pim." I growled as her teeth scraped sensitive skin making another wave of pleasure shoot, begging for a release.

It would be so easy to let her go, to lean back and give in. To spurt inside her expert little mouth and let her take that from me.

But that wasn't how I worked.

I didn't take advantage of people—apart from their money. And I definitely didn't give in. Ever.

"Stop!" Wrenching her mouth off me, I panted as my cock smacked against my bare stomach, glistening with her saliva, pulsating with the need to climb back inside her.

It would be so fucking easy to pull her head back down and tell her to finish what she started.

But the one question I couldn't ignore gave me willpower.

Why had she started this in the first place?

Sitting forward, not caring I remained exposed or she was naked between my thighs, I grabbed her chin again. Her skin was ice beneath my fingers. I refused to look at her breasts or pebbled nipples. I focused on one thing only.

"Why?"

She didn't meet my eyes. Her right hand crept forward and clutched my throbbing cock.

My head fell forward as her palm stroked me with the

lubricant from her mouth, soaring up to squeeze my crown.

"Fuuuck."

Keeping her chin firm in one hand, I grabbed both her wrists with the other, flinching as I yanked her touch away and the elastic of my underwear splatted my cock tight against my belly.

"Tell me why. You didn't want to do this. You don't even like to be in the same room as me, let alone touch me." I shook her a little. "Have I made you feel like you have to repay me? I don't need a pity blowjob."

Her teeth ground beneath my hold, rebellion and secrets in her gaze.

I tightened my fingers, bruising her but unable to stop the frustration leaking through my hand. "Don't touch me, Pim. I don't want that from you."

Her face crumpled before determination replaced her pain.

It was a cruel thing to say, but the truth. Only...not the complete truth. I didn't want subservient sex. I didn't know what I wanted, but fucking her against her will was not it.

Taking a deep breath, I amended, "I don't want that from you unless *you* want it. Do you understand? I'm not going to take from you. Not like him."

She struggled in my hold.

I let her go.

Instead of ducking for the sheet to wrap herself in, she stood seething with reckless calm.

I wished so damn much she'd talk to me, but her silence said everything I needed to hear. I cocked my head, disbelieving the reason I saw in her gaze.

Wait...

I narrowed my eyes, doing my best to see past her anger to the plan gleaming below. "You...you sucked me because you're trying to bribe me...is that it?"

She sniffed, her chin soaring high in the air.

"Why? If not for misplaced need to repay me...then why?" I stopped myself as the answer came. Of course.

Fucking hell, why didn't I realise her thoughts would go in that direction?

Sitting forward, I glowered. "You think if I enjoy fucking you, I'll keep you." My voice lowered. "That I won't sell you."

She locked in place, her kneecaps the only thing trembling when the rest of her was stoic. If I couldn't read her body language, I wouldn't have seen her terror.

"That's it, isn't it? You thought whoring yourself out would make me want to keep you."

Her lips parted at the awful word.

I stood, tucking my pounding cock back into its prison of underwear. "Don't like being called a whore?" I invaded her space, our chests touching, her nipples kissing my dragon's belly. "Then don't act like one."

I couldn't be around her.

I'd do something I'd regret.

This night was fucking over.

"Next time you think you can bribe me to do something by offering sex, remember that I want other things from you. Your body is not my end goal, Pim. Your mind is."

I didn't look back.

Pimlico

A WEEK PASSED.

An awful, terrible week where Elder treated me like a member of his staff. We met occasionally on the deck where the sun shone bright and unhindered, glittering on the ocean all around us, but he merely nodded stiffly and ignored me.

There were no invitations to dinner.

No origami boats or roses.

The night I'd sucked him, I'd relapsed to the same brittle sadness I'd existed in for two years. The shame Elder smeared me with coated everything, and for all the awful attention Alrik bestowed upon me, I wished Elder would at least acknowledge my presence in some way. His temper and judgment over what I'd done drilled holes into me bigger and bigger as each day ticked past.

Not once in two years had Alrik made me feel cheap. He made me wish for death, but he prided himself on telling me how much I was worth and why that value meant he would never kill me.

Elder didn't value me at all.

Was it so wrong of me to use the only skills I had to barter for my safety? Did I deserve to be called a whore?

The moon hung heavy in the sky as I stood on my balcony and pondered just how much I was willing to let this man destroy my soul. I'd already let one destroy my body. I didn't think I could do it again even if the scars weren't visible this time.

The black ocean slipped silently beneath my feet as the Phantom sailed to whatever destination Elder had in mind. We'd been at sea for ten days, and the longer we were away from land and cities, the more he seemed to relax.

But only when I spied on him from the shadows.

When he was aware of my presence, he spiralled tighter and tenser than a fighter ready to battle to the death.

Did I repulse him that much? Where was the man who'd found me intriguing enough, pretty enough, to threaten my owner for one night with me? Why now, that he had me to himself, couldn't he even look at me, let alone talk to me?

Ugh!

I grabbed my hair, rippling in the wind. I didn't want to think anymore.

"Just jump." The two words fell from my lips like a caress. The thought of ending it was no longer powerful but borderline weak. But the sewage inside my mind would never leave. My bones might be healing but would my soul?

My hands clenched the handrail, pulling my body forward. It would be so easy to switch my centre of gravity—push up, teeter, and let the ocean have me.

You survived. Don't give up now.

Sniffing back angry tears, I turned my back on the sea whispering its death-locker sanctuary and closed the door. Quiet descended in the suite, reminding me just how tired I was.

The night we'd set sail from Morocco after Dafford Carlton tried to buy me, the nightmares had begun.

Every time I closed my eyes, Alrik was waiting. He tormented me harder, faster, more brutal than ever before. I'd wake up in sweat-drenched sheets, my heart a chainsaw, and a silent scream lodged in my throat.

Seemed even in unconscious terror, I'd trained my voice not to speak.

Padding to the bathroom, I wrenched on the hot water and climbed into the shower. I did my best to distract my weary thoughts, but washing myself was foreign. My body didn't feel like my own: ridgelines of scars and bumps of broken bones. If I stood too long, heat built in my spine and unwanted aches throbbed in my knees.

I wasn't stupid to think those pains would cease. What I'd lived through had wrecked my young form. But then again, I'd been at war. Whoever returned from war in one piece? Body or mind?

Once I was clean, I dried myself with a fluffy towel and hung it up neatly. Despite the chill of being damp and tired, I didn't dress and climbed into bed naked.

I exhaled heavily and closed my eyes.

* * * * *

"You little bitch. You thought you could run away from me? You can never run away." Master A struck with the chain, slapping it hard with a metal bite against my ass. I bit my lip to staunch my scream as I always did. But it only made him rage harder.

"Speak to me, sweet Pim. Yell. I want to hear you beg."

I tried to curl into a ball, but the ropes on my wrists and ankles prevented me. Tied face down on the bed, I couldn't protect any part of me.

"I know what will make you scream." His chuckle was pure evil. "I know how to break you, pet." His feet thudded on the white carpet as he headed to a remote control on his bedside table.

No.

No. Please.

I squirmed. It only made him laugh.

"Ready for it?" He dramatically punched the play button.

Instantly, classical music rained from the overhead speakers, drenching me in violins and pianos and god-awful melodies.

Master A danced in a morbid sway. "Ah, don't you just love Chopin at two a.m.?"

I bit my lip hard as he came closer, the chain in his hands clinking with every waltz step. "Now *are you ready to talk?"*

I pressed my face into the bedding, hating that I inhaled his scent but begging the mattress to suffocate me and let me go.

I could die like this. I could be free.

But Master A pre-empted me. Dropping the heavy chain across my naked back, he wrapped a thin piece of rope around my throat. "Can't have you trying to run from me now, can we?" *Hoisting my neck up a little, my spine bellowed at the wrongness. The rope throttled me but not enough to kill me. Just enough to prevent my nose from pressing into the sheets.*

The minute he had my head in position, he tied the rope and picked up the chain again.

And this time, I knew he would break me.

Two long years but tonight was the night he would end me.

The music swelled louder, poignant and sad with cellos and drums. Master A's determination became an instrument in the chorus pounding me.

He struck.

I tensed as best I could in my bindings.

"Speak, sweet little Pim."

Another strike, this one so cold and hard my skin split over my kidney, tickling me with blood. "Speak!"

As the music grew louder and louder and Master A's strikes hit faster and faster, I made a decision. He wouldn't let me walk away tonight without hearing my voice. And I wouldn't remain living the moment he heard it.

We were both at the end of our patience.

Tonight, I would scream.

And then, I would die.

"Speak!"

The chain lacerated me. I became ribbons of flesh. Each strike pushed me closer to the blackness I so craved.

Yes, let me die. Please...

"You don't want to speak? Then scream." *Master A hit faster until the blur of connection on my back and the sting of air in the moment's*

reprieve melded into one.
I was dying.
I'll be free soon.
Knowing he could no longer hurt me, that another few more strikes would be the death I needed, I opened my mouth.
The music crescendoed with cymbals and flutes, and I threw myself into nothing.
I screamed.
My throat burned.
My eyes shot wide.
The scream was otherworldly and wrong.
My jaw ached from opening so wide. My ears rang from the noise.
Just a nightmare. Only a nightmare.
Instantly, I began to sob. My scream cut short, and somewhere deep inside me, I realised this was the first time I'd broken my silence unwillingly.
My sadness crested, doing its best to mute the outside world. But something tickled my ears, something harsh and hated and harrowing.
No.
Music.
Classical music.
The notes threw me headfirst back into my nightmare.
He's here.
He's not dead.
He's come back for me.
My back bellowed. My skin sticky from dream-blood and sweat. I couldn't stop my body or the instinct to *run*.
My legs bolted from the bed before my mind even knew I was standing. I flew across the suite, charged into the corridor, and galloped.
I ran and ran, down plush carpet and past expensive artwork.
I careened into walls and clamped hands over my ears for silence.

Yet the music chased me. Threatened me. Warned me that it would catch me, and when it did, I would die.

Sobs interfered with my breathing. I bounced into another wall, shredding my shoulder on an intricate gilded sconce. My blood smeared the neutral paint as I stumbled forward.

I didn't know where I was going. My brain wasn't cohesive. All I could think about was the music.

Music.

Music.

I came to a door. The door opened beneath my fumbling fingers. My bare feet flew up the stairs. Up, up, up. Away from hell. *Fly to heaven.* Where there was no more music or the devil.

Hitting a deck above, the rhythm and classical notes reached a level higher than ever before. The instrument weaving and ducking, playing with me in its sinister way.

I couldn't think.

My hands remained clamped over my ears. My breath sticky in my sob-coughing lungs.

Stop!

I ran down another corridor.

But instead of the music growing quieter, it grew louder, *louder.* It ricocheted in my ears; it reverberated in my skull.

I want it out.

I want it to stop

Please, make it stop.

My arm bled faster as my heart pumped to keep me running.

And then the corridor ended. A dead end. I was trapped.

Alrik's chuckle danced on a cello's string.

I lost it.

Ramming my bleeding shoulder into the door at the end of the corridor, I exploded into a room.

A room where the music lived and breathed.

And in the centre of the music sat the maestro and creator of my worst enemy.

Elder.

The world went black.

ELDER

SOMETHING PALE AND bleeding soared across my threshold.

Part of me noticed and twitched to stop, but the rest of me was captive to my cello. I couldn't stop until the final beat. I couldn't end so suddenly.

My body shook as my fingers held the sweetest note, my bow singing over the strings, the music building louder and stronger and so damn alive it killed me to murder it all in the name of a song.

But I'd reached the end.

It was over.

I tore my callused fingers from the strings; my bow hovered, barely kissing the instrument.

Silence shattered over me.

I looked up just as the midnight interloper collapsed in a jumbled pile, unconscious.

My cello twanged as I caught a string with my bow, launching from my chair.

Pim.

It took three seconds to gently deposit my cello on the floor, two to cross the suite, one to slam to my knees, and zero to gather her naked, clammy body into my arms.

What the fuck is she doing here?

How did she find my quarters? What the hell happened? Violence painted my thoughts. If any of my staff had hurt her, they'd be meeting Moby Dick tonight.

"Pimlico. Open your eyes."

She didn't.

Her lips were slack, her face gaunt and haunted with shadows. Her blood streaked my arm where a small graze on her bicep wept. She was as frigid as ice and as lifeless as a corpse.

"Wake up." Keeping her in my embrace, I climbed to my feet. For a girl with long legs and such fire, she weighed next to nothing.

What was she doing here?

Did she hurt herself deliberately or was it an accident?

My heart raced as questions piled on top of questions.

Was she trying to kill herself?

I'd been an asshole to her for days but only because she'd undone me. I couldn't look at her without feeling her warm, wet mouth or her lips on my cock. I'd told her I wouldn't touch her, but it was for my sake, not hers. I couldn't touch her. I couldn't have her. Because if I did, that would be the end. My issues wouldn't let me have anything less.

But now guilt lacerated me. I'd stolen her to give her a better life. And I'd turned my back on her, telling her she was a whore and not something I wanted.

Shit.

Laying her gently on my bed, I tugged the covers from beneath her and laid them over her nakedness. Her nipples were almost the colour of her pale flesh, the shadows between her legs reminding me she was a woman but still so young. She'd been through so much already. What fucking right did I have to make her feel so belittled?

Tucking her in, I turned on the bedside light and called the kitchen. Melinda, the head chef, answered even this late.

"Kitchen."

Fuck, I wasn't thinking. I should've just called Selix. I didn't need food. Merely someone to gather things to help.

Oh, well. She'll do.

"Please arrange some tea, a hot water bottle, and painkillers to be brought to my room. Better bring a robe from the spa deck, too."

"No problem. Did you want food?"

No, yes, I don't fucking know.

"Bring something that would be suitable for someone who's fainted."

There was no pause or questions. "Sure. On its way."

Hanging up, I sucked in a breath and rubbed my face. What the hell was I thinking stealing this girl? She needed help. More than what I was qualified or able to deliver. I'd been a selfish bastard once again, thinking only of himself.

Leaning forward, I cupped her cheek, ignoring the cool sweat and fear still coating her skin. "You have my word; nothing and no one will hurt you. You're safe here."

She didn't stir.

Not able to sit still, I stood and paced at the bottom of the bed. My room was at the front of the ship with glass on every wall. Effectively, it was a gold fish bowl welcoming sea and sky rather than walls and ceiling. Each pane was quadruple thick and strong enough to withstand pounding squalls. And with one flick of a button, the see-through crystal became shaded with a chemical reaction, blocking the sun but negating the need for curtains.

I looked at my cello.

Up until the night we left Morocco, I hadn't played since Pim came on board. The itch had been there, the drive in my fingers and need in my heart hounded me to become a prisoner to the notes. But Pim had been a fascination worthy of distracting me from my passion. Until I'd shut her out, of course.

The first night we left port, I'd played softly for only a few minutes. The next slightly louder and longer. The next longer and louder again.

Tonight was the first time I let myself go and poured myself into a song; mixing heavy metal with classical, I blended genres and lullabies to create my own.

I was tempted to put the large instrument back in its case. But as I stepped toward it, a rustle sounded from the bed.

Pim thrashed, her lips wide with silent screams.

Forgetting the cello, I dashed back to her and sat on the mattress. Tucking wild hair behind her ear, I murmured, "You're safe. I'm here."

Her thrashing turned worse.

I grunted as her leg connected with my side, but I never moved. My fingers wrapped around her cheek, holding her steady. "It's me. He's not here. Trust me."

Her eyes flew open. In a microsecond, she tore herself away from my touch, ripped off the sheet, and shot to the head of the bed. Wedging herself against the flocked grey headboard, she hoisted her knees up and wrapped her arms around herself, rocking.

She didn't look at me, though. Her fear wasn't directed at me.

I followed her line of sight.

Her terror was toward my cello.

I stood, placing myself between them as if they were two lovers meeting for the first time. "It's just an instrument. It won't bite."

She bared her teeth like a wild cat, a silent hiss on her tongue. Walking backward, I had an odd feeling she would like nothing more than to attack my prized possession and throw it overboard.

I wouldn't let that happen. Under any circumstance.

Widening my stance, I blocked the cello with my body as best I could. "It's just an object. It can't hurt you."

Her eyes flickered from me and back to the thing I prized most in the world. Her chest rose and fell with ragged breaths, a thread of insanity clouded her gaze only for her to shake her head and snap back into the poised and incredibly strong woman I recognised.

Her arms slowly unwound, letting her legs fall to the side. Her breasts danced with shadow from the night sky above, but she made no move to cover up.

A quiet knock on the door wrenched her head to the side.

I held up my hands as if she'd sprout wings and smash through my glass ceiling. "It's only the staff. You've dealt with them before."

Her nostrils flared, her attention distracted between me and the cello as I crossed the room and opened the door. It fucking hurt to leave my instrument unguarded. I didn't trust her.

Melinda stood with a white robe with the Phantom logo of a grey storm cloud, and a barely disguisable figure slung over her arm with a small tray, teapot, two cups, and a hot water bottle.

"Here you go, sir. I didn't bring food; the tea should suffice for a fainting episode."

"Thank you." I took the items.

She reached into her pocket for a packet of painkillers. "Almost forgot."

I took those too. "Appreciate it."

"Not at all." Her lined but pretty face smiled before she turned and headed back the way she'd come.

Closing the door, I faced Pimlico.

She wasn't there.

My gut clenched as I spun to find her.

She'd climbed from the bed so silently I hadn't heard.

My heart leapt into my throat as she stood over my cello, the horsehair bow tight in her hands.

Ever so slowly, so as not to spook her, I placed the tray on my work table before padding softly toward her. "Pim, put it down."

She didn't move.

If she broke it, I'd have to break her.
I wouldn't even think about it.
Her gaze locked with all the hate in the world on the innocent second-hand instrument. The same instrument my parents had borrowed money to buy me. Her hand turned white around the bow. If she attacked it, I'd have to attack her. There was reason in this world and then there was irrationality. My cello was my one irrationality. It had too many things attached to it. Too many bad and good memories, too many scars and stories to allow a twisted woman to touch it.
She would fucking bleed if she hurt it.
"Pim!" My voice boomed as she pulled her arm back, ready to strike. To snap my bow. To shit on my entire past because she didn't understand me.
She didn't listen.
Her arm came down.
She gave me no choice.
I charged.
Grabbing her around the waist, I stopped the arching whistle of the bow before it could strike. Shaking with anger, I wrenched the priceless bow from her hand and placed it gently on the chair where I'd sat to play.
Dragging her away from the precious instrument, I clamped livid hands onto her shoulders and shook. Hard. "Don't you *ever* do that again. You hear me?"
She turned wild in my arms, wriggling and fighting. A growl rumbled in her chest, but she didn't yell or scream.
Her fighting was nothing. I held her effortlessly, but my temper rose to match hers. My insides curled with the urge to hurt. "Just fucking stop it."
She didn't.
Tears sprang from her eyes, tracking down her face.
But she still fought.
She scratched and kicked, connecting with my forearm to gorge tracks and my kneecaps with her tiny feet.
I bellowed, "Fucking *stop*." Holding her ruthlessly tight, I

marched to the bed and threw her onto the mattress.
She winced but didn't stay down.
So I made her.
Slapping my palm against her chest, I shoved her onto her back. "Keep fighting and I will hurt you. You have my fucking word you will be in pain." Breathing hard, I leaned over her, adding more and more pressure to where I held her in place. "Whatever trance or nightmare you're in, wake the hell up. I don't have the patience for this."
She snarled, struggling to sit up. Her eyes once again gravitated back to my cello.
I grabbed her cheeks with my free hand. "What is it? Why are you acting like an idiot?" I dug my fingers tighter. "Goddammit, speak and spit it out."
Her heart hammered beneath my palm holding her down. Her body lurched with terror and rage.
It wasn't an act. Her fear stank my room with truth.
Pulling back, I removed some of the pressure. "I'm going to let you go. But if you go after my cello again, I won't hesitate to do what's necessary to stop you. Got it?"
She ignored me.
My patience wore out.
Pinching her face, I forced her to look at me. "Got it, Pim?"
Her eyes blazed fire.
"Nod for yes. This is one time I won't let you get away with not answering me. Unless you truly want me to hurt you, then that can be arranged."
We glowered at each other.
For a moment, I feared she'd make me hurt her to prove a point. To become like him.
But then saneness finally glimmered; she reluctantly nodded.
I rewarded her by letting her go.
Prowling away, I jerked both hands through my hair, doing my best to figure out what the fuck was going on.

"What were you doing running around the yacht naked and bleeding?"

She slowly sat up, dragging the sheet with her to cover her nakedness. I didn't know why she did. It wasn't because she was shy. Perhaps to make me more comfortable? She didn't hunch, but she did keep her eyes downcast the more sanity returned to her.

Her body language spoke of regret and shame. Of confusion and a lostness that made my goddamn chest ache.

Regret, I could understand—I regretted so much of my life. But shame was not allowed.

Stopping my pacing, I snapped, "I know what you're thinking. It's about the other night, isn't it?"

Her eyes met mine.

"Don't feel shame for trying to show me what we could have together." I gave her a wry smile. "Receiving a blowjob from you—even if I stopped it—felt fucking incredible." Deciding to push her and see just how open she was to discussing sex as a mutual thing, not just an expectation, I added, "Your mouth...fuck, Pim. I dream about your mouth and finishing what you started."

She sucked in a breath, her chest flushing.

"So don't feel shame for showing me what you're worth. I already know what you're worth, and it's a lot fucking more than just sex."

She looked at her hands in her lap.

I couldn't help it.

She thought she could lock me out after tearing into my space and wreaking havoc? The least she could do was listen and communicate for once.

Striding toward her, I once again grabbed her chin, dragging her eyes to mine. "Is this about Dafford? About him trying to buy you?"

She flinched, trying to pull her face away.

I didn't let her.

"If it is, I'll make you a promise right here and now. I

won't sell you. I won't lie and say I didn't think about it. But I give you my word. I won't. You're mine for however long I decide."

Her eyebrow arched as if to ask what would happen when I decided that time was up.

"Then we deal with that when we come to it. Things have a habit of changing. And decisions made now might be obsolete by the time we decide this—whatever it is between us—has run its course."

She scowled as if she didn't do well with open-ended contracts. She liked to see the finish line. To know what would happen in a best-and-worst-case scenario. Perhaps that was why she still held on to the idea of suicide even though she was too strong to ever give up. It was the power in having an end the way *she* orchestrated, no one else.

I could understand that.

Shit, I'd danced with the same possibility myself when everything turned to fucking pieces. But she didn't get to decide that anymore.

"Now I've sworn never to sell you, I need you to swear something in return."

She sucked in a breath, her teeth grinding beneath my hold.

"Swear you won't end it. Don't rob me of the chance to heal you."

She snorted as if that wouldn't be long. She stuck out her tongue, revealing a red line decorating the pink muscle. No more stitches and no more blood.

It was my turn to suck in air. "I'm glad it's almost healed."

She held up her broken hand that'd downgraded from bandage to skin. Her eyebrow rose as she wriggled her fingers.

I frowned. "Why are you showing me your physical injuries? You think now your tongue is functional and your bones are knitted together, I'll decide what to do with you?" A slow smile spread my lips. "Oh, not quite, Pimlico. We have a long way to go before you're healed" —I tapped her temple—

"in here."

She froze.

"Did you think I just wanted you physically fit?" I grinned. "I know damaged. I've been where you are—in a different way, of course. It takes time."

As her eyes narrowed in judgment and questions, a plan slowly unfurled in my head. For so long I had no idea what to do with her. What I could do without damaging my own shaky foundations.

But now... *I think I know.*

"Stand up." I stepped back, letting her go.

She drew in a breath, ignoring me.

I ripped off the sheet and grabbed her wrist, hauling her upright. "When I give you an order, obey. I won't hurt you, but I'll find another way to punish you if you don't."

She wobbled a little. Her hand slapped over her injured bicep, rubbing away the drying blood. Her flat stomach stopped heaving with manic breath, and her gaze only tracked to my cello once before landing back on me.

I waited until I had her full attention.

When her eyes settled on mine, and a sense of calmness filled her body rather than nervous fright, I murmured, "We're going to do something. There isn't going to be a time limit, and I won't answer your questions about why."

She stood taller, curiosity and apprehension budding bright.

"I told you when I first took you that I'd make you worth more than pennies—that you'd be worth fucking millions. Well, it's time I made that come true." My cock thickened with the potential dangerous but delicious game we could play. "I'm going to piece you back together, and once you're whole, then I'll decide your true value. And once that monetary figure has been reached...it will have to be repaid.

"In full."

Pimlico

HIS SENTENCE WAS rude and belittling.

How much I was *worth*?

Who was he to tell me what I was worth? That was for me to decide, no one else.

And to *pay* him for my worth? What sort of sick con artist did I live with?

But I couldn't deny my curiosity piqued. Even if I stood in the room where classical music was created. Even if Elder was the creator of every song that'd tortured my mind while Alrik tortured my body. Even if the cello squatted like a goblin in our midst ready to tear me limb from limb.

I was intrigued enough to fight the shivering need to run far away. I'd never been in this room before, and now it was tainted with notes and pain.

Common sense knew Elder wasn't the one who played when I was raped and beaten. I knew he didn't intentionally rip me to pieces and make me bleed every time he strummed a chord. But I also knew that when it came to my hatred of music, I had no rationality left.

I wanted to burn every violin and rip apart every piano.

I wanted to destroy that cello sitting smugly mocking me. I

wanted to throw it overboard and let the sharks devour it.
No, that's too good for it.
I wanted it to burn and *burn*.
But for the first time, Elder had drawn a line. He'd shown me something he valued enough to raise his voice and put a hand on me. Something that evoked passion in him, revealing a single secret from all the rest that were locked so deep down tight.

He was a mystery, but now I knew his weakness.
His weakness is my weakness, just in different ways.
He had to conjure music. I had to run from it.
Two polar extremes that couldn't survive the other. Was that an analogy for our twisted relationship? Were we too different—from too contrasting worlds to ever find neutral territory?

I didn't have the answers, so I stood, waiting, ignoring the belittling statement and cursing his music and watching him with murderous eyes.

He stuck his hands into his denim pockets, looking like a murderer himself in a black t-shirt and bare feet. He paced in front of me; whatever idea he'd gathered grew and changed with every breath.

"I'm going to give you tasks. Each one will be worth a different value." His voice was hypnotic as he continued to pace. "Each one will push you to take back what he's stolen. Each requirement will force you to find who you truly are beneath your self-imposed silence."

He stopped.

I balled my fists, enjoying the ache for once from my healed bones. *What are these tasks?* And why did I fear them already when he hadn't hinted at what he'd make me do.

His smile was wicked. "You saw who I was in Morocco. You know how easy it was for me to steal that man's wallet. There is freedom in theft, Pimlico. Anxiety and guilt, yes. But an insane rush, too. The power to take what doesn't belong to you and make it yours. There's no greater thrill." His face darkened. "Apart from making music, of course."

I ignored that.

He was deranged. I would never accept his addiction to such disgusting pastimes. Then again, I would rather be a thief for the rest of my life than ever learn to play music.

"The thrill was part of the reason why I stole you. I wanted you, and he wouldn't give me the option to pay." His body tightened. "But I also stole you because it was the right thing to do. Sometimes, stealing is wrongness wrapped up in right." His eyes tightened with age-old despair, dragged into his own black memories. "Sometimes, being bad is the only thing you can do to save the good in your life. And sometimes, no matter how bad you are, even wrongness can't fix it."

Everything he just said was a direct contradiction to the speech he gave when he robbed the Chinese traveller. Could he switch his arguments as he saw fit or did he honestly see the yin and yang of each consequence?

My toes dug into the carpet, not daring to move a millimetre in case it interrupted his trip to his past and forbade me from glimpsing more of him. The longer I spent in his company, the more I witnessed a man I never suspected.

Physically shaking the recollections away with a toss of his head, Elder drew to a stop in front of me. "I'm going to teach you to steal."

What?

"I'm going to teach you how to become invisible, ruthless." His grin grew. "With each task, I'll reward you. With each steal, your value will increase until the next person you're sold to is yourself."

I blinked.

"Get it, Pimlico? You're going to buy yourself back penny by penny, and I'm going to be there every step of the way, no matter how long it takes."

My brain was muddled. I didn't understand what he meant. He wanted me to become a criminal? To use another's possession to purchase my freedom from him? What sort of sick stupidity was this?

Elder didn't care I bristled. He moved toward the cursed cello, picking up the bow from the chair and caressing it as he sat down. "Now that I know what to do with you, let's discuss the reason why you exploded into my room half mad in the middle of the night."

I had no intention of discussing that.

He pointed with the bow at the small tray with tea and a packet of headache pills along with a white robe draped over the back of the chair. "I ordered up some tea for your nerves. If your arm hurts, take a pill." Feathering the bow through his fingers, he murmured, "And I suggest you put the robe on. If you run again, you might want to be dressed this time."

I eyed him warily.

Why would I run?

He saw my question. "Because I'm going to play."

Before I could bolt, he positioned the cello between his legs, bowed his head so a lock of black hair fell over his eye, and strummed the sharpest, soul-skimming note I'd ever heard.

My ears rang. My heart bled acid tears. And my knees wobbled, threatening to chase me to the floor.

He stopped as quickly as he'd begun, cocking his chin, waiting for his previous instructions to be obeyed.

I had two choices.

Yet more damn choices.

Return to my rooms and forget everything that'd happened, or do as I was told and be brave enough to face such an inconsequential but terrifying thing such as music.

"Drink, dress, and sit down in that order, silent mouse." Elder smiled. He looked like a king about to play to his lucky court, his cello a sleeping gargoyle waiting to come alive between his thighs.

Deciding to see how far I could push before my mind snapped once again, I obeyed.

With trembling hands, I poured a cup of fragrant green tea, popped a painkiller even though I didn't need it, and swallowed both.

"And now the robe."

I gritted my teeth against his commandment. Not only was he about to torment me with melody, but he also wanted to torment my body with clothing confines.

Scrunching up my face in disgust, I draped the heavy cotton around my shoulders and slowly tied the belt. Loosely. Not tight. Gaping enough to flare open if I ran. Loose enough to shrug it off if I panicked.

"The hot water bottle is if you're cold. But I have a feeling adrenaline will keep you warm." He pointed at the bed. "Sit. Listen. I want to watch you."

My bones were glass as I shuffled unwillingly to the mattress and sat.

"Tell me why you hate music so much."

I sneered, reminding him in a callous way that I wouldn't speak to him. *Especially* when he made me sit in the same room as that instrument. I couldn't untangle my fear from reality. It made me jumpy and snarly and afraid.

"Is it because of something he did?" Elder's fingers feathered over the strings, spreading wide and elegant over a silent note. "Did he play it while hurting you?"

I hated that he could guess so eerily right.

"I heard it when I arrived that second time. A Chopin piece if I'm correct." His eyes blackened as he played another note, his fingers shifting almost erotically on the cello. "The volume was a tad too loud, not background symphony but a more intolerable interruption."

Alrik always played it loud. Too loud to filter out. But not loud enough to drown the beating he played on my body.

I balled my hands, refusing to look at him. I glared at the carpet, wishing I'd smashed that cello to pieces and Elder agreed to either never have music on the Phantom again or let me rob a bank right now so I could afford whatever ridiculous payment he expected in return for my freedom.

Why does he want me to steal?

Doesn't he have enough wealth?
He couldn't possibly need the money.
It's not about him. It's about you.
It'd been about me for too long. Something sparked inside to fight back. To make this about him. To make him face *his* horrors as surely as he'd made me face mine.

"Don't run, Pimlico. Music can't hurt you." He kept staring while my gaze came up despite myself, locking onto his fingers. I'd never watched a man play an instrument. I'd never gone to lessons or been in a musical family.

Watching Elder stroke his cello was one of the most sensual things I'd ever seen. The way he held it like a lover, so soft and respectful. The way he touched the strings with passion and possession but also gentleness, as if he knew that holding too tight wouldn't deliver the purity he craved.

He consumed my mind. Switching my hatred of what he was about to create into a hypnosis that belonged entirely to him.

My teeth locked together as he shifted in the seat and brought the bow to hover over the strings.

Never looking away, he played a lingering note.

I didn't know what it was. I didn't care. All I cared about was the ghostly fingernails scratching down my back and the bleeding in my heart for every abuse I'd suffered on the frequency of that decibel.

That wasn't a C or D or B flat. That was a rope or chain or whip.

Music wasn't a collection of notes to me. It was a collection of punishment forever wrapped up in an awful tune.

I was glad he'd made me sit. If I were standing, I would've collapsed as memory after memory battered me.

The fists.
The kicks.
The forced sexual torment.
All of it entered the room to thread amongst his chord.
Elder didn't play fair. He hung onto a note far longer than

comfortable only to string into another straight away. I hated every moment, but I couldn't hate him. The way he played...a mask came off revealing the true him.

His eyes gleamed, his face relaxed, and his shoulders flowed into a rhythm that was purely male, purely sex, purely power.

My jaw ached from clenching so hard. I endured the pain while Elder played all because he'd commanded me, too. But also because I was strong enough. Brave enough to shatter the music's hold over me and become entwined with better things.

His head swayed to the song, his body the perfect tuning fork.

As he lost himself to the notes, his limbs became liquid, drowning everything in its power with utter submersion. Faster and faster, more aggressive, more barbaric. He took classical and twisted it into a fantastical combination of metal, Mozart, and Madonna.

He was enthralling.

The fists and kicks faded as my attention switched from Alrik to Elder.

Watching him play was utter magic.

He was free like I wanted to be. Free to open the gates around his heart and live, *to breathe*, before the piece ended. He hung onto every strum, as if begging the note to take it with him when it faded so he'd never have to return to the world where Lucifer resided.

A few minutes. That was all it was.

A few awful, enchanting minutes where my ears screeched and my heart hid behind my ribs with earmuffs, but my mind ignored the fear and focused on his wizardry instead.

And then, it was over.

Elder stood, tenderly placed his cello and bow on the chair, and stalked toward me.

I couldn't move. I jittered and shook and fully expected a fist to my gut because that was what I was trained to expect.

But Elder slammed to his knees before me, his eyes

becoming level with mine where I perched.

Shaking a little, he cupped my face with both hands and pulled me forward. "Forget the past and only remember this."

His lips crashed against mine.

The invasion and heat of his mouth ripped through my memories, forcing new ones to take hold. My hands flew up, bracing myself by wrapping my fingers around his wrists.

He didn't growl at me not to touch him. He permitted me to clutch him like he clutched me—like we'd clutched each other at the white mansion.

His lips moved over mine, demanding but not commanding. My tongue teased the back of my teeth, wanting to lick and taste him again, to see if whatever voodoo he'd filled me with the last time was a fluke or true.

There was no fear to pull away or prediction of worse things. He'd successfully torn me apart to accept this new experience without prior condemnation.

My mouth parted just a little.

He sucked in a breath as he moved with me; the very tip of his tongue ran along my bottom lip.

I was hesitant. My tongue was healed. There was no reason why I couldn't kiss him back. I wanted to kiss him back. *I think*. I was ready to take back this one thing that'd been stolen. But if I did, had he won? And if he did win…what exactly had he won?

My thoughts spiralled into a congested mess as he took the decision from my control.

His tongue speared into my mouth, automatically coaxing mine to meet his in a ritual so timeless we didn't need to be taught.

His breath fluttered over my cheek as he exhaled hard, pulling my face deeper into his as our tongues tangled.

The kiss had no expectations, and that was what made it so heart-warming. Somehow, with the classical notes still hanging in the air, his kiss deleted one tiny memory of Alrik. I had a thousand and one more to go, but he'd taken a sliver and

made it…better? Right? Different?
No, he's stolen it and made it his.
Because he was a thief, and that was what he did best.
And he would teach me to be like him.
All in the name of eventually becoming free.

ELDER

THAT KISS.

Goddammit, that kiss.

I hadn't meant to do it. Michaels would probably shoot me if he knew I'd had my tongue against hers, sharing saliva, running the risk of her healing being compromised.

But I couldn't help it. Ever since she flashed me her tongue in blistering anger—doing her best to taunt me into admitting I wouldn't be keeping her for long because her injuries were on the mend—I couldn't stop thinking about her mouth.

Kisses and blowjobs and sinking inside her were the one-track playlist of my utterly obsessed mind.

I hated her being in my room. I *loved* her being in my room. Instincts clawed, whispering falsehoods that she'd come on her own accord. While she was in my domain, I was free to do what I liked to her.

I was a fucking wreck from keeping my hands off her and myself.

And when I played for her.

Fuck, it had been the biggest aphrodisiac.

I always got hard when I played. It wasn't something I

could control. It wasn't sexual but more of a thrill that gave me pleasure. And that pleasure had compounded to supernova the second I pulled her lips to mine.

And when the kiss ended? Pimlico didn't look as nearly as wild. Shit tons of adrenaline ran through her system from my music, and if I was honest, I shared the same shaky high from her kiss, but when I'd pulled her from my bed and guided her to the door, she hadn't disobeyed. She'd floated as if a tiny piece of the chains holding her down had been snipped.

It took every inch of willpower I had left to kiss her forehead and send her back to her room.

I deliberately kicked her out so I couldn't give into temptation. It would've been too easy to strip the robe and push her backward on the bed. Too simple to spread her legs and lick her; to climb on top of her and take her.

I wanted to sample her so goddamn much.

But sex between us would never be simple. It would be pleasurable for me and pain for her. She'd never been taught how to find enjoyment in fucking. According to her notes to No One *(to me)*, she'd been a virgin. The only sex she knew was with bastards trying to destroy her.

I refused to be yet another one of those.

Sex with Pim would be a labyrinthine of complications, and that reason alone gave me the courage to get rid of her.

If I took her, she'd have to want it too—just like she'd wanted that kiss, even if she hadn't known it until I pressed my lips to hers.

Her gaze when I pulled away hadn't been tear-filled or vacant but soft, as if wondering what the hell happened but no longer afraid of new.

Drawing my mind from yesterday, inhaling deep against the lust I hadn't been able to shed, I turned off the shower and waited as warm droplets cascaded over me. The pounding in my cock hurt and the urge to self-pleasure got harder and harder every day. I hadn't relieved myself since she got on her knees and gave me a blowjob I hadn't asked for.

And now, we'd kissed?

I didn't know how much more self-control I possessed to keep my distance from her.

But today is a new day. Today is teaching time.

I was her master; she was my pupil. There were boundaries in that relationship that couldn't be crossed.

Slinging a towel around my waist, I headed into my suite that was three times the size of Pimlico's and strolled into my walk-in wardrobe. There, I selected a pair of beige shorts and white t-shirt, slipping my feet into simple flip-flops.

My phone said the time was nine a.m., and for the first time since I'd carried Pimlico on board, I wanted to see her. I didn't want to avoid her because she was too complicated and frustrating. I wanted to work with her to earn another breakthrough because, *Christ*, it was rewarding.

Pocketing my phone, I left my quarters and headed down a deck to hers. Stupidly, my hand shook a little as I knocked on her door.

She answered promptly as if she'd been waiting for me.

Once again, she was naked.

No shame or apology.

Her hair hung over her breasts, wet from her shower, her stomach shadowed with muscle, swiftly returning from emaciated to toned.

When she'd first arrived, I was attracted more to her inner beauty. I didn't see the beaten slave or bruises, I saw a worthy adversary.

But now…

Holy fuck.

Now, I saw a woman becoming more and more stunning every day. Her body slowly shed its illness and pain, remembering how to fill out in all the best places. Her breasts were fuller, her hips less sharp. With no jewellery or tattoos or makeup, she was the epitome of natural, and *shit*, she took my breath away.

"You can't do that much longer, Pim." My gaze refused to

unglue from her body. I couldn't stop staring at every exposed inch.

Her head tilted as she held the doorknob, a knowing smile on her face. For a woman who'd been forced to endure sex, she acted as if she enjoyed my eyes on her. As if it gave her redemption as a sexual creature.

I got it.

Having me stare was an exchange of power. I had no way of hiding how my hands balled or throat clenched with desire. She controlled me completely.

Without authority, my hand swooped up, so damn close to cupping her breast and pinching her nipple.

Fuck.

Taking a step back, I growled. "You can't be naked around me anymore."

Her eyes narrowed as if daring me to either touch her or yell at her.

I did neither.

Backing farther away, I commanded, "Dress and meet me in the dining room. We're having breakfast together. And then, we're going to work."

Pimlico

BREAKFAST CONSISTED OF freshly baked croissants, home-made jams, and every exotic fruit imaginable. A small serving of scrambled eggs with hollandaise sauce was our main affair, and by the time we pushed aside plates in favour of steaming coffee mugs, a comfortable silence wrapped us in a bubble no one else could enter.

Not the staff to-ing and fro-ing with dishes. Not the captain when he came in to give the brief on the night cruising and the plan of today's journey.

Elder might look at other people, he might smile and speak to them, but his entire focus remained on me. I sensed him watching, felt him calculating.

The kiss between us lived on my lips, tickling me every time I took a sip of coffee or brought a fork to my mouth. His music corrupted my mind, strumming at odd times, robust in my memory. Whenever I recalled his cello-eloquence, I wanted to silence every note—to ignore he wasn't as gifted as he was; pretend he could delete melody from his life because after that kiss...*wow*.

That damn kiss proved how naïve I'd been even when I believed I was wise.

I didn't want him to love music because it was my enemy.

I wanted him to hate the things I hated. To loath the things I loathed.

I was selfish.

I didn't want to have to face my idiocy or for him to take it upon himself to break me by showing me music wasn't a sentinel being but purely soulful.

He didn't play fair, and his talent spawned so many reactions—emotional, physical, psychological. I never wanted to hear his cello again but at the same time…that was a lie.

I'd been pushed to the brink and managed to stay clinging to the cliff—the next time he played, I might fall.

I didn't want to fall.

I want to fly.

With him.

The liquid in my belly, the hummingbird in my heart—it all equalled one thing.

I like him.

I liked his company, his protection, his friendship. With him, I didn't feel the urge to write every moment to No One. I didn't have the need to curl around my secrets and keep them close.

Elder knew who I was. He'd seen where I'd come from, he'd mingled with the men I'd belonged to. He knew more about me than I would ever tell another stranger, and because of that, there was nowhere to hide, no room to lie—not when we'd met in bitter truth.

But that bitterness is slowly evolving into sweetness….

I was glad when the food was cleared away because I needed fresh air. Needed to be further away from him than sharing a table.

But when he stood and held out his hand, as if expecting me to take it, nerves coiled and rattled in my belly. Despite my willingness to accept my feelings toward him, I wasn't ready for more.

If he wanted to use me, he could. But I couldn't allow myself to like him if he did.

Giving him a hesitant look, I didn't take his hand, but I did follow as he guided me from the dining room through the stately lounge, complete with a piano locked in place. We passed the open-air bar with a Jacuzzi tub set in the polished wooden deck, right to the bow of the boat where a black sail had been strung across the space like a triangle cloud, blocking out the intensity of the sun.

The heat of the day didn't disperse, and the grey dress I'd slinked into did its best to cling to my skin as sweat beaded on my spine.

Elder didn't criticise my wariness or bark commands to come closer. His black gaze pooled with kindness, unable to fully hide the glitter of desire.

My tummy flipped, remembering when he'd come to my door. The way his eyes locked on my nakedness and his body tensed as tight as his cello strings. His raw need ought to have sent me running. Instead, it did weird things to my insides.

Part of me had wanted to slam the door in his face because I knew that look. That look meant having a man inside me against my will. That look meant being used at their leisure and mercy.

However, when Elder looked at me that way...I liked it.

He didn't strip me of power. He made me gather more of it. He became weaker the more desire drenched his blood, while I became stronger, having control to deliver what he wanted or deny it.

It was a dangerous game to make him lust for me. Lust was just another word for evil. But there I was, doing my best to entice him even though I didn't want him to touch me.

Liar.
You do want him to touch you.
Fine.

I wanted him to kiss me again. The kissing was nice. The rest I wasn't ready for. *So you keep saying...*

But a kiss...I could kiss him all day if it meant he'd let me off whatever task he was about to set up.

"Stand here." Elder pointed at the deck in front of him. As I moved into position, he glanced over my shoulder. "Thanks, Selix. Just put it over there."

Selix threw me a half a smile before doing what Elder requested. Placing a black velvet bag on a table bolted to the deck, he left as quietly as he'd arrived.

Strolling toward the table, Elder said, "Lesson one on how to pilfer pockets."

Oh, God. He's serious about that?

I shuffled on the spot.

Reaching into the bag, he drew out a wallet. Unfolding it, he pulled out a hundred dollar note and waved it at me. "This is yours if you can take it from me without me noticing." His teeth flashed. "But fair warning, once a thief always a thief. There's a reason why we don't get robbed ourselves. We know the tricks. We feel the con. You'll have to be sly if you hope to win."

Sly I could do. Sly was just another word for self-preservation: watching and waiting for weakness. I'd become an expert at that.

Light touch, fast movement—those I might need help with.

"Come closer." Elder beckoned me with the wallet as he tucked the hundred dollar note inside. "It's in my right back pocket." Slipping it into the beige shorts he wore, he spun to show me the slight bulge.

My eyes should've noted how high the wallet was, how tight the material, and figure out a way to get my fingers between him and the shorts to steal it. However, all I could look at was the tightness of his ass and the way his left cheek clenched as he bent to look over his shoulder. "Got it?"

My mouth turned dry. But I nodded.

He grinned, brighter and more care-free than I'd seen. "Fuck, I don't know what I'll do when you finally talk to me, Pim."

My body stiffened.

"Even a simple nod from you feels like the biggest bloody reward. I've never focused on a person's voice or lack thereof so much before. It's driving me insane, but I also get why you haven't given it to me yet."

He spun to face me, his hands loose by his sides as if poised to steal. "You're making me work for it. Just like I'll make you work for what I want. It's fair, I suppose." He lowered his face, watching me from beneath his brow. "Another warning, though. You'll break first. And when you do, I'll savour your voice. I'll command you to speak over and over. I'll finally learn what I've been waiting for."

That's what you think.

I smiled, letting mirth mix with a challenge.

We'll see who will win.

He chuckled. "A bet then?"

I nodded again.

A bet to see who would break first. It didn't escape my notice that he'd already broken me to the point where talking nonverbally was now permitted. I willingly wanted to answer because he spoke to me as a normal man spoke to a normal woman.

Elder stroked his chin. "What do you want to bet on?"

I shrugged, giving in to his questions, allowing myself to do more than just nod.

He noticed, of course, his grin growing bigger. "How about one night?"

I jolted.

What?

"One night. The night I arranged before I decided to steal all the nights. One night where you agree to let me do what I want. Where the ultimate thing I want from you is your trust."

Trust?

Well, that was terrible for him to bet on because he'd never earn that. No matter if he gave me a thousand nights. Trust wasn't something I could give.

And he must know that, but he'd asked for it anyway.

Why?
Why ask for the impossible?
I raised my eyebrow, pointing at my chest, breaking all my rules and communicating completely. *And what do I get?*
His eyes tracked my hand, the same look of desire coating his features. Not from my body hidden in a sack-shaped dress but from the fact I'd willingly engaged in conversation.
"You?" His voice cracked. "You get to choose."
My eyes widened, wafting my hand like a bird in flight. *I can choose freedom?*
He nodded. "If want to put your freedom at stake, I'll honour that. One night with me, trusting everything I do and giving me your pleasure *if* you manage to pickpocket a civilian—"
I jolted as my future plans unravelled. I could go home to London. I could find my mother, my friends, my life.
My mind raced. I could do it. I could find a silly girl with her handbag open and slip my hand inside. How many times had I looked at my friends' purses and thought how careless they were?
Elder smirked. "I wasn't finished. Pickpocket successfully and *keep* whatever you steal without giving in to the guilt and returning it, then you've won, and you can have your freedom."
He sauntered toward me, his hands fisting. "However, if you fail and speak before that happens, you give me one night." He shook his head as his hand landed on mine wedged against my chest as if it could contain my suddenly light as a wisp heart. "No, not just one night. You give me your body and mind. You give in to me completely. You *trust* me."
His fingers squeezed my hand, his body setting off alarm bells in every cell.
I took a step back, dropping our linked grasp, holding my head high.
The rules had been drawn. Whatever lightness I'd been filled with at the thought of freedom was dragged down again in what I had to do to earn it. I was afraid but also invigorated.

It'd been so long since someone pushed me to evolve. So long since I'd had requirements other than obedience to follow.

"So?" Elder licked his bottom lip. "Do you agree?"

I wouldn't back down from the gauntlet.

I nodded, sealing my fate and cursing the flutter in my stomach at the thought of him winning. What would he make me do in one night? And why was I terrified but also secretly intrigued about what sex would be like with him?

"Good. Let's get started." Elder took a deep breath, expelling the tension that'd once again thickened around us.

He patted his back pocket, looking so damn handsome in the sun. "Come toward me. I'll show you how to steal then you can practice."

He was giving me permission to attack him? To slip my fingers against his butt and loot him?

Once again, part of me recoiled at the idea of being so close while the rest of me woke up from a two-year hibernation and prepared to relearn that elusive, incredible word.

Play.

ELDER

FUCK, THIS WAS a bad idea.

A really, *really* bad idea.

As Pimlico stalked toward me, her face dancing with an eager but distrusting smile, my cock thickened in need. The more I was around her, the more I wanted her. Especially now as she relaxed into herself, slinking with more confidence and...*is that playfulness?*

I didn't think she'd ever relax enough around me to play.

It hit me right in the goddamn heart to think, despite her disagreement and scorn whenever I used the word trust, she'd already started to do it. She'd allowed herself to soften—if only just a margin. She wasn't expecting me to hit her the moment she came close. She wasn't looking for chains or pain when she walked beside me.

Playing my cello for her last night had been a daredevil move. I worried I'd shatter the rest of her soul and end up sweeping up the pieces. But she'd surprised me. Shit, she surprised herself.

She might've hated every strum, but when I'd kissed her...Christ, she'd kissed me back with a liveliness she hadn't shown before. Our second kiss in weeks and instead of granting a reprieve on my desire for her, it only made it ten times fucking worse.

Drinking in her face one last time, I spun around and stood still. She paused, then her footsteps padded softly again behind me. My skin prickled with awareness as she took her time, judging how best to steal. A quiet shuffle of bare toes and the lightest flutter of touch on my back pocket.

I gritted my teeth as everything roared inside for more. I wanted her hands on every inch of my skin. I wanted her mouth on me. I wanted my cock inside her. My entire body hated me for punishing it with celibacy, bashing against my patience like a dog off its leash.

I throbbed with need as I locked my knees and fought the delicious shudder of her hand slipping into my shorts.

The delicate, sensual flicker of her fingers on my ass—*goddammit*, I almost shot around and grabbed her. Every urge in my blood bellowed to march her backward until her spine hit the deck railing, hook her leg over my hip, and drive my agonising erection against her.

But I didn't.

Because I couldn't get past the guilt of what that would make me and the knowledge she'd let me in just a little.

I could be patient until she let me in a lot.

Forcing myself to focus on why we were doing this and not how hard I was, I stopped breathing and let her finish.

The moment the weight of the wallet left my shorts, I grabbed her wrist without turning around. "Gotcha."

She wriggled as I dragged her forward, plucking the leather from her hand with my free one. "Far too noticeable."

Her chin cocked, dark hair dappling with pinpricks of sunlight from the shade-sail above. I fucking loved the argument on her face, the tenacity and willingness to show what she'd hid along—that she fought for everything and no longer had to pretend to submit to survive.

Clearing my throat from the sudden rush of pride, I said, "You'll learn though. I'll teach you." Letting her go, I replaced the wallet into my pocket and strolled away to lean against the railing. Blue skies glowed sedately, but ominous black clouds lurked on the horizon. I made a note to talk to Jolfer about sailing around if a storm brewed. I didn't mind rough seas, but Pimlico couldn't become afraid of the Phantom. This was her home for the foreseeable future. She had to love it as much as I did.

While I lost myself in the sky, Pim snuck up behind me.

I hid my smile at her attempt to be stealthy.

My ears twitched with her little breaths. My body flinched knowing she came close on her own accord. She moved faster this time; the shadow of her arm snaked over the deck as she reached for the money.

I bit my lip as her fingers crept into my shorts again, sending haywire misfires of what was decent and what was not.

Fighting my shudder, I waited until her touch wedged against the wallet and my ass. Slamming my palm over hers, I kept her hand firm against my flesh and spun around. I corkscrewed into a tangle of bodies—her arm tight and looped over my hip as if she'd half embraced me and summoned me to kiss her.

Everything fell away as our eyes locked.

Fuck, really bad idea.

Her mouth thinned as she tried to snatch her hand back.

I didn't let her go. My gaze danced over her face, committing every freckle and scar to memory. "I felt you coming."

The sentence had a double meaning. Would I ever feel her come? *Could* she come? Could I somehow train a girl who'd traded virginity for slavery and sweep away her horror all in the name of creating pleasure rather than pain when I touched her?

Because it was no longer a matter of *if* I would touch her—my sake and hers be damned.

It's a matter of when.

And when it happened, we were both fucked.

Her forehead furrowed, her lips sucking in a hungry

breath.

I chuckled, dragging her forward until her chest slammed against mine. With a possessive grip, I shoved her hand further into my back pocket, forcing her to grope me.

She shuddered as I lost control a little and locked my gaze on her lips.

Having her so close, feeling her heat, feeling her fingers twitch against my ass, hell it was enough to drive anyone insane, let alone a man who'd made an oath not to touch this woman until she *wanted* to be touched—despite the memories of her mouth on his cock and her tongue on his lips.

We both struggled to breathe, almost as if the world had suddenly dried up of oxygen and we could only survive breathing each other.

"You're right if you think a stranger wouldn't be attuned to your presence like I've become," I murmured, forcing myself to teach rather than imagine her naked and in my bed. "But your shadow gave you away. It's not just a matter of quietness and light of touch—it's about using your surroundings to keep you invisible rather than revealing your crime."

I bowed my head, and hers tipped up as if the same conductor choreographed us.

Sea air wrapped around us, bringing us closer without noticing. My gut clenched as her body swayed into mine, pushing me into the railing.

The irony that I'd just fantasied about pinning her against the same thing wasn't lost on me.

I wanted so fucking much to kiss her.

My fingers unlocked around her wrist, allowing her to pull her hand from my shorts, yet she didn't. She stood exactly where she was, staring at my eyes, my mouth, trapped in the same indecision I was.

My head lowered.

If she wanted me to kiss her, that was entirely different to *me* wanting to kiss her. It meant she invited it not just accepted it. I'd do whatever the hell she wanted.

Her eyes fluttered as our mouths inched closer. My skin heated and prickled while hers broke out in goosebumps. I gritted my teeth in preparation, knowing the moment we kissed I'd struggle to stop at just a gentle caress.

My mind flashed black with images of dragging her downstairs, stripping off that grey dress, and taking her.

She'd let me. But only because she was trained to. She wouldn't fight me. But only because she'd been beaten enough that fighting was no longer an option.

Her breath skated over my lips, sweet with strawberries and mango from breakfast.

I groaned at the barest feather of her mouth on mine.

My mind almost snapped.

And then...she was gone.

The wallet ripped from my pocket and flew with her as she parried backward, a sly grin on her face.

For a heavy heartbeat, I couldn't figure out what the hell happened.

Then she waggled the money holder, taunting me.

Blood rushed from my cock back to my brain.

I glowered at her, anger rising a little that she'd conned me. She'd cheated. But then again...wasn't that the point?

She cheated on her past with happiness. She stood there smiling in a way she'd never smiled before. And the new life in her sombre eyes drowned out my annoyance like a pinch to a matchstick flame.

I couldn't discipline her or tell her she couldn't go around kissing potential marks to distract them from the crime. I couldn't march toward her and grab her and fuck her in reward for using her surroundings to win—just like I'd taught.

All I could do was shake my head and accept that she'd broken my rules and schooled me. Aching with need and smouldering with lust, I threw my head back and laughed.

Pimlico

THAT WAS THE first day but definitely not the last that Elder broke my proverbial chains and taught me how to smile again.

After we almost kissed and I stole the wallet, his captain arrived and dragged him off to discuss the impending storm on the horizon. Elder had looked at me for the first time with reluctance.

My heart skipped with heat. He was as against the idea of leaving me as I was him going. Whatever had made us pay attention to each other back at Alrik's sprang into full authority, tangling us in budding friendship and desire.

He'd stalked toward me and for a second, I'd wanted to kneel at his feet and give him permission to unleash the lust painted all over him. For the first time, I would submit—not because I wanted to, but because he hurt and I didn't like him hurting—not after everything he'd given me.

Once again, I wanted to use sex to repay him because that was all I had of value. But even if I did, even if I locked myself tight and gave him the use of my body, he wouldn't take it.

He'd call me a whore and I'd never let him utter such filth again.

Stopping in front of me, he'd snatched the wallet from my fingers, removed the one-hundred dollar note and deliberately stuffed it into his pocket.

I'd failed to steal with secrecy but I didn't care about the money.

I had something much more treasured. I had a newfound lightness—a more comfortable existence in this world.

His hand had soared upward and didn't stop until it connected with my cheek.

We'd frozen at the contact. His palm comforted me in a way touch never had before, and I'd pressed into him for the barest of heartbeats.

Then he'd gone to deal with whatever nature had in store for us.

Alone on the deck with a smeared watercolour of baby blue and black above, I'd returned to my room to combat the sudden loneliness he left me with.

Now, an hour after my pickpocket lesson, I relaxed on my balcony. Goosebumps from the cold wind replaced the goosebumps caused by playing with Elder. The ocean hovered beneath a thick grey blanket with churning white caps. I didn't understand how the sun could be banished so quickly in favour of such violence.

But I wasn't worried.

The Phantom was sturdy, and Elder was a perfectionist. If I had to be at sea in a storm, there was nowhere safer.

Ignoring my hair snapping around my ears in the breeze, I stroked the origami boat he'd made. I'd scooped it up when I'd entered my suite, needing to hold something of his. An insatiable need to touch him again after I'd squirmed in his arms only an hour ago consumed me.

Another howling gust whipped off the horizon, fluttering the corners of the green money in my hands. The ferocity threatened to tear it from my grip.

My fingers tightened as fear of dropping the little boat increased with every bluster.

Returning inside, I locked the balcony doors and settled on the couch. Already, the normal swell-lullaby of the yacht had been replaced with a choppy rock and yaw.

I settled in to ride it, and was glad of the interruption a few hours later when dinner was served. Along with the maid, two men entered my suite to check the moorings on my table and furniture before nodding respectfully and heading out.

I ate pumpkin fettuccine and vanilla panna cotta even though mild seasickness took hold. As rain lashed at my windows, I did my best to keep my thoughts positive and not let the rapidly deteriorating weather worry me.

I kept staring at the door, hoping Elder would come like he had this morning, but I had no more visitors.

By eight p.m., the water world was no longer below us but all around us. Torrential rain hammered, splashes of fresh liquid mingling with salt in a washing machine churn.

I stayed where I was on the couch, cross-legged and riding the waves, clutching my origami boat in one hand and my bronze genie lamp in the other.

My positivity turned pessimistic, and my muscles were already tired from fighting to stay upright. My healing body was not equipped for a rodeo this soon.

Elder never visited, but he did call around nine p.m.

I'd never received a phone call in my suite, and it took me a moment to figure out where the ringing came from.

Picking up the receiver, I tensed and melted in equal measure as his heady voice licked into my ear. "Sorry, I never came back. It's been a rough day navigating. The storm is too wide. There is no way we can sail around it. Tonight will be bad."

I opened my mouth to reply, two years of silence deleted by a mere phone call. The memory of what to do when holding such a device begged me to speak.

But I swallowed it back.

Not because of the stupid bet, but because I liked whatever was growing between us, but was still wary enough not to trust it.

"I know you won't reply, so this will just be a one-sided conversation. I won't be around tonight. I'm staying on the bridge. Don't go wandering around. Have a shower now if you want before it gets too choppy then get into bed and don't leave. By Jolfer's estimate, the worst of the squall will hit in a few hours. If you get sick, there are bags in the bedside table. I'll come for you in the morning once we're through."

I could barely stand already, let alone have a shower.

Loneliness settled heavier than before. I never normally wanted company, but tonight...I did. I wanted someone to cling to and murmur that the weather wouldn't kill us, even if it sounded like it had every intention of dining on our corpses.

A slight pause once again urged me to fill the silent void.

"Goodnight, Pimlico. I had fun today. I—" He stopped.

My heart shoved aside the howling storm, focusing intently on the phone. I expected him to hang up. I almost wanted him to hang up.

But he sucked in a breath and finished. "I look forward to seeing you again."

The dial tone hit hard and harsh in my ear.

The raging wind gathered pressure. The angry rocking of the yacht did its best to delete the repeating words in my ear.

I look forward to seeing you again.

I look forward not to sex or pain or making me do whatever he deemed acceptable.

I look forward to seeing you...

So simple a pastime but so rare and priceless.

Elder could make me rob a thousand banks and commit a million crimes to pay him back for rebuilding me. But he'd made that an impossible task as he kept increasing my value day by day.

I was right.

Elder Prest was the most dangerous man I'd ever known.

Not because he could kill me whenever he chose, but because he had the power to steal so much more than just my

life.
    He could steal my heart.

ELDER

THE STORM GATHERED in shape and snarl the longer I stood on the bridge.

"Guess we'll be able to put the automatic levelling system to good use tonight, huh?" Jolfer grinned. His face held respect for the sea and the slight insanity of a pirate.

"Let's hope it treats us well." I clutched a handrail as a particularly large crest sent us racing forward. "What ferocity will it climb to?"

Jolfer shrugged. "Harder than the last one."

"That doesn't ease my mind." The last storm had torn apart rigging and knocked over the bulk of the furniture not screwed down. The damn spa tub on the deck had been emptied of its chlorinated hot water and replaced with salty brine multiple times over that night.

"My recommendation is to climb into a chair and ride it out."

Until I'd seen the radar with its hissing black mess and our little red dot bleeping its way into the nucleus, I'd had plans on doing exactly that. Saddling in to ride Mother Nature. I'd pulled myself out of the gutter enough not to want to end my life the way I did when I was younger, but I couldn't stop the small tendril of excitement to see how bad things would get.

I tried to keep my thoughts on my boat and what would soon hit, but they kept trailing to Pimlico. Had she ever been at sea before? Had she ever ridden a storm where the ground became a bronco and the walls creaked and groaned as if desperate to let the sea enter?

If she had, this would be terrifying. And if she hadn't, this would be utterly horrifying.

I can't leave her on her own.

Glancing at the radar, I said, "I'm going to grab something." *Someone.* "I'll be back in ten." My eyes lingered on the captain's chair, and the matching bucket seats soldered firmly onto large steel posts. The shoulder and waist straps would keep us from flopping around when the waves struck, but a quick release mechanism meant we could unbuckle and swim if we capsized.

Not that I think we'll capsize…but you never know.

Yet another reason why I had to get Pim and bring her to safety.

"I wouldn't leave if I were you." Jolfer squinted at the egg-sized droplets obscuring the windows. "Especially to cross the deck."

Admittedly, that was a design flaw. I'd had the boat builders place the bridge towering over the polished deck. They'd insisted there should be some way of internal access from the main floors, but I'd refused an additional lift as I didn't want to interrupt the space downstairs with yet another ascender.

On nice days, even on rainy days, the quick stroll over the exposed wood was a welcome refresher. Today, I would be drenched.

"I won't be long." Pushing off from the control panel where the hand-holds glinted silver amongst the array of glowing buttons and dials, my legs spread for balance as I made my way to the exit.

Blessed with not suffering seasickness, even I didn't like the uncertainty of when the next swell would hit and how big the yacht would roll.

Clutching the doorframe, I battled the hissing elements as I wrenched it open and traded dry for wet. Instantly, the low howl of the storm behind thick plated glass took off its gag and *screamed*.

The noise of wind and rain and thunder hammered me as I shot forward, slipping and sliding across the deck.

My clothes became saturated—a heavy hindrance, robbing me of coordination. By the time I made it to the glassed-in foyer where the lift was, I panted and gasped, my hip throbbing from sliding sideways and falling over.

Not trusting the elevator mechanism in this crazy bucking world, I threw myself down the stairs. Each couple of steps, the boat yawed and yawned, throwing me into a wall then forward then back.

My shoulders ached as I stepped onto Pimlico's level, bruises deep inside from the violence of the squall.

Rather than walk and do my best to balance, I jogged down the corridor, moving with the boat, hitting the walls with a grimace. I wouldn't drag this out any longer than needed.

We need to get back to the bridge.

Reaching Pimlico's door, I didn't knock.

Barging inside, my eyes fell to the messy bed, the coverlet on the floor, but no Pim. *Where the fuck is she?*

I stumbled toward the bathroom. There was no way she should still be in there with hard tiles and smashable mirrors to hurt her.

A loud crash sounded over the mayhem of the storm. Cream curtains billowed as the French doors to the balcony snapped and snarled.

And there, tied to the guardrail with a dressing gown belt was Pimlico.

I slammed to a stop. My knees locked against the roll and buck.

She had her back to me. Her arms spread wide, her head thrown back, and chocolate hair plastered to her naked white body.

In the dark, she lit up in a fork of lightning. Her spine still stark, her bruises still colourful enough to cast mottled shadows over her flesh.

She didn't jolt as another fork split the sky like an angry god. She didn't huddle when thunder answered back with ear-cracking drums.

She merely wedged her feet against the railing and lived.

Pimlico

EXHILARATION.
Life.
Death.
Chances. Choices. Catastrophe.

The storm got worse. I became steadily petrified; huddled in a ball on my bed, clinging to the mattress as I slid this way and that. I thought it couldn't get any worse. That each soar into the sky and every plummet down, a wave couldn't possibly get stronger.

I was wrong.

The wind churned the seas, but the thunder churned the skies, and when the first bolt of lightning arched against the monstrous wet clouds, I had to make a decision.

Scream with terror and think I was going to die or…give in.

I couldn't be afraid anymore.
I'd been afraid for far too long.
I didn't have the *energy* to be afraid anymore.
I'm done.

I'd been willing to die at my own hand. I'd been living in hell where my senses had been dulled, my freedom at touching rain and feeling sunshine stolen. All I was allowed to endure was coldness, nakedness, and pain.

But not tonight.

Tonight, the world was alive. The brutality of existing whispered in my ear to let go of everything and breathe with it. To howl with it. To die with it if that was my fate.

Climbing from my bed naked, I relished the bite of chill because *I* chose it not Alrik. I embraced the fearful scatter of my heartbeat because *I* was the architect of my panic not Alrik. And when I unlooped the belt from the robe Elder made me wear after he forced me to face his cello, a weight somehow unbuckled from my shoulders and fell like a cape around my feet.

I was reckless and stupid and moronically brave as I unlocked the French doors and let them snap back as if alive. I fought the wind, head down, arms up against the rain as I braced myself against the sting of droplets and the caress of tropical gales.

I clung to the balustrade, battling the storm. Unable to hold on against its might, I lashed the terrycloth belt to the balcony, tied it around my hips, and knotted it tight.

I gave my life, not to a piece of towelling and the smite of nature but to fate.

No one—not a person or animal—was in charge of me in that moment. Not even myself.

Facing that was my ultimate fear and my biggest freedom.

I was alone.

I was tiny.

I was no one.

Live or die, the world wouldn't know or care.

Each crack of thunder sent my nipples pebbling and my tummy liquefying with panic. Every deep dark roll of the ocean as it vanished from beneath the boat only to surge upward with more power than any calamity stopped my heart then defibrillated it.

If I could survive this—bare as I was born and open in every way I could possibly be, I could survive anything.

I *had* survived everything.

And this was me claiming that life back by acknowledging that yes, I was small, yes, I was inconsequential, but I still breathed. The world still nurtured me even while its elements did their best to exterminate me.

I was worth living. I was worth surviving. And I would never again let nature or man take that away from me.

My arms spread into wings, wishing the wind would pluck me from gravity and haul me into its angry embrace.

I wanted to fly.

Give me your worst!

"Pim."

The storm knew my name. My fake name. My slave name.

I'm here. I'm yours.

My head fell back in rapture.

"Pim!"

The wind snapped my name to pieces.

Take me. Heal me. Use my true name.

"Pimlico!" Something heavy and cross landed on my rain-soaked shoulder.

My eyes wrenched open.

Elder stood dripping wet, his black eyes wild as the wind. His lips moved, but the gale stole his words.

I frowned, watching his mouth, but he didn't try to speak again. He dropped his gaze down my body, lingering on my breasts and stomach as the rain touched every part of me. His eyes heated every droplet until they sizzled against my skin.

I'd never had someone look at me that way before. A way full of violence but nurturing. Of want but protection. No teenage boy could've looked at me that way and no monster had the capacity to blend such right and wrong and make it undeniably acceptable.

Before I could stop myself, my arm fell, my hand groped for his, and I smiled.

Our fingers linked tight and unrelenting.

Hair plastered against my scalp, clinging like kelp to my

collarbone, but I didn't care. Elder swallowed; his face lit up by rouge lightning, his clothing glued to his delectable body.

His fingers suddenly squeezed mine as if a decision he hadn't even asked himself yet was reached. Pulling me forward, he smirked as the rope around my waist prevented me from sliding between him and the railing.

Still holding my hand he bent down, wobbling as the waves wreaked havoc with his yacht and yanked off his flip-flops. Once bare-foot, he moved toward me.

My heart looked through the chasing raindrops in interest not fear. My body primed from the electricity of the storm, ready to accept touch rather than expect pain.

He wedged his body against mine, his jeans rough against the back of my thighs, his t-shirt unwanted against my naked shoulders.

Clothing. Barriers. Masks.

Letting go of my fingers, he clasped the railing on either side of me, wedging me safely between him.

His protection gave me mixed emotions.

I liked having him there, sharing the power of the storm and being free for the first time in my life, but he'd ruined the rapture I'd felt. His body heat was a trap, warming me when I wanted the rain to chill me because *I* chose it to, no one else.

He'd taken away my choice even after forcing me to make so many.

I did my best to lose myself in the wind again, but it remained tainted. My joy faded as minutes passed. We balanced and tripped, our ears throbbing with howling noise.

Perhaps I should push back and signal we'd go inside.

Maybe I'd tempted death long enough by laughing in the storm's face.

But then, as if my thoughts trickled into him and he read my discomfort, Elder pulled away, letting the wind lash against me with wet-coldness.

I sighed with relief.

Looking over my shoulder, I expected him to order me

into the suite where it was safe or point that he was leaving and to do whatever I wanted.

However, his arms went up and his hands latched around his t-shirt collar. With a black look, he ripped it over his head.

A thunder crash sounded at precisely the same time my eyes fell on his dragon tattoo. His ribs exposed, his organs painted so lifelike he was part man, part skeleton, part myth.

Never looking away, his hands fell to his belt buckle and undid it. Unbuttoning his shorts and unzipping the fly, he grabbed both the waistband of the beige material and grey boxer-briefs and pulled.

He stripped with grace even while fighting gravity, and the moment he was free, he threw away his clothes as if they offended him.

What is he doing?

The question was void the moment I asked it.

I understood.

He understood.

Clothing was not welcome when facing such furious power. We were merely human at the mercy of the weather. Who cared if we died dressed or naked? We had no armament against it—might as well give in to the inevitable.

I shivered and not from the cold as he moved toward me. His right hand landed on the railing where I gripped it. His thumb grazed my pinkie. His erection hung heavy as he took another step, placing himself behind me, aligning our pieces as if we belonged to the same chessboard with a long lost king and queen.

I stopped breathing as his other hand landed by my left. His thumb mimicking his other and pressing my pinkie. He didn't lean forward or wedge his nakedness against mine. He merely stood there, letting the wind nip my spine and the rain lick my shoulder blades. The only contact was my pinkies and his thumbs, but it was the most contact I'd ever had with anyone.

He held me with nothing but his thoughts. He touched me

with something better than hands. He cradled me in feeling and no one—not my mother, friends, or Alrik—had ever done such a thing.

It cracked yet another piece of me, throwing it to the thunder hounds snapping in the wind.

His head came down, his nose tracing the shell of my ear. He inhaled me. I inhaled the sky. I didn't know if I smelled of imprisonment and hatred or freedom and love.

I was blended now.

The storm had taken what I'd been and made me into someone I was meant to become.

It hadn't healed me.

It had purged me.

Leaving me baptised by hell itself in its angry clawing abuse.

A low groan slipped from his chest to mine. My answering shiver was for him, not the storm. My pattering heartbeat for him, not the rain.

I was alive because of him.

I was becoming more than Pim because of him.

A wave surged inside me, breaking over the shore of my mind with the possibility of finally being honest with him, finally giving him my voice, finally admitting my true name.

Before, there was no way I could weaken myself; now, there was a way because it wasn't weakness, it was time.

The softest kiss landed on my cheek, wiped away as quickly as it'd been bestowed.

But it had happened.

I'd felt it.

Time stood still as a man stood behind me, protecting me not molesting me, and allowed me to spread my wings and fly.

ELDER

I OUGHT TO strap her ass for standing so recklessly in the storm.

I should give myself a whipping for doing the same thing.

Where had common sense gone? Where had the fear of a lightning strike or falling overboard and drowning gone?

Who the fuck knows.

All I knew was standing naked with Pim while we faced death with no fear had been better than any pot, better than any drug I could take to calm my mind and let me control my tendencies.

Being that way...free that way...had given me a glimpse into the sort of person I could become if I trusted myself that I wouldn't fuck it up like last time.

An hour we stayed, riding the sea. An hour where my hands slowly slipped over hers, encapsulating her tiny grip while holding onto the rail beneath. An hour where my cock craved to press against her and my heart hammered at being so damn close.

And after an hour, it was as if someone notched up the churn cycle, switching the waves from rodeo to downright berserk. Our feet slipped often, we crashed against the balustrade frequently while I did my best to protect Pim from my weight as we shot forward, bending almost in half as the boat rolled, threatening to kiss the water before springing back and wrenching us into the sky.

Danger turned to potential death. We'd tempted fate enough. I untied Pimlico's safety measure and dropped the belt into the sea. Instantly, the wind snatched it from my hands, a lick of white in the otherwise black sky.

Keeping her hand locked in mine, I dragged her back into the relative safety of her suite. She took one door, and I took the other, both struggling and puffing to shut the wild weather outside and throw the lock home.

Once the wind was banished but the motion was not, I moved to the bed and grabbed the coverlet. Pimlico stood with spread legs, doing her best to predict where the next swell would take us, but tripped forward when the sea decided she'd guessed wrong.

Cocking my chin, I didn't try to yell over the noise. For a moment, I wondered if I'd read our connection wrong outside. When I'd pressed against her fully clothed, her annoyance and frustration screamed loudly from tense muscles. Yet once I was naked and hovered but didn't touch, she'd relaxed as much as she could while fighting a rabid storm. We hadn't been able to talk, touch, or taste—only watch and balance and bow to the ferocity of Mother Nature.

But we'd been linked beyond anything else I'd ever felt.

She'd been in my head. I'd been in hers.

A connection breathed between us now that had no words but was so fucking strong.

Tiredness and muscles ached and throbbed, but we still had a few hours before the storm stopped toying with us. We were soaked past bone and into soul, my teeth locking together from the building shivers.

Moving to the sunken couch, I sat and dug into the cushions. As Pimlico deliberated if she wanted to join me or if I'd overstepped too many of her boundaries tonight, I pulled out the seatbelts wedged in there for times exactly like this.

Fighting to stay upright for the first hour was fine. Fighting to stay seated and not tossed across the room by the fifth hour was not.

Not bothering to dress, I locked the belt around my hips, ignoring that I fluctuated between aroused when I looked at Pim and calm when I looked away. Slowly, she stumbled toward me, grabbing onto bolted down furniture as she made her way across the space.

By the time she flung herself onto the couch, her chest rose and fell with exhaustion. Giving her a smile, far happier than I should be about entrusting our lives to a tyrannical ocean, I reached across her and slid the buckle into its home.

Wrenching the seatbelt tight across her belly, I grabbed the duvet and covered both of us.

I never took my eyes off her face, watching her carefully as the material settled around us, giving instant comfort and warmth on our cold drenched bodies.

A normal person with no aversion to clothing would snuggle in straight away; perhaps even sigh in relief to be draped in softness.

Not Pim.

She tensed. Her jaw worked as she swallowed, wrenching her arms out to press the coverlet down away from her face and neck. She didn't stop touching the soft cotton, but after a few seconds, she forced herself to relax.

I couldn't figure out why she had such an issue with clothing. Yet another question I desperately wanted to ask. I had pages and pages inside my mind. Sheets and sheets of queries and demands that would all have to wait until she was ready.

Her two weeks is up.
You could force her to talk.

My face went slack even as my body continued to tense with wave rocking.

Hadn't I been patient and kind? Hadn't I gone out of my way to build a thin crust of trust so Pim could walk over water

without drowning?
 I'd fulfilled my side of the bargain.
 It's time for her to fulfil hers.

Pimlico

BY DAWN, THE storm hiccupped and decided it'd had enough fun for the night.

Each rock slowly grew less violent. Each gale slowly lost interest. Elder woke from where we'd fallen into pockets of fitful sleep and unbuckled from the couch. Standing naked, he gave me a rueful smile as he strolled into the bathroom and stole a towel.

The boat still skipped and dived, but we'd either adapted to the instability, and our internal gyroscopes handled it better, or he'd taken whatever mystical powers his dragon tattoo had and enlisted its help—unseen wings flapping with power, keeping him airborne even as his feet stayed connected to the Phantom.

I hated how his body no longer looked like a weapon or instrument to deliver pain but something I'd like to touch. I didn't know why I hated the switch of my conclusions. Wasn't it healthy to finally look upon a man and only see a man—no matter how handsome and unique he was—rather than see a killer?

Elder didn't know the jumble of my thoughts or how he distracted me while wrapping the towel around his waist.

Raking a hand through storm blown hair, he said, "I'm going back to my quarters. I have work to do—if, of course, the satellites are still intact." His eyes lingered on mine, then on the bed where snatches of desire smouldered.

I tensed.

If he told me he wanted me, I wouldn't disobey. He'd earned sex after all he'd done. I might even marginally accept it. I wouldn't enjoy it, but I wouldn't loathe it like I had.

Only, he tore his gaze away, shut down whatever he'd been thinking, and rubbed his five o'clock shadow. "Rest. It was a long night." Strolling to the door, he added, "I'll come for you later."

Without giving me time to wave or respond, he left.

The door closed, and every inch of adrenaline keeping me awake popped into tiredness. The thought of sleeping was the best concept ever, so I obeyed his command, curled up on my side with the seatbelt still trapping me in place, and slept a little more.

* * * * *

By midday, the sun took control of the world, burning away the last grey clouds, banishing the rain back to hell.

I woke irrevocably changed from who I'd been before the storm and untethered myself from the couch and my past.

Climbing on stiff joints and bruised bones, I stood on a calm boat and calm soul as if the two were linked with symbolism as well as fact.

The world was tamed.

My memories were tamed.

I'd survived.

Inhaling air still rich and damp from the clouds, I showered, dried, and deliberated whether to stay naked for my enjoyment or dress for his.

I opted to wear the navy and blue shift so I didn't upset the staff who would no doubt be on repairs now the storm had passed.

By mid-afternoon, I found a perfect spot on the lifeboat

canvas and basked in the hot sunshine. It shone stronger and brighter, as if to make up for the messy night before.

I hadn't seen Elder, and I hadn't sought him out. I was happy to be on my own, slowly learning who I was after all this time—now the dirt had been washed away.

By dusk, I retreated to my suite, pulled out the notepad, and opened the door to my heart, ready to converse with imaginary confidant.

Dear No One,
Last night, I was in charge.
Last night, I did what I wanted. I embraced my fear and let it do whatever it wanted to me. It terrified me but freed me. Does that make any sense?
When Elder joined me, I feared he'd tear me away. I expected him to drag me back and slam the doors. But he joined me, No One. It was as if he needed to face his demons in those clouds the same as I did. As if standing together with nothing helped scatter our pieces and realign them into a completely different picture.
I heard him, though. I heard his resolution before he left.
He's run out of patience. Whatever self-control he's exercised won't last much longer because he knows what I do.
I owe him now.
Not just for the safety and time to heal, but for being with me last night. For no demands. For whatever emotion that links us.
Am I ready to answer his questions?
No.
Am I ready to talk to anyone but you?
Never.
Will he force me regardless?
I think so.
He wants my voice just like Alrik.
It's up to me to decide if he deserves it.

ELDER

I NEVER WENT back to her.

The storm had upset the automatic ballast, and I worked all day with Jolfer to fix it. Once that was done, I had important emails to reply to—after I'd reset the communication panels.

By the time night fell, I'd eaten a distracted dinner of lasagne and headed to my room to shower.

I had plans to go to Pim once I'd washed away the salt from the storm, but I wanted to re-centre myself first. I wanted to be sane, so the moment she opened the door I wouldn't shove her against the wall and devour her.

She was playing havoc with my control.

Soon, I wouldn't be able to be in the same room as her without needing to put an end to my frustration.

As fresh warm water cascaded over me, my mind tormented me with her mouth on my cock and the blowjob she'd tried to give. My hand gripped my length, begging to work for a release.

Even though it took every ounce of energy I had left, I pulled my palm away.

As much as I wanted to come, I didn't want to waste the anticipation of whatever would happen when Pim finally did accept me, finally trusted me to do more than kiss her.

I groaned as the image of kissing led to touching led to slipping inside her.

My balls were rock fucking hard.

She's driving me insane.

I needed to focus on something else—something I was immensely good at—before I lost myself to the obsession that would spring into place the moment I tasted Pim.

I'd battled it for too long.

The second I fucked her, I'd be forced to give in and then she'd see the real me. I snorted as I tilted my head to the spray. All this time, I'd been a gentleman. She thought she knew me. She couldn't have it more fucking wrong.

The closer I let myself get to Pim, the harder it was to fight the urge to reveal who I truly was.

Stepping from the shower, I dressed in dark grey sweatpants that sat low on my hips; I didn't bother with a shirt. My wraparound balcony opening onto the main deck glittered with stars thanks to the open doors, and the heat from the aftermath of the storm drenched the air with heavy mugginess.

Heading to the specially designed closet where foam and braces had been painstakingly crafted to embrace my cello, I undid the straps and pulled it free.

If I hadn't installed such a safe place, I doubted the cello would've survived last night's catastrophe.

The weight and bulk were no longer cumbersome, but I remembered a time when the instrument had been a foreign stranger. Then my tutor had played that first note, corralled my unskilled fingers to press on the right strings, and *boom*, the curse in my blood took over.

I played and played and *played.*

Every spare moment, I sat until my legs went to sleep, hunger made me tremble, and my fingers bled for more music. No one could reach me. No one could stop me. Nothing else mattered.

Nothing.

As the cello settled like a compliant lover between my legs, my mind slipped backward into the quicksand of memories.

All my young life, I'd lived with something inside me—something stronger than I was, something that had the power to destroy me as well as save me.

I thought it would decimate everyone I loved until my mother took it upon herself to nurture it. My father agreed, and they gave me free rein to evolve my talent in music. I became obsessed, possessed, and utterly overpowered with the need to be as brilliant as I could. I'd read music until my eyes fogged. I'd practice and practice until my ears rang from the same notes, every second, of every hour, of every day.

Eventually, my tutor spoke to my father. He was afraid of my passion, afraid because I stopped eating, drinking, living. I only existed to master the cello in every way possible.

However, my father understood who I was, and instead of scolding me, he encouraged me.

I became worse.

Origami started much the same. One night, I picked up a piece of my brother's homework left on the kitchen table. His assignment was to make a simple crane for a class project.

It took me all night, but I mastered the entire exercise booklet, leaving my origami creations of cranes and boats and butterflies outside my brother's bedroom, so he woke up in a sea of folded colour.

After that, if I wasn't playing the cello, I was creasing paper into anything I could imagine. I no longer needed guidelines and instructions. I *was* the instructions.

But then, I fucked up.

My childhood disappeared.

And my new life obsession was tracking down those who stole from me and steal from them in return. I'd hunt every person who'd ever put a roadblock in my path and kill them.

And I wouldn't stop until I was the biggest, baddest, most untouchable one of them all.

The entire time my mind ran backward over good and evil,

my fingers flew. Music poured. Violence was shared. Love was created. I didn't play as audiences expected. I didn't keep calm and close my eyes to visualize the notes better.

I let loose.

My body became quavers; my arms double clefts. I lost myself to the dark melody as I maimed and wounded it, changing and designing.

Sweat glistened over my naked chest; my fingers became damp as I struggled to race through a crescendo that made me rock fucking hard and almost at the verge of burning tears.

And then a flutter of motion wrenched my head up.

Pimlico hovered just over the threshold of my room.

Her mouth hung wide, her hands balled. She wore the white robe I'd given her when I'd pushed her from my room the last time. White—the colour of where I'd stolen her from. White—the colour of her innocence that'd been ripped away. White—the colour of lies and half-truths and fear.

My fingers clanged to a stop. My bow dangled, vibrating with the last note I'd played. I'd lost myself so completely I'd shredded half the horsehair. I did this often. I had an endless supply of strings to replace those I broke.

I could never control how deep I'd go, how monstrous I'd play.

And now, I'd done something I didn't want to do.

I'd terrified Pim.

Again.

"Hey..." My throat was barbwire. Gently placing the cello against the chair, I stood on shaky legs. "I didn't see you come in."

I wouldn't have seen a torpedo come in when I was in such a space. But Pim didn't need to know that.

"You okay?"

She couldn't tear her eyes off the cello even as I stalked toward her. The sum of her past darkened her eyelashes, her eyes bright with ghosts.

Ducking in front of her, I murmured, "Music can't hurt

you, silent one."

She flinched as I tried to loop our fingers together. Scurrying around me, she bolted for my cello.

Again?

Balling my hands, I growled. "You know the rules, Pim. Don't fucking touch it."

Take away my cello and you'll take away me. "I need something to play. It's either that or you. Your choice."

She skidded to a stop a few feet away as if the instrument would lash out and punch her. As if the strings would come alive and tie her down while the bow violated her.

Hadn't she climbed over her mountain of hate last time she was here? How could music be so abhorrent on such a deep level?

I played for you...did it do nothing?
You want her answers. She's already telling you.

Moving toward her, I held out my hands as she whipped her head to face me. "I think other methods are required to train that unneeded fear from you."

She gnawed on the inside of her cheek.

Edging around her, I grabbed the cello and sat back down, holding the large instrument to the side. "Come here."

She blanched, backing away instead.

"Don't disobey me. I've been more than cordial. I've been patient and mostly kind. But if you don't start doing what the fuck I want, I'll show you what happens when I get pissed off." I patted my lap again. "Come. Here."

Glowering with temper, she sniffed.

Then grudgingly, unwillingly, she shuffled forward and stood in front of me; her eyes still glued to the cello in my hand.

"At least, that's a start. We'll work on your attitude later." Opening my left arm, I nodded at my crotch. "Sit."

Her eyebrows rose; a barely noticeable shake of her head. It pleased me and annoyed me in equal measure. Since taking her a few weeks ago, she'd built a backbone to verbalize her unwillingness after so long in captivity. That was because of me. After the storm last night, I'd seen where I'd gone wrong. She needed events to push her past her comfort zone. She had to be dragged back to normal by any means necessary. I'd given her the time to find herself again. It was my turn to show her who I was. Then we could move forward together.

Before my desire explodes and I destroy everything.

Her eyes narrowed as I waited for her to obey. Our silence battled and clashed with muted swords, but finally she huffed and turned to perch on the very tip of my knee.

That wouldn't work.

I needed her close. I needed to feel her heart through my chest so I could monitor her terror levels.

"Remember, do what I say, and I won't hurt you." Lassoing my arm around her, I gathered her close, hoisting her from my knee to my thigh. She weighed absolutely nothing, and she gasped as her hip pressed against my cock which was still granite from playing.

I nuzzled her throat. "I'm hard because I play. But now that you're on my lap, I'm thinking of stroking something entirely different to my cello."

Fuck, just hinting at stroking something of hers made every drop of blood swell in my trousers.

She stiffened, froze, then turned lifeless on my lap.

That wasn't allowed.

Resting my bow against my knee, I reached around her nape and gathered her hair to one side, pushing it over her shoulder. She flinched as my fingers grazed her neck. Seemed she still had pressure points hotwired to whatever that cunt had done to her.

Ignoring her tension, I soothed, "I'm not going to touch you. How many times do I need to tell you that?"

Her spine locked even harder, forcing me to admit my contradiction.

"I know I'm holding you close, but you have my word, I

won't touch you anywhere else than where I currently am."

Her nostrils flared, doing her best to suck in a breath.

"Soon you will tell me in explicit detail what scares you so much about melodies—you'll tell me if I'm right about it playing while you were hurt—but for now, we're going to make you the creator, not just the listener."

Her breathing quickened as my bicep bunched to drag the cello between my legs. I wasn't comfortable with her on top of me, and the angle was wrong to play smoothly, but somehow, I knew Pimlico needed to do this if she had any hope of reclaiming yet another part of her.

Holding the tattered bow, I murmured, "Give me your hand." I opened my left palm in invitation, waiting like I would with a scared bird to take a crumb from me.

Sucking in a deep inhale, Pim obeyed as slowly as if the world had stopped moving and one day had stretched to three.

I didn't rush her. I forced myself to be patient. Whatever progress we'd made together from the storm and pickpocketing session had been dulled thanks to my cello.

But when her touch finally connected against mine, she shuddered.

I shuddered.

Fuck, it was like her positive met my negative and created a current, flowing unhindered between us.

Her hand in mine was almost too much. My body clenched to claim more. It took every ounce of willpower to grit my teeth and keep my touch gentle.

Once I'd gathered tattered self-discipline, I fought the urge to inhale her. "Good. Let me control you." I guided her hand to the fingerboard.

She struggled a little as I wrapped her palm tight on the veneer and her fingers pressed against the strings.

"Feel it? It's not alive. It's nothing but a lacquered shell and string."

She shifted on my knee, bumping against my cock.

I locked down my muscles as the anticipation of having

her so close while playing almost tipped me over. "It's not alive until you do this." I reached further around her, guiding her fingers to the right chord. Once she was in position, I softly dragged the half-ruined bow over the strings.

Sound leapt, echoing in the age-old cello—pouring rich and raw around us.

Goosebumps leapt over my skin.

I hadn't had goosebumps from playing in years.

Pim jolted.

Wrenching her hand from mine, she clenched it with the other as if the cello had stung her. Perhaps, it had. Memories stung. Recollections whipped. She had to get past her mind to enjoy such simple pleasures.

Not saying a word, I grabbed her hand and replaced it once again on the fingerboard. She went stiff but didn't try to pull away. She leaned tight against my chest, as if to get as far from the cello as possible. I fought my instinct to kiss her throat and played a B.

My eyes snapped closed as the robust, meaty note quavered. There was no better sound than this. No better magic than this.

She wriggled, but I didn't let go this time. "Stop it. Whatever hold these notes had…let it go. Be that girl in the storm. Remember who you are and who you want to be." I played an A then a D and a G sharp, introducing her ears to a range of highs and lows, savoury and sour notes, sweet and salty. And once we'd done a chord chart, I gathered her closer. "Let me guide you. Don't fight it."

And then, I began to play.

Some notes slipped as our fingers entwined together. Some ended short with my ruined bow. But for the next four minutes and fifty-three seconds, Pim allowed me to drench her in pain-swimming music. She let me drag her back to the depths to pick up the pieces that'd sank so far inside her she would never have had enough oxygen to dive down and salvage them on her own.

The barriers between us melted away and just like in the storm, I *felt* her inside me. I heard her plight. I saw her history. And I understood her on a level I hadn't let anyone enter for decades.

Her spine remained locked against my chest, never softening or submitting, but her fingers warmed beneath mine, accepting not cursing the song we created.

Sexual intensity peaked mid-way when the tune soared high then swooped epically low—a rich combination speaking of abuse and melancholy. The hair on the back of my arms stood up and I couldn't stop my face turning into Pim and my lips caressing her throat.

She winced but her neck arched for me to nuzzle then dropped to prevent an open-mouthed kiss.

We lived in a state of lustful flux where sex plaited itself around us, pulling tighter and tighter, harder and harder to ignore.

Her weight on my leg and hip against my cock drained my energy faster than any sprint or swim.

I was breathless.

I was witless.

I was utterly spent and ripped apart.

The song was an eternity.

The song was a second.

And when the last note faded, I let her hand go and dropped my arm from around her. I needed her gone because if she didn't, I'd fuck her.

Leave.

Get away from me.

She remained frozen on my lap. Her feet planted on the ground, taking her weight even though I would gladly support her—just not when I was seconds away from becoming a savage.

Tears decorated her eyelashes like spider webs, hanging so fine—threading a silver-webbed trap over her cheeks.

How long had she been crying?

My desire switched to rage. Every urge wanted to wipe away those damning tears and find a way to plug her mind from memories, but I let her stay in her thoughts. I didn't force her to return. I gave her the time we both needed to find sanity.

Slowly, her body relaxed from its music-induced statue; she stood from my lap.

I let her go.

I no longer want her to leave.

I never looked away as she paced toward the bed and sat on the mattress with her head in her hands. The cello felt heavy in my arms as I shifted it to the floor, making sure it was safe before going to her.

Now was the time.

This was what I'd been waiting for.

She was vulnerable, shaken, but not broken. She'd never been broken, but now, she had more glue along the hairline fractures and more courage than tears.

"Talk to me."

Her eyes met mine, drying from whatever she'd suffered while we played.

She sat taller.

Towering over her, I commanded, "I've been patient long enough, silent mouse. I've given you things I've never given anyone. It's time to return the favour."

She squeaked silently as I reached for her throat.

I was aware of her fear of having her neck touched, but I didn't let her globe-wide eyes or flinch stop me. She had to learn I would touch her wherever I damn well pleased. She had to trust I wouldn't hurt her like he had.

Clasping my fingers around her throat, I murmured, "Your tongue is healed; you have a working voice box, so sound can come out of your mouth. I know it. I won't beat you. I won't force you. I won't even touch you. But you *will* talk to me."

Letting her go, I spread my fingers. "See? I'm going to put them behind my back. I give you my word. I won't touch you."

I smirked. "For the next ten minutes, at least. If you behave and do what I say, I'll keep my hands to myself for a little longer. Do exactly what I say, and I don't touch you at all."

My jaw lowered. "Don't do what I say, and I'll have to break my promise. Do you understand?"

Her eyes shot darts while her neck contracted as she swallowed.

"Good." Bracing myself, I pushed my legs farther apart and locked my hands behind my back. "Now you know the rules. Let's begin."

Pimlico

WHY MUST HE continue calling me mouse?

That wasn't his to use. Every time he said it in his carnally cruel voice, it sent me careening back to a teenager who wasn't worse than any other teenager but was woefully naïve.

I didn't want to be naïve anymore.

I wasn't naïve when it came to the world of men.

I knew what Elder wanted. I'd felt it the entire time he made me conjure awful sounds from that beast he loved so much. His erection had scalded my hip as if it had a furnace cranked to a thousand degrees.

But if he was going to have sex with you…he wouldn't have promised not to touch you.

The logic didn't soothe me; it only made me more confused.

"Tell me your real name."

Did he honestly think I'd just blurt it out? That two years of silence would be forgotten because he played me one song and stood with me in a storm?

The residue terror from him touching my neck, from *kissing* my neck, overflowed. I'd done my best to keep it in check but if he was about to force me to speak…I wouldn't let him win the battle.

    It was my decision if he deserved my voice.
    He doesn't—not after that awful cello.
    I stood up, chin cocked.
    His face darkened. "Answer me."
    I crossed my arms. *No.*
    "Pim."
    Don't Pim me.

The power and freedom from spending the night wrapped in thunder gave me reckless courage. The music he'd forced into my ears kept echoing on repeat, making me twitchy and wild. Two extremes, slinging together to meet in a mess of frustration, fear, and fury.

    So much fury.
    I was done playing his games.
    I was done playing anyone's games.
    I'll make the rules from now on, you hear me?
    I'd come here looking for the man who played with me on the deck. I'd invited myself into his quarters, hoping he'd kiss me again. I didn't come to be pushed and pushed, and I definitely didn't come to talk.
    I came for fun.
    And you just made me cry.

Elder stood between me and the door. I wanted out. I wanted to run and write to No One. I wanted to toss away his bronze genie lamp because he'd lied about granting me wishes.

If he had the power to do that, he would've taken away my repulsion of touch and kisses and sex, and I could stand before him with heat rather than ice. I could feel his cock against my hip and melt rather than freeze.

After weeks of living with him, I thought I'd be better. He'd promised me he'd find a cure.

    You're a liar.
    Standing, I stepped forward.
    I'm over this!
    His eyes tightened, but he didn't speak as I took another

step and another. My crossed arms wrapped tighter, as if they could shield me from whatever might come next.

I kept encroaching on his space—not caring I went closer to him—my goal was to push past and fly out the door before he could break his promise of not touching me (for the second time tonight) and force me to talk.

"What are you doing?" he whispered, his face cast in shadows. His eyebrows were angry black slashes, his hair tangled from playing such soul-crushing music.

I'm leaving.

A few more steps and our chests would touch. A few more steps and I'd be able to shove him away and bolt out the door.

My gaze kept darting between him, the exit, and that damn awful cello. I didn't care that the first time he'd forced me to stay it hadn't been as bad as I thought. This time—actually feeling the notes quiver and swell beneath my fingers—all I'd felt were Alrik's whips.

Sickness sat in my stomach like a cannonball.

Two more steps and our bodies aligned. I craned my head to stare.

Just let me go.

Elder stood his ground. "Sit down, Pim. We're not done."

Yes, we are.

I didn't second-guess my need to strike him, to hurt him. Even as my hands flew up on their own accord and shoved him backward to give me space, I wasn't fully in control.

Get out of my way!

He stumbled but quickly righted himself. The air crackled with brutality.

"You seriously want to do this?" His voice wavered with violence.

Do what? Let me go?

Yes, let me go!

For all his perceptive patience and cruel understanding, he didn't have a clue what I felt. Did he think he'd fixed me? That his cello was some magical pill and now I was normal?

It doesn't work that way!

I don't want to talk to you!

Nothing about the sudden switch from pickpocket flirting to destroying me with music made me want to open up and have a heart to heart.

He doesn't need a heart to heart.

He read your secrets, remember?

More anger poured through me like hot wax.

All I wanted was to leave and get away from the lingering tingle in my blood from his heat and the sparkling fear from his notes.

I advanced on him; my hands outstretched and ready for war.

He braced his legs, his jaw lowered. "Push me again and see what happens, Pim."

The warning should've been enough to make me sit back on the bed and behave. To open my mouth and utter a single word. But he'd let me get away with other misdemeanours. What was to say he wouldn't let me get away with this one?

I wasn't pretending. I needed to go. Right now.

And you're in my way.

Baring my teeth, I shoved him, putting all my power into the force behind my pummel.

He staggered back, his eyes widening only to go black as death as I darted toward the door.

Freedom.

He was no longer a roadblock. I'd done that. I'd turned the key. Now, all I had to do was cross the threshold and return to my room, and this could all be forgotten.

I took three steps before his hand lashed out, wrapping around my wrist. "I warned you, Pimlico. I fucking warned you not to push me."

He whirled me around, slamming me against his chest. "You pushed and pushed, and I can't fucking take it anymore."

His lips came down on mine, tearing my mouth open and

kissing me deep. My tummy tangled in horror and heat as I squirmed in his embrace.

This kiss was different.

This kiss was *real*.

His past kisses had been fakeries. Elder chose this moment—a moment when I was scattered and jittery—to reveal who he was beneath his masked decorum.

This kiss was utter violence.

Violence, I knew. Danger was what I'd been fed, and violence was what I'd drank for years. My body reacted. Shutting down, it turned stiff and unyielding even as something strange happened. The foreignness that'd been budding from seed to seedling ever since I'd woken in Elder's domain flourished.

The wetness he'd caused in the streets of Morocco returned without permission.

I hated that two women lived inside me. Two personalities, two hopes and dreams and wishes.

The male tongue in her mouth appalled Pimlico. She wanted to bite it, run from it. She hurt with every lick and would forever remain just a little bit broken. She would never enjoy sex because her induction and life had been too traumatic to untangle.

But then there was Tasmin.

A girl who'd enjoyed late-night touches from incompetent boyfriends and was still a virgin to pleasure. A girl who was steadily learning to take back control. A girl who flickered into authority and *felt* Elder's kiss rather than endured it.

My body stiffened then softened. Fought then floundered.

And Elder didn't stop kissing me. His tongue didn't stop dancing with mine, and I didn't know if I licked him back in war or welcome.

His touch hurt but in two ways now instead of one. I was familiar with the bite of fear and unwillingness, but I was new to the heat and fire of his dominance.

His hand wrapped around my nape, kissing me harder.

Part of me wanted to run from his touch, the other wanted to have him collar me so I could feel safe in his control.

My lips bruised. My mind became a washed-up origami sail-boat.

"Fuck, Pim. I'm—I can't stop."

Sweeping me off my feet, he sank to his knees with me in his embrace. His mouth never stopped claiming mine, biting and nipping, forcing me to accept whatever passion he'd held back.

And he'd held back a lot.

I gasped as his hand tore at my robe, yanking it open to reveal my breast. The cool air licked around my nipple. It hardened.

Pim screamed.

Tasmin moaned.

The bondage in my mind reached snapping point.

His hand clamped on the sensitive flesh. Nightmares and flashbacks threatened to take me under. The terror that this was the moment Elder turned into Alrik begged me to cut loose and sink inside myself until it was over.

But Tasmin clung to sensations; she threw back her head and said yes to living.

That strange, unwelcome molten desire licked from his touch into my core, keeping me locked in his embrace. For the first time in my life, I felt a siphon of pleasure beneath the rage of being hurt.

Pim lost a smidgen of power; Tasmin snatched it.

Elder didn't pay any attention to my internal battle. He didn't know how much he affected me, how much he drugged and shredded my mind.

His thoughts weren't on me for once. He didn't watch me, judging how far to take me. He was utterly obsessed with his demons.

"Christ, I need you." His words tipped into my mouth, pushed down my throat with his tongue. Sitting up on his knees, he ripped the terrycloth belt undone and spread the robe wide. The soft cotton had no power against whatever madness lived in his blood.

The moment he'd spread my gown into a cape, he positioned me over his thighs and fumbled with his sweatpants.

His knuckles grazed my inner thighs, nudging my sex.

Pimlico burst into tears, hiding her face, begging this to be over.

Tasmin stiffened, giving into the fear from Pim and pausing for a second too long.

Horror replaced my fascination over how well Elder played my body. I was his cello now. My spine was his bow and my breasts his strings. He created love but violence at the same time.

The back of his hand caught my sex again.

I stiffened even as something inside me melted rather than screamed. I didn't know what he was doing, how far he would go, but everything I'd been trained to expect in sex, every nuance my body had learned to shut out, was achingly sensitive and kept me on a knife-edge of sensation.

A growl rumbled in his chest as his touch turned swift and angry. Blistering heat branded me from his fingers.

My tummy twisted as pants were shoved away. The sight of his cock scared me and like always, my body clamped down against what was about to happen.

Now, Pim and Tasmin were back into one person. There was no more split. Neither wanted this—not like this, not so soon or so quick.

But Elder didn't notice my quaking legs or feel my writhing arms. He was too far gone in lust to notice.

No. Stop...

His hand delved between my thighs, two fingers finding my core and pressing into me.

He grunted beneath his breath, and despite Pim's dryness and unresponsiveness, Tasmin had condemned us both with the slick invitation of wetness.

"Fuck, I never thought I'd get inside you like this." Elder

curled his fingers, sinking deep.

I stopped breathing as his touch withdrew then swirled around my clit, forcing my mind to stay anchored when all I wanted to do was flee.

The longer he touched me, the more my body decided to ignore everything it knew and give in to him. It was too hard to fight. Too exhausting to care.

My mind was a sprinting circus. My blood jumping flees. Something heavy curled in my belly, whispering through my veins stealthy and swift.

It didn't matter that I refused this. It didn't matter I wasn't mentally prepared. My body blossomed beneath his touch. It relished his soft ministration, not agonising punishment. It liquefied for erotic bliss while I rocked in the corner in tears.

He groaned as he touched me again, his fingers sliding in and filling me.

I shuddered despite myself.

My mouth opened in a silent scream.

His lips trailed fire from my mouth to my ear, hoisting me higher in his embrace as his legs bunched beneath mine. "Shit, Pim."

He hadn't put me on the carpet once. Hadn't stopped cradling me once. His hands took control, but there was still a semblance of caring in the way he touched me.

I tried to focus on that, rather than where his fingers were. I tried to remember the laughter when I stole his wallet and not the heavy breath growing thick with desire in my ear.

"Let go…goddammit, let go." His fingers thrust up. "Enjoy me as I'm enjoying you."

My back bowed, and something I'd kept locked deep inside since stepping onto the auctioneer block in QMB floated to the surface. The longer Elder's hands stroked me, the closer his cock came to claiming me, the less flimsy the lock became.

Cracks and fissures ripped like an earthquake.

I hated how unstable he made me.

How I didn't know what was up and down and around. I

clung to him even as I tried to run. And when his fingers slid from my body, and he clutched my frame to hoist me higher over his thighs, I lost it.

I stopped thinking.

I turned catatonic with numbness while at the same time became a firework about to ignite. Two massive extremes. One massive event.

"I need you so fucking much." His legs worked as he positioned me over his cock. His sweatpants clung to his thighs. Clothing hindered both of us—a prison for our bodies while I was imprisoned by fear in my mind.

Fisting himself, he angled upright and slowly lowered me down.

I couldn't fight.

I couldn't speak.

I couldn't breathe.

All I could do was fall forward into his embrace as my body—so well trained from years of abuse—welcomed his thick length effortlessly. There was no obstruction. No denial. The wetness only made his entry smooth rather than agonising.

My teeth clamped on his shoulder, biting as hard as I could as the tip of him nudged the tip of me and whatever lock I'd kept fastened exploded.

With a feral growl, he smashed me into pieces, tore down my defensives, and left Pimlico gaping and bleeding while Tasmin stood over her in newfound power.

The battlefield of my mind quieted as Elder thrust into me victoriously.

He grunted with primal satisfaction then thrust again, filling me so, so deep. "*Christ,* Pim."

I'd never been so stretched; never been so utterly devoured.

And then the tears began.

Deep, endless black tears.

Tears turned to sobs, sobs turned to body shakes, and finally, I got through to Elder in his sex haze.

He instantly stiffened, holding me away from him to look at my face. His cock twitched inside me as disgusted hatred coated his features. "Ah, fuck." Crushing me to him in a hug, he kissed the top of my head as if I was a little girl who'd had a nightmare. "Christ, what have I done?"

The contradiction of such comfort was negated every time his body jerked inside mine.

"Shit, Pim, I'm sorry. I…I—shit."

Gritting his teeth, he pulled me away from him, his legs gathering to push me off.

I couldn't bear to be tossed away after he'd stolen everything. I needed something to clutch while I became completely undone. Throwing myself forward, I gulped and suffocated in tears, drowning in every emotion I'd stopped myself from feeling for so long.

I needed his arms; otherwise, I'd die. I needed him to hold me now he'd decimated the podium I'd stood on and left me in rubble.

I had no one else.

Not even myself.

His arms lashed tight. His lips landed on my scalp again, and he rocked me like an infant. He didn't try to pull out, and the thickness of him coupled with the heaviness of his heartbeat surrounded me until my tears became waterfalls of grief.

I never thought sex would be my undoing.

Sex had been my nemesis for so long, but I'd blocked it out.

I couldn't block him out.

I couldn't stop the knowledge that while he'd taken me against my will, my body had invited it.

Time lost all meaning as he rocked and murmured and gave me a place to come undone.

My hips hurt spread over his. My pussy clenched against his invasion. My eyes blurred the world even as he remained steel-hard inside me.

I ceased to be Alrik's.
And became Elder's instead.

ELDER

WHAT THE FUCK was I thinking?

How had I let myself snap so totally? I hadn't given in to my irresponsible compulsiveness for years, and now, I'd done the worst thing I could ever do.

Pim clung to me, bawling as if I could save her from the awful thing I'd just done. I hated that she still permitted me to be her saviour while I was no better than the men I'd stolen her from.

"It's okay." I stroked her hair, gritting my teeth every time her body shuddered and the delicious fucking way it felt around my cock. "I'm sorry. Fuck, I'm so sorry."

I couldn't do this anymore. My self-control was at its frayed and bitter end. I'd have to sell her or just take her back and give her freedom.

I can't do this.

So what she knew who I was and had enough evidence to have police come knocking on my door? I had to do the right thing for once, and the right thing was letting her go.

"Pim...it's okay."

The knowledge I'd grant her freedom calmed me a little. If I could piece her back together now, she would never have to see me again after tonight.

Taking a steady breath, I whispered, "Sit up, so I can eh..." *What? Pull out. Remove myself from you. Stop raping you.* I cringed against such a word.

Pim hugged me tighter, her shoulders bunched as if she would be swept away if I let her go. Her teeth marks on my shoulder smarted, a faint tickle of liquid hinting she'd drawn blood.

Shit, if it meant she could reverse some of the damage I'd caused by delivering it on my skin, I'd gladly take it.

No wonder my family left me.
They were right.
Look at me.
I truly am a monster.

Holding her was the hardest fucking thing I'd done. I wanted to disengage and give her some space. But if holding her until I died was what it took to redeem myself, then so be it.

I didn't try to rush her.

While she cried, I did my best to deflate my cock but nothing worked. Her strength was what attracted me to her in the first place. Her tears were what made me snap now.

This felt like an end. I'd ruined it. I'd proven to her that my promises meant shit and she was right to look at me with accusation and suspicion. Right to believe I would one day hurt her because what the fuck was I doing now?

I was inside her against her will. I'd taken something she wasn't prepared to give. I'd lost control. Again.

Time ticked onward, but I never stopped stroking or cradling.

The gift she gave by allowing me to touch her after I'd forced myself onto her crippled me.

Slowly, Pim pulled away.

I expected her to stand and physically remove every part of me from her. However, her hands landed on either side of my face, her gaze searching mine as if hearing my grief and regret.

Her fingers were so soft they tickled as she traced my jaw. Tears fell from her eyes, an awful void inside her.

My gut spasmed. "What is it? What can I do? Name it. I'll do whatever you need."

Her touch turned fierce, holding me firm. Her mouth opened to speak.

To speak.

I stopped breathing, my ears throbbing to listen.

She swallowed hard, forehead furrowing with concentration. "El—"

My heart erupted. My cock doubled in size. If I hadn't just taken her on the floor, I would've kissed, and fucking kissed her.

She forced past her unused voice and finished. "Elder…"

My name.

Her first word was my name.

Her voice was everything I wanted and more. Accented, pure, feminine. I needed to come. I had no doubt if she commanded me to come in her perfect, pretty voice, I would.

I inhaled to reply, but she pressed two fingers over my lips and shook her head. She coughed, her eyes tightening against pain.

I obeyed and remained silent.

She sat a little taller. Her pussy gloved my cock with furious heat, and I did my best to push such bliss away. She had no idea how fucking hard it was to stay still and not thrust when every instinct bellowed to drive deep.

Brushing away a fresh river of tears, she gasped. "You hurt me—"

Christ.

I tore my mouth away from her command to be quiet. "I know, fuck, I know. I'm so sorr—"

She clamped her hand over my lips. "I know." She coughed and swallowed, slowly relaxing into the foreignness of speech. "You hurt me, but before that, you saved me."

My nostrils flared, and I trembled with the need to rip her

hand away and talk.

She whispered, "You saved me, and for that I'll be for—forever grateful, but...Elder..." Her eyes latched onto mine, swimming with fresh tears. "Where were you two years ago?"

Earth collided with Mars and Venus and hurtled into my chest to annihilate my heart. Asteroids followed, ransacking my insides until all that remained was a gaping hole my dragon could never hope to guard.

Where were you two years ago?

I understood straight away.

I felt the shredding of my insides, turning into strips of bloody flesh.

Her sobs broke through her strength. Her body rocked on my cock, making love to me all while she gave me her agony.

Her hand fell from my mouth as she curled into my arms again. Her sweet, unused voice repeated into my skin, "Where were you two years ago?" Her fingernails scratched my belly. "Where were you when he killed me?" Her teeth bit my shoulder. "Where were you when he sold me?" Her hand curled into a fist and hit me.

"Where were you?" She hit again.

"Where *were* you?" She struck harder.

"*Where were you?*" She let loose and pummelled me.

"*Where were you?*"

"*Where were you!*"

Where. Were. You?!"

And all I could do was sit there with my body inside hers, cold and ruined.

Answerless.

Powerless.

Destroyed.

www.pepperwinters.com
HUNDREDS (Dollar Series #3)
Coming Late 2016 / Early 2017

NYT & USA TODAY BESTSELLER

PEPPER WINTERS

HUNDRED$
DOLLAR SERIE$

PLAYLIST

Heathern by Twenty-One Pilots
Colorblind by Counting Crows
Demon by Imagine Dragons
Bones by MSMR
Defying Gravity by Idina Menzel
Time is running out by Muse
Last Hope by Paramore
Safe and Sound by Taylor Swift
Bring me the horizon by Throne
Hysteria by Muse

ABOUT THE AUTHOR

Pepper Winters is a multiple New York Times, Wall Street Journal, and USA Today International Bestseller. She loves dark romance, star-crossed lovers, and the forbidden taboo. She strives to write a story that makes the reader crave what they shouldn't, and delivers tales with complex plots and unforgettable characters.

After chasing her dreams to become a full-time writer, Pepper has earned recognition with awards for best Dark Romance, best BDSM Series, and best Dark Hero. She's an #1 iBooks bestseller, along with #1 in Erotic Romance, Romantic Suspense, Contemporary, and Erotica Thriller. She's also honoured to wear the IndieReader Badge for being a Top 10 Indie Bestseller, and signed a two book deal with Hachette. Represented by Trident Media, her books have garnered foreign and audio interest and are currently being translated into numerous languages. They will be in available in bookstores worldwide.

She loves mail of any kind: **pepperwinters@gmail.com**

THANK YOU FOR READING!

Printed in Great Britain
by Amazon